The Last Brontë

The Last Brontë

The intimate memoir of Arthur Bell Nicholls

A novel

by

S R Whitehead

© S R Whitehead, 2017

Published by Ashmount Press
www.srwhitehead.com

A CIP catalogue record for this book is available from the British Library.

ISBN 978-0-9552835-1-2 (Mobi)
ISBN 978-0-9552835-2-9 (ePub)
ISBN 978-0-9552835-3-6 (Paperback)

Book layout by Clare Brayshaw

Cover design by Emma Charleston

Prepared by:

York Publishing Services Ltd
64 Hallfield Road
Layerthorpe
York YO31 7ZQ

Tel: 01904 431213

Website: www.yps-publishing.co.uk

for Jenny

'The truth is, of course, that there is no pure truth,
only the moody accounts of witnesses.'
Laurie Lee
I Can't Stay Long

Prologue

I woke that morning filled with foreboding. A soft light was entering my room and a breeze lifting the curtains. The martin chicks were chirruping in the eaves and the sparrows in the yard but, in the house, all was quiet. I reached out for my watch. It was half past five, still early, but I could not lay awake weighed down with fears so I rose and dressed and then sank to my knees and prayed.

"Oh Almighty God, Father of all mercies, preserve and keep thy obedient and humble servant Anne that she might be restored to health to serve Thee whom she loves above all things. In the name of thy Son, our Saviour, Jesus Christ."

Down in the house, a door sneck clicked. That would be Mary, I thought, going down to the kitchen. I didn't want to meet Mary, nor anyone else, until I had seen the mail, so I crept downstairs and let myself out and set off for a walk on the moors.

I strode up the lane past the school and the parsonage, heading for Penistone Hill. It was a fresh spring morning. The sky was high, the fields were sparkling with dew and new life was bursting around me but, though I walked in Eden, my heart was full and my mind a blank. I didn't want to think. I didn't dare; not until I had seen the mail.

Coming back an hour later, I saw William Hartley. He was sauntering up Parsonage Lane with his bag on his back and when he turned into the parsonage garden, I stopped on the hillside to watch him. He went up to the front door and handed in the mail and then, when he came back, I told myself I must wait for a respectful passage of time but my heart was thumping so hard in my throat that I could not wait. I ran down to the lane and into the parsonage garden and stood at the open front door. I could see up the hall to the kitchen where Mr Brontë was standing with his back to me. I quietly walked in. Martha was by the kitchen table and Tabby in her chair, both staring down at the flags. Mr Brontë too was looking down and when I saw the letter hanging in his fingers, I knew. Time stopped. Later, I would be angry with Charlotte for leaving Anne at Scarborough, but not then. My anger would come like the roar from a distant cannon, hitting the ears sometime after the shot has left the cannon's mouth and at that moment, when the shot struck, I felt numb.

Mr Brontë said prayers for Anne's rest, his usually resonant baritone flattened by grief, while Tabby and Martha wept: Tabby in her chair by the range and Martha by the table with her shaking fingers twisting the strings of her apron. After the prayers, Mr Brontë blessed Tabby and Martha and then left the kitchen for his parlour next door. I touched his arm as he passed and tried to follow him but he raised his hand and closed his door leaving me on my own in the hall – on my own, that is, until the dogs found me. Keeper, Emily's big old mastiff, had howled for a week when his mistress had died and now Flossy, Anne's spaniel, was looking at me. He sat and swept his feathery tail across the flags. 'Where's Anne?' he was asking. 'It has been six days.' Keeper sidled up to me and I stroked his broad head.

The dogs wanted me to tell them that everything was alright but everything was not alright. I was not alright. My legs felt weak and my head began to spin. I pushed back the dogs and ran out to the garden where I sat on the bank with my head in my hands and I wept.

I had loved Anne Brontë. Not from the beginning, as in a romance, although even then I'd liked her, but over the years of our acquaintance I became her friend and her confidant and then, in the end, when it was too late, I found that I loved her. I loved her ringlets and her violet-blue eyes. I loved her courage and her intensity, her piety and her selfless kindness because it was Anne who extended her hand to me when I needed it, four years earlier, when I was newly arrived in Haworth. Dear God, where did those years go?

CHAPTER ONE

May 1845

"*Toleration* is our watchword here, Mr Nicholls. This is not Ireland. We have no Romanists here." We were standing in Mr Brontë's parlour. It was a bright May morning of 1845, the occasion of my introduction to the Haworth cure and dusty sunbeams were slanting in through the windows that looked out to the church. Mr Brontë extended a hand towards two wing chairs by the windows and I went and sat down, only then to be wrong-footed when he remained at his hearth. "We have Methodists," he went on. "They are entrenched, but they are bred of the Anglican Communion and they are good Evangelicals. Baptists also abound but, there too, some of the most neighbourly kindnesses extended to me over the years have been from Baptists." He raised a skeletal finger at me. "*Toleration* for the sake of high principle and also, I am afraid, for the sake of low necessity because although we are the Established Church we are in a minority to Dissenters here."

Mr Brontë was tall and straight. His black clerical coat was tight-buttoned in the old-fashioned style and he wore a long white cravat wound tightly round his neck. His hair was white and close-cropped to his skull, his face all tenacity and bone and with cataracts clouding his deep-set eyes, he addressed me down the length of his nose.

"Lean on our sexton for support," he advised me. "John Brown knows every stone of the church, every family of the village and every sod that he shall lay them under." Mr Brontë spoke with the fluid clarity of a moorland rill. His delivery was clipped and his syntax old-fashioned and, even after forty years, his Down accent still strong. He came over now and sat with me, locking his fingers in his lap.

"You will know that I have been unwell," he confided. "I am prey to bronchitis and it has been so persistent this winter that I am quite weakened by it. I suffer other degenerations appropriate to my age that I shall not trouble you with but the fact of the matter is that if I am spared two years more I shall have attained my three score and ten and I can no longer do the things that I could … and my eyes …" he looked sadly down at his hands. "For correspondence and the news I rely on my daughters … my sermons I devise from memory … I am a shrinking man, Mr Nicholls." His eyes remained in his lap for a few moments but then, of a sudden, he sat up. "What I need is a strong, young curate." He raised himself from his chair and strode back to his hearth. "You may have heard that your predecessor was negligent and since his departure I have been forced to rely on our neighbours."

"I am ready to serve, Sir, and to learn."

"I shall not over-tax you. I know that Haworth is your first cure and that you have yet to master your calling but, as our school master and mistress have also just left us, I must first ask you to take charge of the school." He took a piece of paper from his pocket. "Also, the village of Stanbury …"

It occurred to me as Mr Brontë spoke that he had been anticipating this interview for so long and his plans for me were so firmly laid that there could be no gainsaying him.

I was to take charge of the National School, have pastoral responsibility for the village of Stanbury and two hundred outlying farms; I was to join the roster of officiants at services, commencing that Sunday, I was to take a wedding on the Wednesday and see John Brown about a funeral on the Thursday.

"And you will need, of course," Mr Brontë concluded, "the names of those currently in receipt of parish relief." He held out the piece of paper. "And I have also listed – on the back – you will see – the gravely ill whose salvation will hang in my judgement upon your early intercession." I rose to accept the proffered note and as I took it, Mr Brontë clasped both my hands. He lifted his head and searched for me down his nose. "I am accustomed to *doing*, Mr Nicholls. Incapacity does not suit. If God wills it, I shall regain my strength. Until then I fear I can offer you little more than my advice. Please seek it freely at any time." Then he released my hands and drew back to ring for my hat.

I might have felt daunted by the duties laid upon me that morning and, if I had been older and wiser, I dare say I would but I was not old and wise, I was twenty-six and completely inexperienced and, if Haworth fell short of my Trinity dreams, it was the only cure I'd been offered so, if that was God's will, Haworth was where I would serve. At eight-thirty the following morning, I presented myself at the National School.

Classes had been taken by a roster of temporary helpers since the master and mistress had left: a roster that included our chapelry clerk, Mr Redman. I had understood — wrongly as it turned out — that on that particular morning, Redman was to have taken the class but, when I walked in, the class was of girls and no mistress was present. For a moment I hesitated but then, as it was gone half past eight and thirty pairs of eyes were upon me, I decided I'd introduce myself and so strode up to the rostrum.

"Thank you girls!" I called out over their heads and silence descended. "To your places please." The girls spread themselves out along the desks. "Please be seated." As a body, they sat, all save one girl at the back who stayed standing. "There is a place over there." I waved a finger at an empty space but she did not move. She was wearing thick-lensed spectacles and I wondered if she perhaps could not see me. "Do you see?" I waved again at the space and the room went quiet. "Are you ..."

"Mr Nicholls!" she called back at me. "It is Mr Nicholls, is it not?" I was taken aback and I looked to see what kind of a girl might address me so boldly. "If you wish to be acquainted with my class," she continued, her voice breaking with rage, "have the courtesy to introduce yourself firstly to me." And she advanced up the room. She was the height and build of a ten-year-old girl but, when she came forward, I saw she was wearing a crinoline and her features were not those of a child, but of a grown woman.

"I beg your pardon, Madam." I gathered myself as best I could. "You will be one of the temporary helpers?" She stepped up onto the rostrum. She only came up to my collarbone and she was slender as a child but her hair, drawn back into the nape of her neck, was no child's and nor was the look she was giving me from behind her dense lenses.

"The only temporary helpers we get in Haworth," she whispered acidly, "are curates." She examined me closely, her small square face red with rage, and so close I could smell her breath.

"Madam," I said, with as much dignity as I could muster, "you already have my apology. Do me the courtesy of accepting it." I looked down at her as firmly as I could, my reputation in her hands. "You evidently know who I am and what my business is here and there you have the advantage of me. Please, will you step down and let me introduce myself to the class?" Charlotte, for she it was, then turned to the class.

"Girls," she called out in a now steady voice, "this is Mr Nicholls. He is my father's latest curate and he will take prayers." Then, gathering up her books from the rostrum, she strode out of the room leaving me on my own with the class.

It was not the best start to a career: insulting your employer's daughter and looking foolish in front of a class of girls. I'd soon re-asserted myself with the girls but Charlotte was another matter. At that first meeting, I had perfectly confirmed her prejudice that all curates are fools and that she could cheerfully shun me which, for years to come, she did. I was sorry about that. I wished I'd done better. The social pool in an out-of-the-way place like Haworth is small enough without alienating my employer's family. Mr Brontë had two more daughters besides Charlotte, and a son – all of them around my own age – but the son and youngest girl were working away and the only other family member at home, Emily, was, if anything, even more hostile to me than Charlotte. I supposed that Charlotte had warned her off me after the schoolroom debacle because, whenever I ran across Emily, she too shunned me. The incident with the geese will illustrate.

To the rear of Haworth Parsonage there is a small drying field and, setting out later than I should one morning, I cut across it on my way up to a prayer meeting at Dimples. Washing was already on the line and, as I slipped through the field gate, I noticed Emily pegging out linen from a basket. I hurried up the field and bid her a 'good morning' but then, without a look or a word, she set down her basket and went and opened the door to the peat shed, releasing her geese. Now, I know about geese: we'd had them back home. Victoria and Adelaide, as Emily called them, took one look at me in their field and came for me. The field was steep and I was only halfway up it, I had no chance of beating them to the wall, so I turned and stood and faced them off. It was a risky stratagem and not guaranteed to succeed but I felt I had no option. I stood, four-square, and glowered at them and though they honked and hissed, they furled in their wings and reluctantly turned aside. Emily, with her hand still on the shed door, was watching me and, for the first time ever, our eyes met. Emily was tall and slim like her father and her unkempt tresses framed her father's long face but her eyes were not her father's; they were fierce as an eagle's and, at that moment, full of anger. I too was angry. Releasing her geese had been a hostile act and I stared Emily down as hard as I had her geese until, after a few moments, she too turned aside. I was not in Haworth for social reasons, I realised that, I was there to assist Mr Brontë in his ministry, but a little common civility from his daughters would not have gone amiss. I thank God that there also was Anne.

CHAPTER TWO

Anne

I first met Anne on a sunny Saturday afternoon in June. I had been in the chapelry about a month by then and was still struggling to get to grips with the incongruity of a squalid industrial township bounded by square miles of moorland and farms. Not that I was complaining; I welcomed the challenge. I was glad, after my years of training, to have the opportunity to work, to prove my worth to myself, to Mr Brontë and to God, but I am no zealot, and when I got the chance to take an hour out, I took it. That afternoon that I first met Anne, I had just finished my dinner and was sitting on the bench outside Sexton House with Mary and her four-year-old, Hannah. Sexton House adjoins the National School in Parsonage Lane. It faces south over the burial ground towards the fields and moors beyond and, with the church immediately below and the parsonage above, I regarded Parsonage Lane as our private close – our haven from the bustling township below the church. Mary had been quietly knitting at her end of the bench and Hannah talking to some stones in the lane but I was content just to bask. I had closed my eyes against the sun but then, hearing the parsonage gate, I looked up. Flossy, the parsonage spaniel, was wagging down towards us with a young woman. She was small and neat and carrying a basket.

"Miss Anne!" Mary set down her knitting and jumped to her feet. "So, it was you last night. We heard the carriage just after we'd gone to bed and John said it'd be you and Branwell." Mary smiled up the lane at Anne but Anne's eyes were fixed upon Hannah. She reached out to her.

"And who can this big girl be?" she teased her, "not young Mary! She's thin as a pin and this little girl's plump. Let me get hold of her." Hannah squealed with delight and ducked behind her mother's skirts but Anne caught hold of her and lifted her into the air. "Goodness what a weight!"

"Aye. That's our Hannah," Mary smiled with pride. "Six months is a long time at that age." Anne planted a kiss on Hannah's forehead and the little girl squealed again.

"So," Anne asked her, "how old are we now to be such a big girl?"

"I'm four."

"Four in April," Mary confirmed and then, for the first time, Anne noticed me. I had stepped back, to give the women space, but Flossy had found me and now Anne gave me a severe look.

"You won't have met Mr Nicholls," Mary said and Anne's eyes softened. She put Hannah down and offered me her hand.

"Papa has told me about you." Her hand was small and soft but the grip, firm.

"Oh dear!"

"No *oh dear* about it," she said, "Papa had nothing but praise. *Heaven sent* he said you were." These sisters knew how to surprise. That first look and the grip had been fierce, but now her hand hung gently in mine and her smile was warm. Anne was not conventionally beautiful: her brow was too broad and her chin too small but her eyes were beautiful – almond-shaped, violet and large – and she tied up her hair so that ringlets danced on her cheeks.

"I hear you are with us for a holiday," I said, and she let go my hand.

"Branwell is. For a week." She looked away over the burial ground. "I might stay longer."

"Oh?" asked Mary, "shall you be with us for the summer then? Not going to Scarborough with your family?"

"I don't know," Anne frowned, "it might depend," and then we heard the shout.

"Aha, sister! What ho! Eyeing-up the new curate?" It was Branwell, striding up from the village. He put out his hand. "You will be Nicholls."

"Mr Brontë's son?" I took his hand, surprised. He was small and ruddy, not a bit like his father.

"And heir." He swept me a theatrical bow. Branwell was like an actor: expressive and full of zest. His eyes were small but they sparkled behind wire-framed spectacles – spectacles the colour of his receding copper hair that he brushed up like laurels.

"So," he asked, "how do you find our little metropolis? Your salver will be swimming with cards I dare say."

"Oh, I'm paddling through them," I replied in kind, "not getting my feet too wet." He laughed and slapped my shoulder.

"You'll shoot I dare say."

"Er, yes. Back home. Just rough stuff."

"You must come shooting with me. These moors are full of grouse and I know all the squires with the rights. I'll introduce you."

"Branwell." Anne sighed at Mary's side. "It's June and you don't have a gun."

"The Taylors always have a gun for me. And they'll have one for you too Nicholls." He took my arm and turned me aside. "Have you met the Taylors yet?" I had met the Taylors. They were an important Church family out at Stanbury with farms and interests in the textile trade but, before I could answer, Anne repeated,

"But it's June." Branwell's eyes flashed. He spun round at Anne and threw out his arms.

"Alright, rough stuff then!" He glared at her angrily. "Carrion, rabbits, rats. Would that be alright?" Anne held his gaze with a level look till Branwell had to defer. She picked up her basket.

"It was nice meeting you, Mr Nicholls," she gave me a smile, "if you will excuse me, I have business in the village," and, ignoring her brother, she touched Hannah's hair and set off with Flossy down the lane. Branwell, embarrassed, put his hands on his hips and puffed out his chest.

"Seen the worshipful master, Mary?"

"John?"

"I've been down to the lodge but he's not there." Mary nodded up the lane.

"He's in the barn."

"On a Saturday afternoon?"

"He's a lot on. He's putting the new baby on the Ramsden memorial."

"Hmm." Branwell frowned respectfully at the ground for a moment then looked up again at the barn. "I'll go dig him out." He flashed me a smile. "Good to have a sportsman in the lane, Nicholls. I'll fix that shoot with the Taylors." Then he too strode off and left us.

Hannah had wandered indoors once Anne had left and, as Mary and I resumed the bench, a smile flicked over her lips.

"Something amusing you, Mary?"

"Nay, it's just them two."

"Anne and Branwell?"

"Aye. She's got him right there, did you see?" She pressed down her thumb on the bench.

"I saw there was a bit of an atmosphere. Are they always like that?"

"What? Big brother and baby sister? I should say not." Mary took up her knitting. "There's something happened at Thorp Green." She gave a firm nod. "That's why she's not goin' back. He's got himself into bother and Anne's mad at him."

"Mary. I have no idea what you're talking about."

"I've known them two from being childers and I'm tellin' you: what you just saw was Branwell in bother." Mary flicked her knitting out over her lap. "And now he wants John."

"And what has John got to do with it?"

"Branwell always runs to John when he's in bother. He'll be wantin' him to drown his sorrows with him down at the Black Bull but he's picked the wrong day."

"I must say, Mary, you read an awful lot into a brief exchange. If you're right, I'll be impressed."

"Oh, I'll be right, but only because I've seen it before. Branwell's jobs always end in bother and Anne got him this one so that's why she's mad at him."

"There could be any number of reasons why Anne's not going back – and anyway, that's not what she said – she just said she'd be staying at home a while longer." Mary huffed.

"She'd know if she were spendin' the summer with her family at Scarborough." Mary sniffed and resettled herself on the bench. "Anyway, whatever she does, she'll not stop at home for long. There's nothing round here for her now, not since Mr Weightman." Mary's ball of wool rolled onto the ground and I bent down to retrieve it.

"Mr Weightman?"

"Another young curate before you."

"And what was he to Anne?"

"They were sweet on one another, that's what. It broke her heart losing him."

"Did he leave for preferment?"

"No. He died of the cholera, sick-visiting down Stubbing. You'll see his memorial in the church, next to Mrs Brontë's."

"Goodness! The poor fellow! How old was he?"

"Twenty-eight." *Twenty-eight*! Two years older than me. I'd done plenty of sick-visiting down Stubbing myself. A chill shivered through me and Mary changed the subject.

"Have you found anyone to take over from Charlotte yet?" She nodded towards the school. "For next door?"

"No, not yet."

"Then why don't you ask Anne? If she is going to be around for a bit she might help you out." The church clock struck one. It was time I was moving.

"Do you know, Mary? I might just do that."

Anne had intrigued me, and not just with her beautiful eyes, but with her manner: her paradoxical mixture of softness and steel, her command of her brother, her easy warmth with Mary and Hannah and her welcoming of me – so different from her sisters. I did need a teacher for the girls in the school and, if Anne were prepared to do it, then 'who knows?' I fancied, 'I might yet make a friend!' I went up to the parsonage the following morning where Martha had answered the door.

"He's not in." Martha was John's and Mary's second daughter. She was seventeen by then with four years' service already behind her.

"Good morning, Martha," I greeted her cheerfully, "I am not here to see Mr Brontë. Will you please ask Miss Anne if she can spare me a moment?" Martha, her hand resting on the door knob, affected incomprehension.

"Miss Anne? What do yer want with 'er?"

"I think that's my business, don't you?"

"I'm sweepin' the master's parlour. I don't know where she is." At Martha's back, the dining room door opened and Charlotte appeared.

"What is the matter, Martha? Why the commotion? You know I am at my desk." Charlotte must have seen me in the doorway but she gave me her shoulder and addressed Martha.

"It's Mr Nicholls, Miss Charlotte. He wants to see Miss Anne."

"Why?"

"I don't know. He won't tell me. You ask 'im." Martha let go the door knob and returned to Mr Brontë's parlour, leaving Charlotte in her doorway and me in mine. Reluctantly, Charlotte turned to me.

"May I ask your business with my sister, Mr Nicholls? Perhaps I can help you. I would not want to inconvenience her unnecessarily." Yorkshire, I understood, was not King's County where the common courtesies are observed but Charlotte was being deliberately rude.

"My business is with Miss Anne," I told her firmly and now she feigned indifference.

"I merely wish to save you from wasting your time." She removed her spectacles and called down the hall. "Tabby?" We both stood in our respective doorways listening to lame old Tabby lumbering across the kitchen to the hall door where she put out her head.

"What's up wi' yer?" she demanded. "Yer legs is younger na mine. Callin' me out like some chit." Tabby was a heavy woman in her mid-seventies with a square face and firm jaw and a mass of white hair poked out from every side of her cap. Charlotte was apologetic.

"I am sorry, Tabby. I did not mean for you to come out. Do you know if Emily and Anne are back yet?"

"Don't yer think yer'd know if they were back?" Tabby was leaning against the door frame, taking the weight off her bad leg. "Mornin' Mr Nicholls." She gave me a nod.

"Good morning Tabby." She eyed me curiously.

"Is that you comin' in or goin' out?"

"I have come to see Miss Anne."

"An' no one's asked yer in?" She gave Charlotte a sour look. "Come through to t'kitchen. I've just seen the dogs an' lasses comin' down off Penistone Hill. They'll be here in a minute." Charlotte returned to the dining room and, closing the front door myself, I followed Tabby into the kitchen.

"Sit yerself down." Tabby sat down heavily into her high-backed chair beside the range and indicated that I sit at the table. She nodded towards the scullery. "I've seen 'em through the winder. They'll be here in a minute." There was the smell of fresh baking. A dozen discs of haverbread were hanging from the creel and in the niche beside the range two loaves of bread were cooling with a tray of currant teacakes. "I'd offer yer some tea but yer'll be gone before kettle's boiled."

"No, thank you, that's alright, Tabby. I've just had my breakfast." I put my hat on the table and pulled out a chair but, before I had chance to sit down, I heard Emily, Anne and the dogs come tumbling into the scullery.

"Rags are on the side!" Tabby shouted to them. "I'm not havin' them dogs shakin' their selves in here." I watched through the open doorway while Emily and Anne each towelled a dog.

"Go on then." Emily released Keeper, her cross-bred mastiff, who made straight for the bread behind Tabby.

"No yer don't!" Tabby grabbed him, "Lie down! Lie down!" and Emily walked in.

"Did yer tek bread out?" she called to Tabby in a course Yorkshire accent and Tabby nodded at the loaves. "Thank God!"

"Good job one of us 'as a brain in 'er 'ead," Tabby chided, and then Emily saw me. She froze and stared at me as at some deathly apparition.

"Where's Charlotte?" she demanded of Tabby.

"Dinin' room. At 'er desk." Emily's stare passed through me to the hall and she followed it, out of the kitchen. "Take no notice of 'er," said Tabby, "she's what they call *in character*."

Anne came through with Flossy who jumped up to me, wagging his tail.

"You have a friend," she said.

"Flossy's everyone's friend." I scratched his ears.

"That's true." Anne hung up her cloak on the back of the door and Tabby nodded at me.

"He's come to see *you*."

"Oh?" Anne looked at me, surprised, and, for a moment, I couldn't think what to say.

"You've got 'im tongued-tied," Tabby chuckled, "take 'im out into t'garden. Fresh air'll loosen 'im up." Anne put out a hand towards the hall,

"Shall we?" and with Flossy at our heels, we walked through the house and out to the garden.

The parsonage garden was a square allotment the width of the house and half a dozen steps led down to it from the front door. It was sadly neglected. There were signs there'd been borders in front of the house but they were now overgrown, as were the banks either side of the steps. A circular path ran round the plot, bounded on the outside by shrubs and fruit bushes while, in the middle, a hawthorn sheltered an old rustic seat. I asked Anne if the neglect were perhaps due to her absence.

"Oh no," she'd laughed, "I never had any sway here. The garden is Emily's domain." She looked at the neglect. "One of her realms."

We took to the path and I saw, as we passed, Emily and Charlotte at the dining room window.

"Is that why Emily is watching us?" I nodded towards the house. "Are we trespassing on her realm?" Anne glanced at the window.

"No. That's just my sisters watching over me."

"Oh!" I felt the sting of another social gaffe. "I'm sorry. I didn't think when Tabby said … would you rather one of your sisters walked with us?"

"No I would not!" Anne laughed again. "Thank you, Mr Nicholls, but I have been looking after myself for six years.

I do not need the protection of my sisters." We came again to the front of the house. Children's voices were ringing in the lane and little Hannah appeared at the gate. She smiled broadly to see us together and climbed up the two steps to the path. Anne bobbed down to greet her and Flossy fussed her and then Hannah's three sisters appeared. They hesitated at the gate and the eldest, Eliza, called in,

"Hannah, you've to come out!"

"Oh don't worry about that," Anne told her, "you can all come in if you want to." Gingerly, the girls climbed up onto the path but then, from behind us, there came the cry,

"Eh! What do yer think yer doin'?" It was Martha, out on the top step brandishing her broom. "Yer know full well yer don't come through that gate. Even I don't get to come through that gate and I live 'ere! Be off!" and she swept her broom at them. It is unwise to intervene in family disputes, however doubtful the justice, and so Anne released Hannah and the four crestfallen sisters waddled back to the gate and the lane. Anne stood up and smiled.

"Big sisters," she said.

"Big sisters," I agreed and, as we set off again round the path, I added, "six girls though! What are the odds of that?"

"We were five girls and a boy once," Anne said, "till our two oldest sisters died, twenty years ago." She looked up at me. "So, in Parsonage Lane, the odds are short."

"I had five sisters once, but then I had four brothers as well so we were all square."

"*Had*? Have you lost sisters too?"

"All of them. And three of my brothers."

"Oh Mr Nicholls!" Anne's face crumpled in concern and she put her hand on my arm. "That's terrible. How could that be?"

"Oh, they're not all dead. At least, not as far as I know, but I haven't seen any of them in twenty years and after so long, I don't suppose I will now."

"But what happened? I don't mean to pry – if it is too painful …"

"No, no, that's alright. It was, like your loss, a long time ago. We had a small farm in County Antrim. It was too small to support five sons and so my brother Alan and I were sent a hundred miles away to live with our uncle in King's County. He had a school there and could give us an education. Neither Alan nor I have seen our family since." Anne looked appalled.

"In twenty years?"

"Yes."

"Do they write to you?"

"Not for years." Anne's hand was still on my arm. "I was upset at first, but you learn to adapt and anyway, I gained a second family with my Bell cousins."

"And you still had one of your brothers."

"I did, but Alan and I were never close. He was one of those boys in a hurry to grow up – you know – to be a *man* – while I quite enjoyed being seven so, while he made friends with the boys in the school, I made mine with my little cousins, of whom there were legion." Anne's hand slipped from my arm and her eyes to the path. She was easy to talk to this third Brontë sister, so much more sociable than the others. I decided to come to my purpose.

"So," I said, kicking at the gravel, "you might be staying with us for a while."

"Why do you say that?"

"Because didn't you tell Mary that? That you would not be

returning to Thorp Green? Some difficulty?" Anne stopped in her tracks.

"I don't think I said anything about a difficulty."

"Didn't you?" She was giving me her stern stare. "Perhaps it was Mary who said that." Anne looked pensively away to the house, to the windows where her sisters had been watching, but their faces had gone. She turned back to me.

"Then Mary was right; there is a difficulty at Thorp Green, a considerable difficulty that has caused me a great deal of pain." A dark frown clouded her brow. "I have told my father so the news will be out soon enough: I have resigned my position at Thorp Green. I shall not be going back." She gave me a firm look but I didn't know what to say. I had no wish, on such short acquaintance, to be party to Anne's private problems.

"I'm sorry to hear that," I offered, "and after such long service." But then her frown melted and she started to smile.

"Oh, don't worry, there's nothing to be sorry about." She looked over to the rustic seat beneath the hawthorn. "Shall we sit down?" We crossed to the seat. It was spangled with white blossom which I cleared with my hand and we sat down looking out over the burial ground to the church.

"Do you believe in Providence, Mr Nicholls?"

"Ooh," I settled myself on the seat, "there's a big question for the time of day."

"I do." She turned and looked at me. "I think that by removing me from Thorp Green, God has shown me his purpose. I have been a governess for six years now and in that time I have witnessed some very unpleasant things of which this recent is only the last. Do you know, Mr Nicholls, that a governess occupies a very singular position in a house?" I raised an interested eyebrow. "Shunned by family and servants alike, she occupies a position of cold isolation, but one from which she has a clear view of the rest of the household and I intend to turn that to account." She was sitting up straight with her hands in her lap, her gaze as straight as her spine. "Over the last few months, I have felt a growing compulsion to expose the inequity of the governess's life and now that I am released, I can do so. I am going to draw on my experiences to write a didactic romance – a story, fictive but instructive – in the hope that, when it is published, it will expose the governess's plight and provoke reform." She relaxed her back and smiled. "So, you see, Mr Nicholls, you have no need to feel sorry for me. It is an exhilarating prospect that I see before me and, I am sure, God's purpose."

"It is a gratifying thing to have found God's purpose," I cautiously agreed.

"Is that the voice of experience?" She cocked her head at me. "Have you found God's purpose for yourself?"

"Well, yes, I believe I have," I confessed, "after offering me nothing for a whole year, I am bound to think that God was saving me for Haworth."

"And you profoundly feel that?"

"I think so, yes."

"And so you will have ambitions for Haworth, as I do for my book?" Anne, like her sisters, was direct. I did have ambitions for Haworth, but they were still half-baked and not ready for sharing.

"It's early days." I sat back and raised a knee, locking it in my clasped hands.

"You do have ambitions then!" She sat forward to make me look at her. "Tell me about them." I really did not want to tell my employer's daughter about my ideas for his chapelry but Anne had been so frank herself, she gave me no choice.

"I could wish that the Church stood more firmly against Dissent," I told her; "I cannot be satisfied that we are in a minority here."

"And what could you do about that?"

"Many things." I let go my knee and turned to her. "I believe that our Low Church practices offer too little contrast to those offered by the Wesleyans and Baptists. I think education is key: there is, for instance, no church or church school in Stanbury, a village of five hundred people with five hundred more dependent on it. The Wesleyans have a very active school there, which they are extending, while we offer nothing." Anne was watching me keenly. "We just don't get out enough." I put out an arm. "Take the Whit Walks. In two weeks' time, it will be Pentecost. Every Baptist and Methodist chapel and school will be parading their choirs and bands with their banners flying but where will the Established Church be? Are we too proud to go out into the highways and byways with our congregations? To give thanks and praise *en masse* amidst the glories of God's Creation?"

"You think that the Church should put on a Whit Walk?"

"I do, yes, show the flag."

"Then speak to Papa. You have only two weeks, and who knows where any of us will be by next Whitsuntide?"

CHAPTER THREE

The Whit Walk

Anne had tripped me into organising the Whit Walk. She had thrown down the gauntlet and I'd fallen headlong right over it. I hadn't needed another challenge, God knows, I had enough to do without organising a procession and picnic but, Anne's violet eyes had rested on mine and, well, what could I do? I had wanted to impress her, show her I was a man who could get things done, crass, I know, but interesting women were scarce as saints in Haworth and I wanted Anne to like me so I was ready to do what it took. I went to Mr Brontë and he gave me his qualified consent. The Church had always had a Whit Walk, he told me, but the custom had been dropped during a dispute with the Dissenters over their paying of Church rates. At the time, Mr Brontë had thought the parading of the Church's authority insensitive and, though the rates dispute had been settled, the walks had never resumed. *'Toleration'*, Mr Brontë had told me and I'd answered, *'can lead to domination'* and, with the caveat that I liaise with the Dissenting ministers, he'd consented.

Branwell was positively jubilant. 'We shall have a massed band,' he'd declared, 'I am thick with the Merralls. They have a brass band in their mill and together with the church band we'll blow those Ranters to kingdom come'. But then

Branwell remembered he'd be back at Thorp Green by Whitsun so that idea fell. Anne's support was more concrete. Before I'd left her in the parsonage garden, she had agreed to take the girls' classes and now she took charge of the girls for the walk. Unsurprisingly, Charlotte and Emily declined to help but, as Whit Tuesday approached and our plans became firmer, I started to see how positive this Whit Walk might be: the revived demonstration of the Church's authority and I marching out at its head. It was a timely opportunity to make my mark.

The morning of the walk and Parsonage Lane was thronged. The weather was fine with a high sky, perfect conditions, and the bustle that had started at seven with John setting up tables and urns in the schoolroom expanded, through the morning, to the length of Parsonage Lane and the croft. The walk to Stanbury and back would be followed by a picnic in the croft then thanksgiving in the church and many hands had been brought to the tasks. Churchwomen brought baskets of pies, buns and biscuits that Mary and Martha stowed in the school while, at the same time, serving beer and macaroons to the arriving Church Councillors and Patrons. Anne and I had to play host to these dignitaries between marshalling the children in the lane and all this to the sound, coming down from the croft, of the church band rehearsing their hymns.

As the hands of the clock closed on twelve, everyone was in his place: I, in front, in my full canonicals, beneath the church wardens' banner and Anne at my back leading the girls, all in white. Behind the girls came the Sunday School teachers, then the boys, all in black, then the band and, in the rear, a couple of hundred men and women of the congregation, all dressed in their finest attire. We filled the lane from the church at the bottom to the field gate at the top and, as the church clock struck the first chime of twelve, the parsonage door opened and Mr Brontë crossed his garden to address us over the retaining wall.

"What a sight is this at my gate?" He stretched out his arms over the length of the lane. "My flock of good sheep, penned and ready to march under the banner of Christ." He smiled down at the faces turned up to him. "I wish I were marching with you," he told them. "Time was when I would have leaped this wall and led you round the bounds of Stanbury, Withins and Oxenhope, but not today. Never mind." He sniffed and drew himself up. "You have my blessing and, it would seem, of the good Lord too – has he not sent us a perfect day?" A murmur of 'ayes' rippled through the lane. "Give thanks to Him for it," he told us, "and all the rest of His Creation that you will pass through between here and Stanbury and, if you run across our Dissenting neighbours, remember that they will be giving thanks too to the same Beneficence; we are all brothers in Christ." He closed his eyes and lifted his palms. "May the Holy Spirit of God, that descended in this season upon the apostles in their grief, go with you. In the name of the Father, the Son and the Holy Spirit." A loud 'Amen' rose up from the lane and then, as Mr Brontë turned back to his house, the bells of the church clashed out, the band struck up *All hail the power of Jesus' name* and the Church Whit Walk set off.

I don't know when I had felt so happy. Less than two months into the cure and there I was, striding out in my best shovel hat and gaiters, ahead of a band of four hundred churchmen, women and children singing out their praise of the Lord. It was a moment to savour. I was Pompey, King Billie and the Duke of York leading my troops to salvation. In Kirkgate, at the bottom of Parsonage Lane, a crowd had gathered to cheer us on: the diners from the King's Arms, the White Lion and Cross Inn were out with their drinks and napkins and, as we crossed into Ginnel, a group of rough lads ran tumbling and laughing beside us. The church band was splendid and every bit a match for so great a choir and, as we entered the confines of Ginnel, *There join the everlasting song and crown him Lord of all* cannoned off the walls and brought my heart up into my throat. I looked round and saw Anne. She was singing out loud with the rest and she gave me a wide smile. 'Pursue your ambitions,' she had told me, and I had.

At the junction of North Street, more knots of people were waiting to watch us pass, some waving and smiling and others stone-faced, Dissenters I supposed, but I saluted them all the same. Why would I not on such a day with the music of praise at my back? Even when we got into West Lane and passed the Baptists' new chapel and, a hundred yards on, the old Wesleyan chapel that was due to be pulled down to make way for a larger, I found their challenge uplifting: the Church was on the march again and my opportunities were great.

Praise my soul the King of Heaven followed *All hail* as we passed out of the village along West Lane towards Stanbury. The rollicking lads were still with us. There were more of them now, up to a dozen, keeping abreast of us along the hillside path. I recognised a couple of them as Dissenters' lads, but they were laughing and larking as any boys will on a holiday and all in good jest.

The road descends steeply at the end of West Lane, from the margin of the moor down towards the lush pastures of the Sladen Valley. It is one of the few verdant corners of the chapelry and, on that bright summer's day, I looked across it to Stanbury and the hump of Pendle Hill, twenty miles beyond.

"Look." Anne touched my shoulder.

"Look at what?"

"Coming down the road from Stanbury, on the other side of the valley." I looked to where she was pointing and saw, what I had missed before, a procession like our own winding down the hill towards Sladen.

"A Dissenters' Whit Walk," I suggested.

"Methodists."

"How can you tell?"

"There aren't that many Baptists in Stanbury."

"Well," I gave her a smile, "we shall see who's in the better voice."

The bridge over the Sladen Beck was wide enough for a cart but not two processions and, as the road narrowed between high embankments, the only passing place I could see was on a piece of ground just beyond the bridge so, as we were the nearer, I decided that we would cross first.

"Put on a pace," I told the wardens bearing the banner, and then, turning to Anne, "put on a pace. We shall cross the bridge before them." Then I went back through the procession to tell everyone else.

"Speed up? Why?" asked the band master.

"The Methodists are coming down from Stanbury. We'll beat them to the bridge."

"Hah!" he cried and, as I strode back to the front, the marshal blast of *Rule Britannia* burst over my head and, come the chorus, four hundred voices let fly.

31

The road being steep, the quickened pace sent the girls and boys almost running down the hill and, rather than hastening the procession along, the wardens and I had to try to hold it back. The jostling rush and the stirring song seemed to fire the lads on the hillside who ran on ahead of us laughing. The sight seemed also to fire the Methodists across the valley because they too now put on a pace and I could see why. They didn't want to meet us in the narrows any more than we did so they were making for the open ground but then, when they gained it, they kept coming, straight onto the bridge, just as we were entering it too. The collision was inevitable. Anne and I and the wardens were borne forward like foam on a wave of girls and boys pressed on by the adults behind them who, I am sure, couldn't know what was happening. The Methodists' front ranks were not girls, like ours, but a phalanx of men and, first among them, was their minister. He and I were thrown together amidst oaths from the men and gasps from the girls as the wind was knocked out of them.

"For pity's sake," I told him, "get back off the bridge."

"Don't *pity's sake* me," he answered, "*you* get off the bridge. We are giving praise here. Offering thanks to the Lord for the gift of his Grace."

"As are we," I told him, pressed to his chest, "we are all brothers in Christ and …"

"Brothers in Christ!" He was a heavy, bearded man with wild eyebrows that now shot up. "Does a brother in Christ mount an assault such as this? You do not have the right. We have marched this road for sixty years and you come at us like this!"

"We are not *coming at you*. I wrote to tell you."

"No you didn't."

"I wrote to your superior, Mr Moorhouse."

"The Revd Moorhouse is not my superior. *He* is my Brother in Christ." A sod of earth landed on his shoulder spraying both of us with soil. "What the!" I wiped the soil from my face and looked over the side of the bridge to see where it had come from. The village lads were grouped on the hillside, pointing and laughing and tearing up sods, the girls were crying and the men shouting while both bands continued to play and the people at the back kept on singing.

"Mr Nicholls!" Anne squeezed up to me. "You must get the children off this bridge." A sod now landed among the girls. They screamed with fright and I challenged the minister again.

"You must back off the bridge – onto that rough ground. There's nowhere else to go and those lads have to be stopped." He looked over to the lads on the hillside and then back at me.

"*Your* lads, aren't they? You brought 'em." And he set his jaw. He wasn't going to move. It was obvious.

"Mr Nicholls!" Anne shouted again, "For Heaven's sake!" I pushed past the minister to the side of the bridge. It had a low parapet and I jumped down into the shallow beck. I waved to the boys to jump down too, and to the bandsmen at the bridge's end and gradually, as the boys ran up the hill after the ruffians, the rest of my Whit Walk ebbed from the bridge to the beck and the sides of the road so the girls might come off and the Methodists go on their way.

There was only one casualty that day: the Brown's six-year-old, Mary, who hurt her ankle. It looked like a sprain so I carried her all the way back on my shoulders. It was an arrangement that met both our needs: Mary's for consolation and mine for a cross to bear.

* * *

"No, really, Mr Nicholls, you should not blame yourself." We were sitting on a couple of children's chairs in the schoolroom after Anne's Thursday class.

"Why not? Your father's made it very plain that I am to blame and it's his opinion that counts."

"The Church doesn't blame you. Everyone who was there blames that dreadful Abraham Soyland. It was obvious he'd done it on purpose. He had timed it perfectly, you could see, and don't tell me those rough boys from Haworth didn't know what to expect. Why else did they shadow us all the way there, giggling and larking? They knew full well they could expect rough sport. No. It was all planned. You were the victim, the injured party and everyone agrees you handled it well."

"John Brown doesn't." I hung my head over my clasped hands.

"Oh, little Mary wobbled her bottom lip at him and, like all fathers, he fell soft. You carried her all the way home, didn't you? I'm sure Mary doesn't blame you?"

"No, Mary's been generous."

"There you are then. No harm done."

"Except with your father." I sat up and sighed. "He told me that my predecessor, Smith, had let him down and that he hadn't had a reliable curate since …" I was about to say 'since Weightman'. It was what Mr Brontë had told me when he was tearing a strip off me – that he hadn't had a reliable curate since Weightman – but I balked at the name because hadn't Mary told me that Anne had loved him? Anne's cheeks coloured. She'd seen that I knew. I felt my own cheeks colouring too, it was an awkward moment but one that Anne quickly saved.

"My father has high standards," she said firmly, "but you'll find him forgiving. You consulted the Dissenting ministers, didn't you?"

"Ah, well," I rubbed my hands together, "not quite. Your father said 'liaise' and I wrote to their leaders in Haworth."

"Perhaps it would have been better if you had talked." Anne was right about that. I had known at the time that a personal approach was what was required but I was the new curate and they were Old Haworth. I had taken the coward's option.

"It would have been better," I agreed. "It's always better to talk." Anne gave me a smile which I returned. Her smile was so generous and her concern so sincere, I felt drawn to her, uncomfortably drawn. I averted my eyes and Anne rose to her feet.

"I have to go to York tomorrow," she picked up her basket and books, "Emily will be coming with me and we shall be gone for a few days."

"Oh?" I stood up too, "York? Any particular …?"

"Don't worry, Mr Nicholls, I shall be back for next Thursday's class." Then she walked out of the room and left me.

I didn't think I'd annoyed Anne. I hoped I hadn't. It was bad enough feeling Mr Brontë's ire after the Whit Walk fiasco without annoying Anne as well. I need the friendship of women. At home, I had had my aunt and my girl cousins – my sorority of sense against the bumptious boys – and I needed that friendship in Haworth. I began to worry, while she was gone, that I *had* annoyed Anne, and as soon as she got back, I determined to know.

My opportunity came a couple of days after she got back. It was a drizzly morning of late June and, as I was coming out of Sexton House, I saw Anne hurrying up the lane.

"Miss Brontë!" She was wearing a poke bonnet and had to turn round to see who was calling. Her expression was severe and it did not soften when I caught up with her. "How was your holiday in York?" She did not answer. She returned her face to the setts and continued walking. It was not a good start but I kept up with her and, heeding, I suppose, the need to be civil, she said, after a few paces,

"It was not a holiday, Mr Nicholls."

"Oh I'm sorry, I supposed it was."

"I had business in York."

"Ah." I felt now some movement. "With the Robinson family I dare say." She stopped and, for the first time, looked up at me. It was not the open, friendly face that I'd been carrying in my mind's eye.

"Why do you say that?"

"Well, isn't Thorp Green near York? And your brother still living there with the Robinsons?" Anne examined me, her eyes scanning mine, then she withdrew back into her bonnet and set off up the lane again. I was walking on eggshells. It was not the conversation I had hoped for and, with my heart sinking, I tried some firmer ground. "Still, I'm sure Emily must have enjoyed York. Being less familiar with the city than you, she must have found it interesting." And I added, "very different from Haworth."

"Not to Emily it wasn't. She was in Gondal from beginning to end." We had reached the garden gate. Anne mounted the two steps but, before setting off up the path, she hesitated and, frowning down at me, said,

"Forgive me, Mr Nicholls. I'm sorry. Charlotte is leaving for Derbyshire and I must see her before she goes." Then she hurried off into the house.

It was not the exchange I had hoped for. Where was the fellow-feeling in those big violet eyes that I had enjoyed in the schoolroom and the parsonage garden? I had annoyed her after all, I decided. My feelings for her had, for a moment, run deep and she had noticed; that was why she'd jumped up in the schoolroom but, though it would be another two weeks before I found out, I was not the centre of Anne's universe; there was a larger reason for her coolness and it concerned someone infinitely more important to her than me.

CHAPTER FOUR

A family crisis

The crisis broke in the middle of July. Just a month after his return to Thorp Green, Branwell was back in Haworth. He too had left the Robinson's service but Branwell had not resigned his position as Anne had, he'd been dismissed. The exact circumstances of his dismissal remain a mystery but one thing was immediately clear: his failing was neither professional nor financial, it was moral, and Branwell came home in disgrace. Mr Brontë was furious with him and he did not care who knew it. I had tasted Mr Brontë's wrath myself, after the Whit Walk, but I was not his son and my failing not moral; his anger with Branwell was visceral.

"He has a right to be angry," was Mary's judgement, "John would be if it were one of ours. Mr Brontë's spent twenty-five years making his name good in Haworth and Branwell's chucked it back in his face."

It was the conventional view, but Mary was wrong about John; he did not condemn Branwell, he supported him, as I myself saw, a day or two after Branwell's return.

It was going up to midnight. I had been working late at my desk and was just getting ready for bed when I heard footfalls in the lane. They stopped beneath my open window and then, after a few moments, there was a loud knock at the door that John quickly answered.

"Old Knave!" It was Branwell. "Will you admit me, John? Or will you turn your face from me like everyone else that I have loved?" He was drunk.

"Nay lad," answered John. "What yer doin' here this time o' night? Get up off my step an' hold yer noise." There was scuffling as John tried to lift Branwell.

"Invite me in, old friend, and we shall share a bottle of what you have."

"No chance," John told him. "Mary's downstairs an' anyway, yer looks as if yer've had enough. I'll give yer an 'and 'ome." Branwell started sobbing.

"I am loved, John, by a lady. This is my crime. For daring to glimpse through the gates of the garden of happiness I am reviled by Papa and shunned by Charlotte. I have seen paradise John and the lady who stands within is beckoning me still though the lock is turned against me. Do you condemn me John? For seeking my portion of happiness?" There was again the sound of scuffling as John tried to support Branwell.

"Come on now lad. I'll 'elp yer 'ome."

"No! Tell me John," Branwell sobbed. "Tell me that you stand against me or tell me that I am allowed to be happy with the lady I love. Tell me John. Tell me." There was a moment's silence and then John answered,

"Not if she's already wed, no. Now come on. I'll get yer up 'ome."

"Wed to a tyrant!" Branwell cried. "No husband he! No penner of poems nor singer of sweet songs. No lover."

"No. But wed."

"Then I am wed too," Branwell proclaimed. "Providence has arranged a match for me to a certain woman robed in black and calling herself Misery. She walks by my side, she hangs on my arm as affectionately as if she were my legal wife and our contract shall be unto death." Again, there was scuffling. I went and looked out of the window. John had his arm round Branwell and was staggering him up the lane. At the parsonage, a solitary lamp was burning and when John got to the garden gate, Emily came out and took Branwell from him, carrying him in and closing the door.

The following morning, Mr Brontë sent down for John. I saw the two of them sitting together at the parlour window and they talked for a long time. When John came back, he told me that he had agreed to look after Branwell and as soon as arrangements could be made he would be taking him away from Haworth for a holiday in Liverpool.

Charlotte finally arrived back from her three weeks in Derbyshire the following evening. Mr Brontë was deeply upset by Branwell's dismissal but he was, by then, equally upset at the breach it had opened between them. I felt for him. He was sixty-eight years old and almost blind with enough other troubles to bear. I prayed for them both and when I told Mr Brontë, it must have moved him because, quite unexpectedly, he invited me to join his household that evening for family prayers. It was an invitation I was pleased to accept after the Whit Walk debacle but, in hindsight, one I might have declined.

Prayers were held in Mr Brontë's parlour. Mr Brontë had delayed them that evening in the hope that Charlotte might join us but, when she was not back by nine, he started without her. We followed the Order for Evening Prayer. All present joined in The Confession and then listened in silence while Mr Brontë recited The Absolution. All minds, I am sure, were on Branwell.

"*Almighty God the Father of our Lord Jesus Christ, who desireth not the death of a sinner, but rather that he may turn from his wickedness and live ...*" We heard the dogcart pull up in the lane. Mr Brontë continued with The Absolution but I and everyone else turned to the window to see Charlotte hurrying up the path. "*... He pardoneth and absolveth all them that truly repent and unfeignedly believe His Holy Gospel. Wherefore let us beseech Him to grant us true repentance and His Holy Spirit, that those things may please Him which we do at the present ...*" Charlotte appeared in the doorway, flushed and bare-headed and carrying her bonnet. "*... and that the rest of our life hereafter may be pure and Holy, so that at the last we may come to the eternal joy; through Jesus Christ our Lord.*"

Charlotte joined in the 'Amen'.

"Where is Branwell father?" Mr Brontë had not seen Charlotte arrive and he was surprised to hear her voice.

"Charlotte?" He lifted his head and looked down his nose in her direction. "You are home?"

"Yes father. Where is Branwell?"

"Branwell is in the care of John Brown."

"John Brown!" Charlotte stepped into the crowded little room. She looked quickly at Martha, "I am sorry Martha," then back to her father, "but is that wise? John is as familiar with the inns and beer shops as is Branwell. I hardly think that John Brown ..."

"Charlotte," Anne whispered, at her side, "you know perfectly well. I wrote to you." And Emily sniggered,

"The return of the Princess Nekayah!"

Charlotte, clutching her bonnet to her breast, lifted her face to the ceiling.

"I should have been here!" she wailed, but Tabby merely clucked while Emily and Anne dashed each other a look. Charlotte then turned to Anne, her face hot with ill-temper. "If I had been here I would have managed the situation. No one need have known. He has humiliated me. What could I tell Ellen? What shall I tell Ellen's mother and her brother? Branwell has behaved abominably."

"Charlotte, Charlotte, Charlotte," Mr Brontë tried to soothe her, "your brother is guilty of a sin sure enough but it is a sin of frailty. The abomination here is not Branwell's, it is the unscrupulous employer's – she who took wicked advantage of her son's tutor. Hers is the abomination."

"You mean Mrs Robinson," Charlotte said, and again Emily and Anne exchanged looks.

"Yes Charlotte. Mrs Robinson. The consort of a Minister of the English Church. The woman shall answer." Charlotte's head dropped forward.

"It is too bad," she sighed. "I am too tired. I shall have to retire."

"You shall pray with us first." Mr Brontë pressed his palms together under his chin. "*Our father …*" and Charlotte stayed with us to recite the Lord's Prayer.

As I have said, Charlotte's arrival from Derbyshire in the middle of family prayers was an incident I'd have preferred not to witness, I felt compromised, but there was a positive coda: the following morning, Anne came out to see me.

"You are owed an apology, Mr Nicholls. Last night's was an unseemly exhibition and you should not have been exposed to it. I am sorry." She had followed me into the garden after my morning meeting with her father. Apart from the briefest of exchanges in the schoolroom, it was the first time she had spoken to me since her last apology on that same footpath, two weeks earlier. I was cautious.

"I had no wish to intrude on your family's private business," I told her, "but Mr Brontë did invite me …"

"Mr Nicholls, your prayers are appreciated believe me – and needed – but you should not have been exposed to the theatricals."

"Charlotte was tired," I offered, "I would never style her concern for her brother as *theatricals*." I was at the gate ready to descend to the lane. I really did not want entangling in a family dispute; I was struggling, as it was, to regain Mr Brontë's trust without further snares, but Anne had more to say.

"Oh it was theatricals." She waved her hand at the house. "It is all theatricals. Branwell has criminally disgraced himself and so invents a romantic cover; Charlotte makes a show of outrage because her hero has again shown himself flawed and Emily makes sense of it all by transposing it into her fantasy world."

"You mean the Princess Nekayah?"

"A Gondal character. A fantasy."

"Ah," now I made the connection, "so when you said that, in York, Emily was in Gondal …"

"Gondal is Emily's fantasy world. I shared it with her when we were young but I have been six years in the real world while the rest of my family continues in its own. I am sorry Mr Nicholls. I did not intend to burden you with my family's troubles but sometimes I have to talk to someone sensible and this morning it seems to be you."

Someone sensible! It might not have been the most affectionate epithet ever bestowed but it was on the right side of indifferent and after two weeks of walking on eggshells, I took heart from it. Obviously, the family was upset about Branwell's dismissal and Anne especially so because she had been at Thorp Green and knew the truth – the truth so dark that she too had felt she must leave. I understood Anne's priorities – family will always come first – but if I were her sensible someone in whom she could place her trust, I'd settle for that.

Two days after Charlotte's return, John and Branwell left for Liverpool. They were gone for a week and the holiday was only a partial success. Branwell was less fevered on his return but his malaise remained and the small progress that was made in Liverpool would probably have been made in Haworth. John had done his best to amuse Branwell with excursions and a boat trip down the coast but Branwell was not for being amused, he wanted only to sit in ale shops and talk of his misery. Anne had made mention of some 'criminal' disgrace but John knew nothing about that; he'd heard only the version of events that Mr Brontë had accepted, that Mrs Robinson was the cause of his son's downfall, the senior partner in an illicit liaison that had been discovered by her reverend husband. The version that Mr Brontë accepted was a scandal but, to a fabulist like Branwell, it was a romantic scandal and so tragic.

After the dry spell in June, the weather broke. Days of rain turned the roads into mires and the mires on the moors into treacherous bogs and even when it wasn't raining, the air was leaden and the village stank. Haworth did not have piped sewerage. The night soil was piled into middens that the rains loosened, swilling their contents down the streets to settle in stagnant pools. The air was fetid and sickness soon spread. Diarrhoea, scarlet fever and measles all raged that summer, adding danger to my burden of work. Thank God, I managed to stay well, and a good thing it was, because Mr Brontë continued poorly and what help I did receive came from the neighbouring clergy, most especially Joseph Grant of Oxenhope.

Oxenhope, a village two miles to the south, had just been hived off from Haworth as a chapelry in its own right and Grant was the Curate-in-Charge. He was, like me, twenty-six, unmarried and new to the district and what else we had in common we discovered when he invited me over for tea. Until there were funds to build him a parsonage, Grant was living at Marshlands, the school master's house in the hamlet of Marsh, halfway between Haworth and Oxenhope. It is a pleasant fifteen minutes' walk from Sexton House, part of it under the canopy of an ancient elm avenue, and, after heavy rain in the morning, the afternoon's skies were clear. When I walked up his garden path, Grant was on his haunches assessing the damage.

"Ah Nicholls." He rose to his feet. "What am I going to do with these?" Grant was tall and willowy with large kind eyes.

"The peonies?"

"Is that what they are?"

"You'll have to support them. Bend some beech twigs into a frame and tie them up. Either that or cut them back till next year." I gave him a smile. "Just another job for you." He frowned down at the peonies.

"They'll make a table posy." He bobbed down and started cutting at the blooms with his penknife. "I've invited Sutcliffe Sowden to join us. I hope you don't mind."

"Sutcliffe Sowden?" The name meant nothing to me.

"Curate-in-Charge of St James's, Mytholmroyd. Mytholmroyd's a new chapelry, like Oxenhope, so there's a lot he can tell me. Well, well, well!" Grant nodded to the lane where a stocky figure with tousled red hair was striding towards us. "The very man!"

"Has he walked all the way from Mytholmroyd?"

"Ten miles is nothing to Sowden. He'll probably want us to go for a walk with him after tea before he sets off back." Sowden turned into the gate and nodded at the peonies.

"Those for me?"

"If you like." Grant stood up and put his hand on my shoulder. "I don't think you've met Arthur Nicholls. Brontë's new curate?" Sowden gripped my hand.

"A full chalice, Haworth," he fixed me with his steely blue eyes, "even without Oxenhope."

"Not a poisoned one I hope."

"I would never say that, but full."

"Full of opportunity then." Sowden flashed me a smile and Grant held out his peonies.

"Shall we go in?"

The dining room at Marshlands was high and airy with tall sash windows that looked out over the hay meadows to the dun-green moors beyond. Grant had given the peonies to his housekeeper who set them on the table in a bowl. They brought a splash of colour to an otherwise Spartan apartment dominated by a black granite fireplace and furnished only with the table and chairs. The high tea was good: beef and vegetable soup, cold calf's tongue and early potatoes with pickles followed by a rhubarb pie and cheese. Sowden was quiet during the meal, more interested in the food than the Haworth gossip that Grant and I were peddling, but when I touched on Mr Brontë's toleration, he interjected:

"His mother was Roman Catholic."

"Really?" replied Grant, "I never knew that."

"I had it from Morgan in Bradford. They're old friends. Brontë's as firm as the rest of us against Romish superstition but I think his background inclines him to social toleration."

"Social toleration can be argued in Ireland," I cut in, "where there is social stasis – each side staying bound to its inherited religion – but I see no such stasis in Haworth." I paused while the housekeeper cleared our plates. "Haworth seems to me to be all in flux with the Dissenters expanding and the Church contracting. Have you seen the Baptist's new chapel in West Lane?" I asked Sowden. "Five Hundred seats! And the Methodists, a hundred yards away, about to start on their new chapel with six hundred and fifty seats *and* a brand new school to go with it – and these in addition to the Particular Baptists at Hall Green and the Primitive Methodists on Mill Hey. And this is only the village! There are Dissenting chapels in Stanbury, Hawksbridge and here in Marsh." Sowden pushed back his chair and crossed his legs.

"Welcome to the reality of the Pennine front line."

"But not a reality we have to accept surely?"

"No, not at all," Grant answered, "that is why Oxenhope was hived off. My brief here is to establish a new church and school to serve some of the communities you mention. The Church is not indolent Nicholls; work is going on; look at Mytholmroyd." He held out a hand to Sowden. "You're expanding aren't you Sowden?"

"We are. Our congregation has grown fifty per cent in the past four years and I too am planning to build."

"I am delighted to hear it," I told them, "and I congratulate you both on your leadership but where is the leadership in Haworth? Where is the Vicar of Bradford? The Haworth chapelry is a part of his parish but I never hear his name from one week to the next, let alone see him, and Mr Brontë has not the strength."

"Brontë built the National School, you know. All his own doing."

"I know, I know, but in the years since then, all the initiative has been with the Dissenters."

"Then perhaps," said Grant, smiling across at me, "what Brontë needs is a vigorous young curate."

"Funny you should say that. That's just what he told me."

"Well then."

"Well then?"

"It sounds to me as if Brontë's looking to *you* to give some leadership. You're clearly a man with ideas; what do you think the Church should be doing in the Haworth chapelry?" *What should the Church be doing in the Haworth chapelry*? I didn't need to think about that.

"We need a mission church and school in Stanbury. The Methodists hold it as a private fief. Five hundred souls and five hundred more in the farms around it. That's where I would plant my flag." Grant raised his glass.

"Then amen to that."

Grant re-charged our glasses from the decanter and, as our conversation broadened, so did our agreement.

We lamented the departure of the Wesleyans from the Established Church and all the other ruinous schisms. We gave thanks for the Thirty-nine Articles and the authenticity of the Anglican Communion and we discussed how the Church might regain its leadership and the more we talked the more we found we agreed: leadership demanded authority, it demanded liturgical discipline and it demanded the unequivocal acknowledgement of the Eucharist as central to our mystical communion – we were agreed, in short, on our admiration of the Oxford Movement and its leader, John Henry Newman.

It is a grand thing to make new friends over good food and wine and I walked home that evening with a spring in my step. Midsummer's eve was almost upon us, dappled moonlight was lighting my path through the elms, my future, I felt, was in my own hands and I sang as I made my way home:

> Rejoice today with one accord,
> Sing out with exultation;
> Rejoice, and praise our mighty Lord,
> Whose arm hath brought salvation.

I raised the question of Stanbury with Mr Brontë the next morning. I knew the interview would be difficult after the Whit Walk fiasco but Grant and Sowden had inspired me and besides, I wasn't going to let Soyland triumph. We sat in the chairs by the window.

"You do not think," Mr Brontë suggested, "that passions might be running a little high for another Stanbury adventure?"

"Oh, I agree." I was relieved that he would even talk about it. "I am not thinking of a public campaign, nothing confrontational, (a good word I thought) I was just thinking, to begin with, of one or two exploratory approaches to the funding bodies – you know: the parish and diocesan treasurers, the Churches' Committee, the National Church Society."

"And the people of Stanbury?"

"The people of Stanbury? I thought we wanted to avoid confrontation."

"Are not your proposed mission church and school meant to serve the churchmen and women of Stanbury? You don't think your exploratory enquiries should be of them? It would be wise to desist for the next month or two, certainly, until passions have cooled, but it is the support of the Stanbury churchmen you are going to need. It is with the Taylor and Robinson and Ramsden families you are going to need to talk – and I would go further – you should get them to pay."

"Get them to pay?"

"Yes. Never mind taking the offertory box to third parties; it is the commitment of our Stanbury members that you want because where their money goes so their hearts will follow – but not yet – hold off until the New Year." We heard a commotion in the hall: it was Branwell shouting,

"Out, out," and his toe-caps click-clacking down the stairs.

"But out where?" Martha asked him, "Master'll want to know and yer haven't had no breakfast."

"Just tell him *out, out*, like the brief candle," and, slamming the front door behind him, Branwell left the house, passing beneath our windows on his way to the lane. I looked across at Mr Brontë. He hadn't seen Branwell passing his window but he had heard him. He straightened in his chair and lifted his head.

"How is Branwell?" I asked him.

"Tormented," he replied. "Punishing himself and punishing those who love him for deprecating his lapse. I have tried admonition and now reason but he will not return to the prescribed path. I invite him to pray and his lips stay shut." Mr Brontë rose from his chair and I followed. "You pray for him Mr Nicholls," he put his hand on my shoulder, "ask God to show my son the path to redemption because he will not hear it from me."

Branwell spent as little time as he had to under his father's roof. He passed his days walking on the moors or, more often, languishing in the village inns where he could numb his hurt in less critical company. He was drinking heavily and not just ale and gin; he was buying opium at threepence a phial and making up laudanum that numbed his days but ruined his nights. Martha told John that Branwell raved through the nights, keeping the whole household from sleep. I rarely saw Branwell; he was still in bed when I paid my calls but one morning I saw him – or heard him at least – trying to restore his old closeness to Charlotte.

Mr Brontë had gone out to the privy and I was sitting in his parlour waiting for him to come back. The door was ajar and, though I could not see into the hall, I heard Charlotte when she came out of the kitchen, and Branwell, when he came down the stairs. His step was light and he sounded cheerful.

"Dear sister."

"Good morning," I heard Charlotte answer. "If it still is." She must have gone to the dining room door because next Branwell said,

"I do know what you're doing in there you know."

"We are working, Branwell, only working."

"You are all scribbling novels aren't you?"

"Branwell …"

"No, no, you have no need to be shy," he told her. "I am really very pleased for you. It has been years since you and I wrote anything together. You were not going to give up just because I was away, no, I am happy for you. You have had Emily to write with this past year or two, and now I see you have brought Anne into your little circle, which is fine. But you must not be shy Charlotte; if you need advice – any of you – on plot, characterisation, dialogue or even publishing, I can help you with publishing, I am very well in at the *Halifax Guardian* for poetry, and my own novel is coming along terribly well. I am in correspondence with Macaulay about it you know. Yes. He wrote me a most complimentary letter; very complimentary indeed, he thinks it will do very well when it is finished." There was silence then for a few moments, before Charlotte said,

"You look as if you are going out."

"I thought I'd go for a walk. I don't suppose you would like to join me?"

"We shall take our walk this afternoon as usual. I am busy at the moment."

"Right." Again, there was silence. "If you'll tell Papa I've gone out then?" Charlotte must have indicated the parlour door because, a moment later, Branwell's head came round it. He gave me a smile.

"Papa not in?"

"He's out the back. He'll be back in a minute."

"Just tell him I've got the sovereign thanks and I'm going for a walk." Then Branwell left. I watched him pass the windows to the gate. He was wearing his good coat and a cravat but he did not turn left into the lane, as he would if he were going for a walk, he turned right down into the village. The sovereign had been given him by his father to settle a debt and the next time I saw Branwell was two days later. It was eleven in the morning and he was in the kitchen still in his night shirt. He was pale, haggard and shaking, crouching by the range and crying uncontrollably for his late Aunt Elizabeth. Anne, like the rest of us, was worried about him.

"Branwell needs to get another position." I had called in at the schoolroom to help her tidy up after her Thursday class. "Home is the worst place for him. Papa's anger might have cooled but Branwell knows he has failed him and he's punishing himself."

"Mr Brontë is a strongly principled man," I offered, closing the top windows while Anne collected the slates. "It can be hard for a son to live up to."

"Which is why he needs to get away, and not just from Papa: Charlotte is constantly sniping at him, telling him he's a disgrace and she can't invite her friends here."

"I saw Charlotte was angry."

"Because it's personal. Charlotte always put Branwell on a pedestal and she doesn't like her heroes to fall."

"And Emily? Is she berating him too?"

"Oh no … Emily?" Anne gave a little laugh. "Emily doesn't judge. If Branwell chooses to drink himself senseless, Emily thinks he should be allowed to get on with it."

"Not very helpful."

"No, it isn't, which is another reason why he needs to get away: find his feet again and achieve something." Anne had gathered up all the slates and I went and opened the cupboard for her.

"Find his purpose," I suggested.

"Yes." I took the slates from her and stacked them on the shelves. "We all have one, don't we? That positive contribution that we must make while we are here? I worry that Branwell is leaving it too late to find his."

"Too late? He's only twenty-eight, isn't he?"

"Men can die at twenty-eight." A dart of pain shot through Anne's eyes. Weightman: he had died at twenty-eight. Always, around Anne, there hung the spectre of Weightman. I closed the cupboard door.

"And *your* purpose," I asked, moving the conversation on, "how is your *magnum opus* progressing? I never see you these days but through the dining room door."

"Oh, it is progressing, but not quickly enough. Charlotte and Emily are also writing."

"I know. I see them at the table with you."

"Their stories are very different from mine but I find it helpful, working together; we give each other impetus." She picked up her basket and a frown creased her brow. "I had been wanting to talk to you actually, Mr Nicholls." She looked up at me. "If I am going to finish my book by next spring, I shall need to devote all the time I can to it and I wondered if you'd found a teacher yet – for the girls. We did say that my help would be temporary."

"Another teacher!" I was knocked back. I didn't want to lose Anne. We'd just nicely become friends – even confidants – but if she gave up Thursdays, when would I ever see her? "No," I told her, "I'm afraid I haven't." She raised an eyebrow.

"I believe May Wright might be interested."

"May who?"

"Jonas Wright the carpenter's eldest? She's perfectly well qualified, and available. I think she'd do well."

CHAPTER FIVE

Of faith and doubt

And so I lost my Thursday friend. Why, after railing to me against her sisters for living in fantasy worlds, Anne had closed herself up with them to write her own work of fiction was a disappointment at least and at worst a betrayal. I had thought we'd become friends: that, living so close, we would be constantly running across one another and passing the time of day but it didn't happen. Every morning, when I called at the parsonage, she was shut up with her sisters in the dining room. When she went out for walks, she went with her sisters and they went together to church. On the rare occasions that I did see Anne out alone, she was head down, wrapped in her cloak and hastening off on some errand with never the time to speak. It was disheartening but, if I missed Anne, I hadn't the leisure to mope because the demands of the cure, far from easing as I worked myself in, grew increasingly great.

The summer and autumn of '45 were unremittingly wet. As a result, the harvest was poor and food prices rose. The wet weather aggravated the already squalid living conditions in the village adding all kinds of sickness to the miseries of the poor. Food prices and the public health were grave problems but they must be viewed also against the background of the continuing depression in the textile trade that had persisted throughout the forties. Markets were shrinking, mill-hands were being laid off and already low rates of pay were under downward pressure from the abundance of idle labour. There was widespread want among the working poor and the Chartists, who had already rioted in Bradford, were agitating in Haworth. As the autumn slipped into a miserable winter, there was a pervading sense of unease and, at times, it was my faith alone that sustained me.

If times were hard in Haworth, they were worse back home. The weather had been warm and wet in Ireland too but the harvest of the small farmer's staple, the potato, had not just been poor, it had failed. The wet, warm soil had proved the ideal breeding ground for a blight that spored and spread so quickly that it infected the entire national crop and as winter set in, in great swathes of the country, the people had nothing to eat. Starving families abandoned their farms and poured into the workhouses that quickly became crowded and diseased. My brother Alan, in Dublin, sent me newspaper accounts of mass graves in the countryside covered with lime, of cabins demolished over the remains of their tenants and bodies ravaged by starving dogs. I prayed for Ireland and any satisfaction I allowed myself at being useful in Haworth was tempered by guilt at not sharing the suffering back home. Mr Brontë felt it too of course for he had brothers and sisters and nephews and nieces and we prayed for our homeland together. That winter was, as I say, a testing trial of my faith so when that faith was undermined, I faltered.

John Henry Newman, the guiding light of my generation, went over to Rome. I was incredulous. Newman had awakened us to the torpor of the Established Church and sent us out to celebrate the Anglican heritage. Through him we had returned to the great common themes of Protestant churchmanship: the shared tradition and the patristic texts. He had brought us to believe in an Anglican Communion whose traditions are every bit as deep as Rome's and whose leadership of Protestantism might finally outface the ignorance and superstition of the empire that he himself had once described as 'crafty, obstinate, wilful, malicious, cruel and demoniac.' And now he had joined it.

As soon as I had time, I hurried over to Oxenhope to see Joseph Grant and he was as incredulous as I. The newspapers were full of it. Their editorials and letters columns addressed little else for days and the whole Anglican Communion was split over it. Some ministers of the Church followed Newman to Rome but not many, that was not the point. The hurt was that for twenty-five years a large body of churchmen had hung on Newman's every word and now they had been betrayed. As an old Evangelical, Mr Brontë, I knew, had little time for Newman and so I tended to avoid Church politics but Newman's defection so dominated the news that the issue couldn't be avoided. When I went in to see Mr Brontë, he was philosophical.

"Your friend Newman is ahead of you, Mr Nicholls," he said, smiling over his newspaper, "but then, he is your leader and you are his disciple."

"Mr Brontë?" I didn't follow him.

"Your hope that Protestants might unite around a common heritage that ante-dates the Reformation does rather ignore the conclusion of its own logic. Newman has simply followed it through."

"And how is that, Sir?"

"Well. Once you have decided that all the myriad Protestant Churches, sects and 'isms' must unite around traditions that ante-date the Protestant Reformation, you have only the Roman Church left. Newman is simply pursuing his own logic to its conclusion. I suspect he may not like that conclusion, but he is an honourable man and he must, after a lifetime of advocacy, live with the consequences."

I was tired. How much of my despondency was due to the miserable winter and over-work and how much to my crisis of faith I did not know but my faith had been my main support and now it was weakened. I needed to reinforce it, but with what? Joseph Grant had decided he would keep faith with the Oxford Movement and support Newman's successor but Sutcliffe Sowden and I were not sure. Mr Brontë's simple observation had troubled me. He was, as usual, right, but surely there was more to it than that. I think I was the only Christian in Haworth, at the beginning of '46, who was not triumphant at Newman's defection so there was no one in the village with whom I could talk – no one, it transpired, except Anne.

Within the same week of February '46, Tabby had a fit and Martha developed an inflamed knee. Tabby's fit was not serious but Martha's knee was so painful that we had to bring her down to Sexton House to be nursed by her mother. I gave up my bedroom for her and slept in my parlour on a truckle and on the evening that Martha moved in, Anne Brontë called to see how she was. I was working in my parlour and had no idea that Anne was in the house until I heard the light tap on my half-open door.

"Come in." Callers to my room were invariably members of the Brown family so I was surprised to see Anne. I leaped to my feet. "Miss Brontë!"

"I just wanted to thank you, Mr Nicholls." She was in her heavy winter cloak and carrying her bonnet and gloves.

"Come in, come in." I was only half dressed. "I wasn't expecting … it has been so long." I slipped on my boots and set about buttoning my waistcoat.

"Yes it has and I'm sorry. I have been busy."

"I know," I said, buttoning furiously, "I see you every day in the dining room." I pulled my waistcoat straight and pushed my fingers through my hair. "I expect you have come to see Martha."

"I have seen Martha."

"And how is she now?"

"The knee's still giving her pain but, with the weight off it, I expect we shall see an improvement." Anne's eyes rested on the truckle bed. "It is very good of you to give up your room." I moved to try to cover the bed but of course that was impossible.

"It will be scrubbing the stone flags," I suggested, ignoring the bed, "the cold must strike through to the knees." Anne was standing on my threshold, watching me. Should I invite her in, I wondered, to a single man's study? I hesitated, and then she said,

"How are you Mr Nicholls?"

"Oh, well enough," I tried to sound light, "better than most this long winter." Then she asked me again.

"How are you? I was sorry to hear about John Henry Newman." Her words dropped like a trap. They were so unexpected. Everyone else in Haworth had teased me about Newman but Anne was not teasing, she meant it. I put out my hand to the Windsor chair by the fire.

"Won't you sit down?" She skirted my bed and perched on the edge of the deep-seated chair while I sat on the chair by my desk. "I will admit it was a shock."

"It was a shock to everyone, but to those good churchmen who had put their faith in him ..." she inclined her head sympathetically, "and you, here, alone with no family," she gave me a searching look, "I think Newman must have been important to you." How could she know that? I don't think we'd talked about Newman above once, and to conflate him with my family ...

"Miss Brontë." I clasped my hands together between my knees. "You must not think that I have no family. I have a wonderful family in my aunt and my cousins."

"But no father. We all need a father." She maintained her watch of me.

"Newman as a father-figure?" I forced a laugh and sat back on my chair, "I think you flatter him." Anne turned aside, aware, I think, that she had embarrassed me.

"Well," she said, this time more genially, "perhaps there is another movement in which you can place your trust."

"Another movement?" I was relieved she had moved on from Newman but wary of where she was leading. "I thought you distrusted religious movements, as your father does."

"Certainly, God dwells not in institutions but in our hearts. There is no more personal relationship than the one we have with God but there is a place for Christian fellowship, and unity is preferable to discord, so I wondered what a good churchman might be thinking." *What a good churchman might be thinking!* Was this about Church politics – which I had never ever heard her mention – or was it about me? For one so forthright, Anne could be elusive.

"You are referring, I suspect, to the International Movement of Evangelical Christians." She nodded.

"It is Protestant and Universalist. I read that, on the Continent, the movement has attracted ten times more converts away from Rome than Newman has taken to it. I thought it might appeal to you."

"To a degree," I answered carefully, "but the movement's rejection of the newly discovered patristic texts is a problem. We cannot pretend not to know what we have learned." Anne stiffened.

"You would allow your faith to be qualified by modern scholarship?"

"The four gospels are our essential witness statements, but we now know that others are extant – the testaments of Thomas and Judas for instance – they can only add to our understanding of Christ's time on earth." Anne bridled.

"You would weigh the testimony of Judas with those of John and Matthew? And admit Thomasian doubt into the gospels?"

"Philological discoveries do show …"

"Apocryphal nonsense!" She sprang to her feet. "'*Add thou not unto his words lest he reprove thee and thou be found a liar.*'" She cracked the last word like a whip. "I am very surprised at you Mr Nicholls, and disappointed." Her face was flushed with anger. "If ever I was tempted to think that scholars and clerics could be anything but a hindrance to the attainment of Grace, you have settled the matter." She hurried from my room and, before I could speak or stop her, disappeared down the stairs to the lane.

She had given me no chance to explain. In any exchange, a party has a right of reply but Anne had given me none.

Suddenly, she was cross and upset and then she was gone. I was upset too. Though I'd seen little of her since she'd started writing, I still valued her friendship and to be damned so flatly, on so esoteric a point, seemed barely credible but then, the next morning, I met her again. It was dawn and I was just coming out of the house. The air was cold and, hearing a cough from the top of the lane, I looked up and saw Anne, wrapped in a shawl and hurrying towards me. After our meeting the previous evening I had no wish to meet her but she gave me no choice.

"Mr Nicholls," her voice sounded reedy, "I have been worried that I offended you." She came up close to me, her breath condensing on my lapel. "Are you not afraid to doubt?" she frowned. "You cannot have faith *and* doubt. God's message is very clear isn't it? *Lord, I believe, help thou my unbelief*? I prayed for you last night that you would abandon doubt." Her breathing was wheezy and she coughed again.

"Are you alright?" I asked and she shook her head.

"It's just my asthma. I'm not good on cold mornings."

"Then go back home," I told her, "you shouldn't be out here."

"I will," she nodded, but then, frowning anxiously at me, she added, "I just wanted to tell you." Then she pulled the shawl over her mouth and turned and went back to the parsonage.

I had a parcel delivered that spring that did not belong to me. I had come home late one evening and found it on my desk. It had a note attached from William Hartley, the postmaster, explaining that, while the addressee was a Mr C.

Bell of Parsonage Lane, he knew no such person but I was called Bell so he thought that it might be for me. I could see Hartley's logic and so opened the parcel and in it found three identical copies of a book handsomely bound and evidently straight from the press. '*Poems*' read the title on the cover, '*by Currer, Ellis & Acton Bell*' and below it '4/-'. I took up one of the volumes and turned it in my hands. It was bound in dark green cloth with gilt lettering and there was a geometric design around the edge. The contents of the volume were one hundred and sixty-five pages of sixty-one poems by the three Bells. I was sure that these books were not meant for me. I had never heard of Currer, Ellis or Acton Bell and Hartley would have to look elsewhere for the intended recipient but it was by then beyond Hartley's hours of business so I did not return the books until the following day, by which time, I confess, I had read the poems.

They were attributed and ordered by turns so that a poem by Currer Bell was followed by one by Ellis, then one by Acton and then another by Currer. As I read, the different qualities of the poets became apparent and before I was halfway through, I believe I could have identified the writer of any of the works without the attribution. The poems by Currer and Acton Bell I thought largely unremarkable, although one or two by the latter had a musical quality, but the poems by Ellis Bell were of an altogether different order and it was they that kept me turning the pages, reading and re-reading and writing out copies late into the night. If this was new work, as it appeared to be, then there were among these few poems by Ellis Bell, some of the most spiritually moving I had ever read. The poet demonstrated a love of God that was a revelation to me. He wrote in terms that were comfortable and intimate with the Creator while at the same time in full awe of His power. In all my life, I don't think I had ever been so spiritually moved. The only comparable literature I could think of was the Revelation of Saint John itself and I commit no blasphemy in saying that.

The following day I returned the parcel of books to Mr Hartley. I told him that they were not intended for me but that I would be interested to know who Mr Bell was when he found out. Two days later, Hartley stopped me in the village and told me that Charlotte Brontë had called for the parcel and she had asked that any future mail for Mr Bell be delivered to her.

I was intrigued, it was a mystery, but not for long. It soon struck me that Currer, Ellis and Acton Bell were the thinly veiled *noms de plume* of Charlotte, Emily and Anne Brontë; the initials were the same and listed in the order of the sisters' seniority. I knew that the sisters were writing novels, but nothing about any poems, and what intrigued me now, and I found difficult to accept, was that the sublime verses of Ellis Bell could have been penned by Emily Brontë.

It was an impossible notion. Emily had always paraded – to me at least – a wholly irreligious temperament. She only came to church out of loyalty to her father when she would hide in the corner of the parsonage pew with her head in a book she brought in for the purpose. She sang neither psalms nor responses and it seemed to me, as I observed her across the pews, that her presence in church was more of an insult to her father than a support. I found it incredible that Ellis Bell should be Emily Brontë but my doubts were dispelled two weeks later when I ran into her by Sladen Bridge.

I was on my way up to Stanbury. I had seen a small paddock there, right in the middle of the village, that would make the ideal site for my mission school and, what was better, it was owned by George Taylor, Stanbury's leading churchman. I had an appointment with Mr Taylor, I was hopeful, spring was in the air and, as I strode along under a clear blue sky, I sang aloud as I went,

> 'A thousand thousand gleaming fires
> Seemed kindling in the air;
> A thousand thousand silvery lyres
> Resounded far and near:
>
> Methought, the very breath I breathed
> Was full of sparks divine,
> And all my heather-couch was wreathed
> By that celestial shine!'

– till I came upon Emily. She was sitting on a little stool beside the beck with a pencil and paper in her lap. She stared at me, mortified, and I stopped and stared back, but only for a moment, then I hurried on up the hill towards Stanbury.

During the same week that *Poems* was published, the Revd Edmund Robinson died at Thorp Green. He was forty-six and he left a widow, Lydia, his heir Edmund, formerly in the charge of Branwell, and the three daughters formerly in the charge of Anne. Anne was deeply affected by the news and wrote letters of condolence to her former charges. Branwell too was affected. For four days together he stayed drunk, he did not eat, he barely slept, he wept, shouted and raged and whenever his poor father, half-blind and ill as he was, attempted to pacify him, Branwell repaid him with threats of suicide. It was an extravagant show of self-mortification but how much of it was sparked by remembrance of his injury to Mr Robinson and how much by his sisters' appearance in print, only Branwell would know.

CHAPTER SIX

Seeing some light

Anne stayed shut up with her sisters all summer. There was no doubting their commitment. After morning chores with Tabby and Martha they retired to the dining room and closed the door. They took their dinners in there, emerging during the afternoon for their walk with the dogs, then back again through tea until prayers and then, as often as not, they'd return to burn midnight oil. I was saddened to lose Anne to her sisters. Hadn't we been friends? She clearly cared for the future of my soul so she must have cared something for me but the times I saw Anne on her own that summer, I could count on the fingers of one hand. But then, I too was busy. Not so much in the school by then; Anne's protégé, May Wright, had proved excellent, and we had engaged a full-time master to relieve me of the boys so, if Anne had been about in Parsonage Lane, chances were, I would not have run into her. My duties in the village were all-consuming and what time I could spare I spent up at Stanbury and the outlying farms trying to raise funds for my mission school. George Taylor had given me a wonderful start with his donation of the paddock and I was eager to build on that so, with one thing and another, I saw little of Anne until late August when, with her father and Charlotte away, my duties brought us together.

Charlotte had persuaded her father – or bullied him – into having one of his cataracts surgically removed. She had found a practitioner in Manchester who had developed a new technique. There were declared risks to it and convalescence would be slow but Mr Brontë had, in the end, agreed and so, at the end of August, Charlotte travelled with him to Manchester where they would stay for six weeks.

The parsonage felt strange without them. With the king post and a major spar removed, the edifice felt insecure – especially with Emily and Branwell at home – but Anne was there too and, when I called each morning to go through the mail there was always the chance I might meet her. For the first few days I was disappointed – she remained shut up with Emily – but, on the Wednesday of the second week, I was surprised when it was Anne who opened the door to me. She was cheerful and welcoming and she followed me into the parlour to help me sort through the mail. She did the same on the following day too and on the day after that, she was light-hearted and wanting to talk, which suited me: it was all I had wanted all summer. She asked me what I had been doing, especially in the school and at Stanbury. When I asked her about her own summer, she said 'oh, just working' but then, round about the middle of September, she received some news about her work that she shared with me. I don't think she had intended to share it with me but time and place were so aligned that, in the end, she could not resist.

We had been talking about Emily and *Poems*. I had decided I wouldn't mention the poems – I wasn't sure I was supposed to know – but then, in the middle of September, I saw a review of them in such an unexpected quarter that I couldn't help but tell Anne. The review was in my alma mater's journal, *The Dublin University Magazine*. The magazine is devoted to the interests of the university's alumni so I was surprised – nay, astonished – to find in its columns a review of *Poems by Currer, Ellis and Acton Bell*. I took the magazine up to the parsonage and showed it to Anne while we opened the mail. She had taken it to the window to one of the chairs and I pulled up the other to sit with her.

"Ah, they have printed my poem, *A Reminiscence*." She smiled at the page and then laughed. "'*The tone of all these little poems is certainly uniform …*'" She shot me her smile. "The reviewer thinks we are one author. '… u*niform in a sort of Cowperian amiability and sweetness, no-wise unfragrant to our critical nostrils.*' Well I shall be satisfied with Cowperian, Mr Nicholls. What do you say?"

"I should be very pleased with Cowperian," I told her. "Congratulations." Anne passed the magazine back to me and I folded it into my lap. "But the reviewer should have noticed the different styles."

"Ah, so, you have read the poems."

"I have, yes." I rested my hands on the magazine.

"And did you discern different styles?" *Did I discern different styles*? How to answer that? I crossed my legs and looked out over the burial ground.

"The poems of Ellis Bell …" I began, choosing my words, "there is a oneness with nature in them, a oneness with the Creator that I found transcending." I looked back at Anne and opened my hands. "I am making no comparisons here," I told her, "what I might say about Ellis Bell's poems implies no criticism of the others, far from it, but I was moved by Ellis Bell's poems, they soar above Cowper's hymns, even, I would say, to the language of prayer." I looked back out over the burial ground and then, after a few moments, added, "but I do wonder at the mind that created them." Anne did not blench.

"You wonder at Emily." I raised an eyebrow and sat back in my chair. Now it was Anne's turn to look out of the window. "I like your word *oneness*." She said with emphasis. "Emily never could understand why she might need a third party to achieve oneness with God – not a priest, not a Church, certainly not an international movement of Churches." I took the touché. "But where is salvation in Emily's work? She loves God, of that there is no doubt, but where is Christ the Saviour? In all her work you will not find Him. Emily loves God's Creation to be sure and she articulates its power as effectively as any poet that lived but no amount of empathy with this world will prepare Emily for the next. Nothing in her poetry suggests to me that she has any privileged knowledge of what is to come. All that Emily can know is what the rest of us know and that is written in the scriptures – the scriptures that she shuns." Anne frowned down at her hands. I was expected to respond but, if Emily had lapsed, I knew better than to come between sisters.

"We are not to judge." I offered.

"No. But we can advise those we love. Show them the way to the truth." She shot me her penetrating look. "Are we not *required* to save souls?" Here was Anne, the saver of souls, reminding me of my ordained duty, but I couldn't reach Emily Brontë.

"No one will be more concerned for Emily than your father, Anne, and no one is better qualified." It was the coward's answer and Anne's eyes still held me.

"But you will pray for her?"

"Yes," I conceded awkwardly, "I will pray for her." Anne lowered her eyes and I turned in my chair in relief. "So," I said, returning to the poems, "you continue at your desks. Does this mean that we can expect a second volume of poems sometime soon?"

"Oh no," she waved the idea away, "no more poems. That was Charlotte's idea and a complete waste of money, no …" she bit her lip and her cheeks coloured as if suppressing a smile.

"Something amusing you?" She put back her head and looked up at the ceiling but her smile would not be suppressed. She looked out of the window.

"Can you keep a confidence, Mr Nicholls?"

"I think you know that." She turned back to me.

"I have learned this week that my novel has been accepted by a publisher."

"Well, well, well!" I slapped my hand on my knee. "Congratulations! No wonder you look so pleased with yourself. And your sisters? Are their novels to be published too?"

"Mr Newby – that's my publisher – he has reservations about Emily's story. He is asking her to do more work to it."

"And Charlotte's?"

"The Professor?" Anne rolled her eyes. "I told Charlotte from the beginning that she couldn't write in a man's voice but she wouldn't have it. I am afraid Mr Newby has rejected Charlotte's altogether."

Which was why Anne had time for me. Her novel was off her desk. She had no father to read to and no Charlotte to dance to. Emily was still at home, but busy reworking her story, and Branwell was lost to oblivion so Anne joined me with the mail in the mornings and then, in the evenings, sat with us at Sexton House. She would come down after tea to enjoy the late sun with Mary and the girls and, if I were at home, with me too. I was so pleased to have her back with us and those September evenings of '46 are some of my sweetest memories of Haworth: the accumulated warmth of summer radiating off the Sexton House wall; the fullness and stillness of that pendant season and the happy banter of the girls. Anne was in her element with the girls.

"I just love the little ones," she confided one evening watching Hannah, "I sometimes wish they'd never grow up and now Mary won't have any more."

"But you will have your own children," I'd told her, and that wistful shroud had veiled her eyes.

I enjoyed those six weeks in charge – occupying the parsonage parlour as if it were my own and Anne at my side – it felt so natural. We sorted the mail together and chatted at our leisure about the chapelry and my work and Anne's hopes for her book while the soft autumn light slanted in through the parlour's sash windows. It was a time for us both to reflect on how far we had come. Anne was drawing on her experience as a governess to be a published author – ahead of her sisters – while I, after eighteen months' intensive induction, could survey the chapelry content there was nothing with which I could not cope. I had had a baptism of fire and, as if in confirmation, on 20th September, I was ordained priest. I had been ordained deacon just before I arrived in Haworth but now, along with twenty others, I was to go to Ripon to become a full priest. It was the culmination of my life's ambition: a day heady with ceremony and holy mystery but when I went down on my knees before the Lord Bishop, it was not holy mystery that flooded my mind but Anne Brontë. When Bishop Longley asked me, '*Are you persuaded that the holy scriptures contain sufficiently all doctrine required of necessity for eternal salvation?*' I heard Anne's rebuke: '*We already have God's Word and Christ's message, they are inalienable truths.*' Before God and my bishop I could answer in truth, '*I am so persuaded.*'

Mr Brontë came home at the end of September and there was a wonderful change in him. I went up to see him the day he arrived. He looked fit and well, although his left eye being blue while his right remained white, disconcerted. He stepped forward from his hearth to examine me.

"It is good to see you Mr Nicholls."

"It is very good to see you Sir."

"You know," he observed, scrutinising me, "for an Antrim man, you're not a bad-looking fellow." We laughed and moved together to the chairs in the window. Mr Brontë was eager to learn everything he had missed: who had died and who was on relief, what was the state of trade and the school and how was I doing in Stanbury? It was marvellous to see him so hungrily gathering back to himself the reins of control and, over the next few days, he visited every corner of the village, seeing sights he'd not seen for a year or more and then, when he got back to his parlour, he wrote. He wrote to the vicar and the bishop demanding their concern for the plight of his flock; he wrote to colleagues and friends, simply because he could, and he wrote to the newspapers. Spurred, no doubt, by his experience in Manchester, he wrote to the *Leeds Mercury* advocating the use of sulphuric ether as an ocular anaesthetic. He wrote to the *Leeds Intelligencer* twice: his first letter proposing salaried sub-deacons and his second compulsory education, and, in a flourish of boyish enthusiasm typical of his new mood, he wrote to the Master General of the Queen's Ordnance outlining plans for a projectile that could penetrate the hulls of ships. It was wonderful to see him so miraculously restored and back in control.

'Now, Mr Nicholls, you must take yourself off for a holiday,' he told me, 'go home to your family and enjoy your earned rest.' It was an offer I was pleased to accept.

It had been eighteen months since I was last in Ireland and what I found there shocked me. The landscapes I rode through were strangely deserted. The grey stone walls still marked out the patchwork of fields and cabins but there was barely a soul to be seen. In Banagher itself the population had shrunk from three thousand to two and those that were left looked oppressed. People had moved to the larger towns simply to find food, or further, to the ports to leave Ireland for ever. It was a disaster of Old Testament proportions, Ireland was changed for ever but, as I was driven past the lodge and up the lime avenue, I found Cuba House quite unchanged.

Cuba House had been my uncle's house. It went with his position of Master of the Royal Free School that occupied buildings on the estate. It was a Palladian mansion of six bays on four floors built in the 1730s for the retired governor of Cuba and it had been my home since I was seven. My Uncle Alan had died in '39, since when another master had been running the school, but my aunt and cousins still lived in the house and Aunt Harriette's welcome was full of maternal concern.

"Mr Brontë's sound an eccentric brood," she observed one evening after supper. "I think you must exaggerate in your letters just to amuse me." We were taking coffee in her small parlour. It was the old housekeeper's room that she had adopted as her private sanctuary and, while my cousins entertained themselves in the rest of the house, we talked. I pooh-poohed the charge that I exaggerated.

"Mr Brontë is a good man – generous, broad-minded, astute – and an exemplary Christian. If he is eccentric it is only because he cares more for the Word than the Church."

"I meant his children seem eccentric. The daughter that snubs you and the one that wanders off in all weathers and the louche son – there seems to be only one that is normal." She sat back and raised an eyebrow. "I think you are fond of Anne Brontë."

Fond! Now there was a coaxing euphemism! I took a drink of my coffee. I would freely admit that Anne and I were friends, but in the way that Aunt Harriette insinuated?

"She's a lot more friendly than her sisters," I hedged, "and good – good in the village – visiting the sick – and she's very good with children – Anne cares about people. Why are you smirking?"

"Watching you babble."

"I wasn't babbling … was I?" My aunt laughed.

"Bless you, Arthur. You can be so gauche." She took up her coffee. "So … there is a rude one, a wild one and one who's a saint."

"I didn't say Anne was a saint."

"Nor did you say she was pretty." Aunt Harriette raised her eyebrow again and this time I had to smile.

"Yes aunt, Anne Brontë is pretty. She has large, violet eyes, a small chin and rosebud lips."

"There you are then. That wasn't difficult was it? How old is she?"

"Anne?"

"Arthur!"

"Err … twenty-six?"

"One year your junior. That's companionable, but getting late for starting a family." I leaned over my knees and groaned. My aunt had just leaped three fences ahead, further than I intended to follow but she bore on. "You say she cares about people?"

"Everyone. She's a very caring person."

"Does she care about *you*?"

Does Anne Brontë care about me? My aunt was unstoppable but I knew she'd have to be answered. I sat back in my chair. Anne and I were friends, I was sure of that. I had been the 'someone sensible' to whom she had unburdened herself when Charlotte came home; we had confided our ambitions to each other and she worried about the destination of my soul, but did Anne care about *me*? I thought about our walk round the garden and the touch of her hand on my arm, and then how she'd withdrawn from me, writing her book, then come out to chastise me only to be friendly again while always there was that veil, that shroud shielding her sadness. I could only answer truthfully.

"I don't know."

"Do you care about her?" I looked back across the hearth at my aunt. Despite her bereavements and struggles to raise her family alone, she was still beautiful: tall and straight, her grey hair tied back to frame fine bones and eyes that demanded the truth.

"Yes," I told her. "I believe I do."

The Haworth I returned to was already blanketed with snow and a bitter easterly was cutting up Parsonage Lane. Everyone was coughing: John Brown from his stone-dust, Branwell from neglect, Charlotte and Emily with head-colds and Mr Brontë and Anne were confined to their beds – he with influenza and she with her asthma.

I'd thought a lot about Anne on the journey back. I had always hoped that I would someday marry and have children of my own, but with Anne? I could imagine it: the clerical daughter as the clerical wife, the gifted teacher as an exemplary mother, the published author as a source of worldly pride – and I knew it would take nothing for me to fall in love with her – if she would let me – if she could raise her gaze from a dead curate to a living one. I decided, as my train neared Keighley, that I would be bolder with Anne; I would show her that I cared for her and was ready to stand by her so, when I got back to find that she was unwell, I immediately penned her a 'get well' note and took it up to the parsonage. Martha was in the kitchen with Tabby and, after we had exchanged pleasantries about doings in Haworth and Ireland, I asked Martha if she would take my note up to Anne. She said that she would but then, just as I was putting the note into her hand, Charlotte's head popped round the door.

"I am going up to Anne," she told Martha. "Is there anything to take up to her?" Had Charlotte overheard us? Had she been listening at the door? Considering that it was the first time she had set eyes on me since I got back, her manner was exceedingly brusque, even for her. Martha darted me a look but I said nothing.

"No, you're alright," Martha told Charlotte, and Charlotte looked down at the note. She hesitated.

"Here y'are." Tabby turned in her chair and lifted a saucepan off the range. "Take her a posset up if yer goin'." Tabby poured the warm milk into a tall cup then added a little wine from the cupboard. "Tell her to drink it warm." Tabby stirred the posset and pushed it across the table to Charlotte who, stiff-lipped, came forward to take it. She still wasn't acknowledging me.

"Good morning, Miss Charlotte," I said.

"Good morning to you," she replied, still not looking at me. "I trust you enjoyed your relatives." And she was gone.

What was it about Charlotte that she always managed to wrong-foot me? I had done nothing wrong and yet I was left feeling guilty. Because I had baulked, for a second, at allowing Charlotte to deliver my innocent note, the servants sensed intrigue and volunteered themselves into a conspiracy which Charlotte picked up on, putting me, in her mind, in improper collusion with them. Martha delivered my note, but I never got a reply.

Anne continued ill throughout that hard winter. In the three months following my return from Ireland I don't think I once saw her out of doors; the snow was too deep and the fogs too damp for her fragile lungs. Anne's asthma was weakening her and I worried about her but worry was all I could do because I could not get near her. After that golden interlude in September, the parsonage was again bustling with people and when Anne did eventually come downstairs she retired to the dining room with her sisters. I wondered what she was doing in there. Charlotte and Emily would be re-drafting their rejected novels, I imagined, but what kept Anne in there? I never heard another thing about her book being published. Perhaps something had gone wrong. Perhaps Anne's novel too had, in the end, been rejected. I didn't know and I couldn't ask. Again, I felt I'd been shut out.

The heavy snow in December turned to steady rain in January and conditions in the village slid from miserable to awful. For want of fuel, the homes of the poorest ran with damp and cellar dwellings flooded with filth. If one household suffered consumption another suffered typhus or dysentery and there was much sad work for John and me in the burial ground. Conditions were no better down in Keighley where the senior physician there, Dr Milligan, gave a series of lectures on the diseases of his poor with recommendations on how to avoid them such as clean water and piped sewerage. Milligan's lectures drew wide support, including that of the Rector of Keighley, Mr Busfield. Similarly, in Bradford, our vicar, Dr Scoresby, wrote a book exposing the squalid condition of his poor parishioners and so Mr Brontë and I decided that we too should campaign for improvements in Haworth. Obviously, there would be expense: surveyors would have to be consulted, plans drawn and the ratepayers persuaded. I approached our young physician, Dr Wheelhouse, to canvas his support for the enterprise and he suggested that we meet at the Black Bull, which was where I found him, one February evening, just finishing his dinner.

The bar parlour was quiet when I walked in and Wheelhouse was at a table by the fire having his plates cleared away by the landlady .

"Mr Nicholls!" He waved to me. "What will you have?" Ordinarily, I do not drink in the village inns but the occasion demanded it so I said I'd have porter. "Fetch Mr Nicholls a pint of porter will you, Hannah?" He balanced his brandy glass on the landlady's plates. "And you might as well fetch me another of those."

John Wheelhouse was about my own age and lived in lodgings in West Lane, although he dined in the Black Bull. He was heavy built with thick auburn hair that hung lank on his collar and his devotion to his calling was drawn in dark rings under his eyes. We sat over our drinks talking about the public health and the prospects for improvements and Wheelhouse was supportive. He told me he was fully persuaded of the connection between inadequate sanitation and disease and he said he would support our campaign in any way he could. It was an encouraging start and, as I was inwardly rehearsing my report to Mr Brontë, his son walked into the bar.

"Ah, Wheelhouse!" Branwell cried across the room. "What ho, what ho! Applying leeches to the curate's purse?" His face was flushed and his eyes glazed and he staggered unsteadily towards us.

"Hello, Branwell," I greeted him flatly. "Actually, I am Dr Wheelhouse's guest." Branwell slumped into a chair and smiled stupidly at us each in turn. We weren't going to be able to continue our conversation with Branwell in that condition so I made ready to leave but Branwell stopped me.

"I wager you think I've come to coax a drink off you." He fumbled in his pocket and pulled out a shilling. "Well you're wrong! See!" He held up the coin between forefinger and thumb and twisted it like a jewel. "Earned wages these! Commission from Wilson Greenwood at the King's Arms for persuading a brace of travelling gents to put up for the night." He brought his flushed face up to mine. "Know ye not the Guytrash?" he snarled. "The great hound howled yester 'een on Crow Hill on the moor road over to Colne." He gave me a lurid grimace then sat back in his chair. "I told 'em stuff like that. Tales of travellers lost, their entrails dragged along the turnpike and dumped in Nan Bog." He threw back his head and laughed; laughter that brought on a coughing fit. "I made more of the tale than that," he added, holding his chest, "two pints with chasers it cost them before they were frightened enough to put up for the night." He turned the shilling in his fingers. "And this for me from Greenwood." He gave me a smile. "I'm off to the bar." He scraped his chair across the flags and pointed at Wheelhouse. "Don't go away."

Branwell fell into conversation at the bar and I dared to hope we were rid of him but, five minutes later, he came back with a tankard of ale in one hand and a gin in the other. He had picked up on our conversation.

"Are you two talking about sewage?" He sank heavily into a chair. "Is this then *le sujet de la mode* among the educated classes these days? Did our intellectual fancies soar so high that our wax wings melted and we fell into a mess of sewage?" Branwell took a sip of his gin and then, returning it carefully to the table, asked to know what we were talking about. Wheelhouse outlined for him the detrimental effects of poor sanitation on the public health – a connection that Branwell seemed to apprehend – and then he told him how we hoped to introduce measures that would improve things in Haworth.

"Laudable!" he said. "Who will pay?"

"Given the improvement in public health that proper sanitation will bring," I told him, "we think there will be no extra cost to the ratepayers beyond the initial investment."

"So the ratepayers will have to find the capital investment?"

"That's right. There is no other source of finance and the improvements would be in the ratepayers' interest." Branwell thought for a moment.

"No." He shook his head. "They won't buy it. Half the ratepayers these days are in default and most of those that aren't live outside the village and have their own springs and cesspits so why would they pay for what they don't need?"

"It is not a matter of private needs," I explained. "It is a matter of everybody recognising the public good, the improvement to the general health of the whole community."

"Altruism?"

"Yes, and enlightened Christian charity. It is how our society functions."

"That may be, Sir, in the generality," Branwell leaned in to me, "but who in Haworth do you think will pay for his neighbours' drains?"

"There are men of means in Haworth who are also good Christians."

"Name three," Branwell challenged me, and I began to protest. "No, no. Indulge me," he insisted, "as you say, there are some wealthy Christian gentlemen in Haworth – I could name them all – but indulge me – name any three."

"All right." I thought for a moment. "Joseph Greenwood of Springhead, James Greenwood of Bridgehouse and Michael Merrall of Syke." Branwell visibly brightened. He sat forward on the edge of his chair and took a draught of his ale.

"An intelligent choice, Nicholls." Branwell's eyes were dancing. "An interesting combination. Two men of trade and an aspiring gentleman: a Dissenter and a Churchman and another who has changed his stripe, but all wealthy and all active in their chosen religion. Let us see if we can forecast their response to your sewerage scheme." Branwell drained his tankard and chased it down with the dregs of his gin. "Get me a pint in will you, Wheelhouse? I'm working rather well here." Dr Wheelhouse looked over to me. I covered my tankard with my hand and he took Branwell's and his own empty glass to the bar.

"Joseph Greenwood, Justice of the Peace, Lord of the Manor of Oxenhope, retired spinner and aspirant to the status of Gent. You will certainly get nothing from him." Branwell tapped the table with his knuckle. "Well, you might get the famous five bob that he gives to every public cause so that his name will appear on the subscription list. Joseph Greenwood detests public spending: it is the driving passion of his life." Dr Wheelhouse came back with his brandy and a fresh tankard of ale for Branwell who immediately took a long draught.

"I'm sorry," I told Branwell. "But I must tell you that, in my experience, Joseph Greenwood is an extremely conscientious public figure. He sits on the boards of schools and charities and as to the current issue, I cannot think of a subscription list on which his name did not appear."

"Yes! Five bob Joe!" Branwell nodded vigorously. "He sits on charity and school boards so that he can oppose expenditure." Branwell took another draught of his ale. "Who else did you say? Oh yes, his brother James, Master of Bridgehouse Mill. He won't pay. All his properties are down in the valley, he's no interest in the village, but the Merralls might, as long as they can see a profit in it, business is business after all." Branwell looked aside into the flames of the fire. He sat pondering for a few moments, chewing the inside of his cheek, then he said, still into the fire,

"Wealthy Christians." He looked up at me. "Do you not see the irony of it, Mr Nicholls? The oxymoron? The camel and the needle's eye? No man who takes the meagre comforts of his neighbour and heaps them upon his own gross pile can properly be called a Christian. Joseph and James Greenwood – and yes – the Merralls, they've all learned to suppress their charitable instincts and, like the King of Phrygia, turned to the worship of gold." I exchanged a look with Wheelhouse who sat back to distance himself.

"There were five hundred handlooms in this valley when I was a boy," Branwell went on, "and what he made from his loom kept the weaver in his own home and on his own land but he cannot do that now. Since the Greenwoods and the Merralls and the rest of them erected their satanic mills, the yeoman weaver of the Worth Valley has had to abandon his sturdy cot, move off his ancestral land and put his wife and children to work for a master's pittance, living in a master's hovel with neither light nor air nor place to dump his filth." Wheelhouse nodded gravely at this while I – perhaps more used to warm words – stayed impassive. "You think me a rambling romantic, don't you, Nicholls?"

"No," I told him. "Dr Wheelhouse and I are here to address some of the problems you allude to but James Greenwood, Dissenter though he is, is neither Godless nor callous and nor is Mr Merrall."

"Because they support Chapel and Church you mean?"

"Well yes, and their moral conduct besides." Branwell sat up to the edge of the table.

"How moral is it to employ children when their fathers have no work?" I did not answer. "Well I don't think it is. James Greenwood worked his children from six in the morning till eight at night until the Factory Act stopped him, and for less than five shillings a week. The Merralls were prosecuted for working their children beyond the permitted hours and it is not only their time and labour that the masters want, they demand their hands very souls." I had listened to Branwell's tirade out of respect for his father but I could not permit blasphemy and I told him so.

"You think I blaspheme?" he bridled, "how long do you think you would remain in James Greenwood's employ if you didn't attend the Baptist Chapel twice every Sunday? Or the Merralls' if you didn't go to Church?" He jutted his chin at me. "And why do you think the mill masters insist on that?" He looked fiercely from me to Wheelhouse and back to me but it was a rhetorical question. "For you to put the fear of God into them. That's why. Keep their people docile, keep them in dread." He sat back in his chair. "Blasphemy indeed!" He scoffed. "You are in an unholy alliance, Mr Nicholls. You and Papa and the Dissenting ministers are the mill owners' beagles, their whips to keep their hands in hand, that's the only reason they support you, so don't expect their charity, for drains or anything else."

There would not be many more occasions when I would find Branwell so lucid. His tortured nights left him exhausted and he generally slept during the day but one morning, not long after his tirade in the Black Bull, I met him again and I shall always remember it as his final surrender.

I was leaving Mr Brontë's parlour when Branwell came down the hall. He looked unkempt and hollow-eyed and he was wearing his burgundy coat that, by then, looked as battered as he. I was on my way to church to conduct a memorial service and we walked together as far as the gate. The passing bell was tolling.

"Who's that for?" Branwell asked me, his eyes on the path.

"A memorial service for Katherine Holmes. She died of a fever in London and her employer had her buried there." Branwell looked up at me.

"Katherine Holmes of Middle Laithe?"

"Yes."

"Poor Kate." He frowned. "She was pretty. What was she? Twenty-five?"

"Twenty-six."

"Poor Kate," he said again, "I liked her." Branwell returned his gaze to the path.

"Come and join us then." I suggested. "Her family, I'm sure, would be glad to see you there." But Branwell shook his head.

"No eulogies. I *knew* Kate. I don't need her memory filleted by someone who didn't."

"Then at least come and pray for her." We stopped at the garden gate and Branwell turned to me.

"You pray for Kate, Mr Nicholls. I'll see her soon enough." He put up his collar and gave me a sad smile. "Until then, I shall hey me off to high Cithaeron and join Dionysus' dance until *I* reach the Elysian Fields." Then he thrust his hands into his pockets and set off for the moors.

CHAPTER SEVEN

The novels of Currer, Ellis and Acton Bell

Anne was prostrated with her asthma throughout that winter and it was April before she ventured out on her own. I saw her occasionally: huddled between her sisters in the parsonage pew, or crossing the hall when I arrived for my morning meetings. She would give me a smile and a word when we met but it looked like an effort; she was stooped and breathless and I think she just hadn't the strength. I worried about her. She was clearly unwell and, if her permanent frown were anything to go by, unhappy too, but then who would not be, confined indoors for four months? Coming back from Ireland I had vowed I'd be bolder with Anne but what could I do? There was no chance of a proper conversation with her; not in the parsonage with her sisters in one room, her father in the other and Tabby ruling the kitchen so we did not get beyond smiles and pleasantries until the warm westerlies drew her out for short walks and to church, which was where, eventually, we met.

She had waited back for me after evensong. I had preached on Isaiah 53, '*And to whom is the arm of the Lord revealed?*' It was not uncommon for one of our combative parishioners to wait back to challenge me on some aspect of my sermon but when the diminutive figure, swaddled in bonnet and cloak, turned out to be Anne, my heart rose.

"I enjoyed your sermon, Mr Nicholls," she called to me as I walked up from the vestry, "but you raised an important question that I don't think you fully answered." The church was empty and almost dark. The only lamp still burning was over the north door and Anne was standing beneath it.

"What question is that, Miss Anne?"

"Is faith in the gift of God?" It was a question to shake the church floor and not one I'd have chosen to rekindle our friendship but the set of Anne's brow left no choice.

"Yes," I answered, joining her under the lamp, "faith is the greatest of all God's gifts." In the lamp's low glow, Anne still looked frail: dark shadows sagged from her eyes, her skin was dry and her brow knitted with worry.

"Then it is a gift that God can both bestow and withhold?"

"Ah," I now recognised the argument, "you are worried by the Calvinist heresy that God elects some people to Grace and abandons the rest to damnation."

"Let us not confuse the issue with words like *heresy*, Mr Nicholls; this is a matter of the most fundamental importance. If a sinner – any sinner – fervently repents, even at the eleventh hour, will they be admitted to Grace?" I smiled reassuringly.

"Isaiah 53. It is there in the last verse. '*He was numbered with the transgressors and He bore the sin of many and made intercession for the transgressors*'. It is why God sent us his Son."

"Then Christ will intercede with God for anyone who genuinely repents of their sins? Even at the last hour?"

"Even at the last hour."

"But to be redeemed we must have faith?" I nodded. "And faith can be found by anyone who seeks it." I nodded again. "Then if that is true, if faith is universally attainable through the effort of man's free will, it is not in the gift of God."

So, that was what was worrying Anne: her old anxiety about faith and doubt; the same anxiety that she had brought to me all those months ago in my parlour and then stormed out. I wasn't going to let that happen again so I tried a fresh tack.

"Miss Anne." I gave her a warm smile. "I understand that you were close to the aunt who looked after you when your mother passed on, the late Miss Branwell?" Anne's frown deepened.

"How does that signify?"

"Your aunt was a Methodist was she not?"

"And my father is an Anglican. What are you saying?"

"I merely wish to say that you are more likely to find comfort in the teachings of your father, a trained and experienced minister, than in the nursery lessons of a Dissenting maiden aunt." Anne's face flushed.

"Is this your advice then? On the gravest question that any of us has to face? Listen to a man before a woman?" Her eyes scanned mine, darting from one to the other, searching for some hidden truth that I did not have. I felt stupid. 'Be bolder with Anne' I'd promised myself yet on this – of all issues for a priest – I seemed destined always to fail her. My heart sank. I didn't know what to say. I could feel her drifting away from me – *again*. I threw out my arms to her.

"I just don't think you need to worry," I told her. "I have not the trace of a shadow of a doubt about the destination of your immortal soul." She looked desolate.

"I am not worried about myself. I am worried about Branwell. And about Emily." She was on the verge of tears and I didn't know what to do. Nothing I could think of to say seemed adequate. I wanted to hold her, it was the only response, to enfold her in my arms and melt with my warmth the furrows from her brow and those deep-grained anxieties that deprived her of peace but of course I could not.

"*I* am worried about *you*," I told her. "I am worried that you worry about others while you are careless of yourself. I am worried that you are so unwell." She lowered her eyes to the flags.

"That is kind of you, but spring is almost here. I am always better in the spring."

"Then you must promise me you'll come out in the spring. Leave your desk and get some fresh air. Let us all see you more – let *me* see you more." She raised her eyes and, at long last, smiled.

"I promise," she said, "when my book is finished."

"But your book is finished. You told me six months ago that it is to be published."

"This is another book, a more important book, more important to me than my health so, thank you Mr Nicholls, please, yes, pray for Branwell and Emily – and pray for me."

I felt rebuffed. I am not a demanding man, God knows, give me a glimmer of hope and I will shoulder my load and trudge on for months – as I *had* trudged on for months – battling through snow to sit with the sick and the dying, warmed only by the hope that, when she was well, Anne would leave her desk and be friends again. Only now, Anne would not be leaving her desk, she was writing a second book, so where now was my glimmer of hope? How long does it take to write a book? A year? Longer? And when that book was finished, would there not be another – each one more important than the last and more important than her health? I despaired for her; I despaired for myself.

The sisters' routine continued: chores after breakfast then into the dining room till afternoon and their walk. I did see Anne from time to time, when, in passing, she would give me a smile and a word, but it was not till late spring, when Miss Nussey came to stay, that we next were able to talk. It was Miss Nussey's first visit to the parsonage in two years. Charlotte had been so ashamed of Branwell that she had debarred her friend from coming, but now Branwell was so little in evidence that Charlotte had raised her embargo. The afternoon was hot, I remember. I was returning from a meeting in Stanbury where six more of our members had pledged funds for the school. I was calling to give on Mr Brontë the good news and, when I entered the parsonage garden, I saw Miss Nussey and the sisters sitting under the hawthorn with the dogs. I tipped them my hat as I passed and bid them a good day. Miss Nussey had smiled and Charlotte and Emily ignored me, so it had fallen to Anne to respond.

"Mr Nicholls," she called out, "have you a moment?" I stepped onto the grass and walked over to them while Flossy, without lifting his head, banged his tail on the grass. "Let me introduce you to Miss Nussey." Miss Nussey was sitting between Charlotte and Anne on the rustic seat while Emily sat facing them on a kitchen chair. Emily rose and plucked up her chair by the rail.

"Oh, don't go, Emily," Miss Nussey pleaded, but Emily nudged Keeper with her foot.

"Keeper's too hot," she said. "Stupid dog won't go in until I do." Keeper looked up at Emily and rolled heavily onto his feet. She clicked her tongue at him and, ignoring me, took him and her chair into the house.

"Ellen," Anne said. "This is Mr Nicholls."

"I thought it must be." She gave me a smile. "How are you Mr Nicholls?"

"Hot, if I'm frank." I glanced round the base of the tree for signs of tea but there were none. "I have just walked down from Stanbury." Anne jumped to her feet,

"Then let me get you a cordial," but Charlotte was quicker.

"I'll get it," she insisted and she hurried off into the house after Emily.

"Come and sit in the shade." Miss Nussey patted the bench beside her and Anne resumed her seat. Miss Nussey was short, about Anne's height. She was plump and fair as an English peach and she glowed with health and contentment. Like Anne and Charlotte, she was wearing white lawn with embroidered collar and cap. I felt large beside her, and very hot.

"How are you coping with our Yorkshire ways, Mr Nicholls?"

"Oh, well enough I think. I've just about got the measure of the people here and they of me."

"And you subscribe, I understand, to the Oxford Movement."

"Ellen!" Anne scolded. "Where have you got that from?"

"No, no. That's alright," I insisted, "I did once but not anymore."

"Oh? And what turned you? Mr Newman's defection I dare say."

"Really Ellen!" Anne said again but I did not mind.

"Yes, Miss Nussey, it was. As far as I am concerned Newman was too important a leader to lose and I think now that the movement is adrift."

"I agree with you, Mr Nicholls. Newman is principled and brave. I admire him."

"You admire his move to Rome?" Miss Nussey laughed.

"Heavens no! I? Who was schooled by Moravians? I have no more truck with Rome than Charlotte has but I admire strongly principled men and Newman is an heroic example." Charlotte arrived with the barley water and I stood to accept it.

"Now then, Ellen," Charlotte said, wiping her hands together, "if you are ready. I promised Mr Greenwood I would show you to him, we are expected for tea."

"Which Mr Greenwood is that, Charlotte?"

"Joseph Greenwood of Springhead."

"The bald one with the spinning mill?"

"He was a spinner, yes, but he has retired from trade. He is a gentleman now."

"A *gentleman*?" Miss Nussey pulled a face. "I thought he was a Baptist!"

"He was a Baptist but he has joined the Church, and the Tory Party, to become a JP."

"Well, well, well!" Miss Nussey looked up at me and raised an eyebrow. "A *gentleman* in Haworth! Were there ever such times? I shall have to be on my best behaviour shan't I, Mr Nicholls?" I returned Miss Nussey's knowing smile and Charlotte stepped up to her.

"Yes, you will, now pick up your reticule." I passed Miss Nussey her reticule and she took my hand.

"It has been very nice meeting you, Mr Nicholls."

"And you too," I told her, then the friends linked arms and went off to the village leaving Anne and me on our own.

"Miss Nussey seems nice," I said, resuming my end of the seat.

"Forthright," said Anne.

"I don't mind *forthright*." I put my empty glass down under the seat. "I am quite used to *forthright* by now." I looked over to the gate where we had last seen the two friends. "Miss Nussey and Charlotte seem very attached."

"Oh yes." Anne too was looking at the gate.

"I was about to say 'like sisters' but the epithet is hardly apt in your case."

"Nor in Ellen's. She is the youngest of twelve and her mother still has two more daughters at home besides Ellen." Anne lowered her head and absently examined her boots. "More like Darby and Joan."

"Darby and Joan? I thought they were an old married couple?"

"Well," Anne absently turned her feet to put her toecaps together. "Charlotte does like Ellen to call her Charles." She looked back at the gate. "It's nice for Charlotte. She loves Ellen. They make each other happy. I sometimes think that if she and Ellen could be together always, Charlotte would be quite content."

Anne looked so well now, I thought. It was hard to believe how ruined she had looked just a few weeks before but, even as she gazed at the gate, she still frowned.

"Are you alright Anne?" I said, and you might have thought I had struck her. Her face crumpled and her shoulders sank. I didn't know what I'd done. I didn't know what to say. I sat looking at her and then, with tears glistening, she said,

"I am in conflict with Emily."

"With Emily? Over her apostasy?"

"Over her novel."

"I thought it had been rejected."

"She did some more work to it. Newby is going to publish it now." She turned to me. "Mr Nicholls, it is so un-Christian. So vicious. It offers nothing to the world but depravity – depravity and despair." Her tears spilled. "It is an abuse of her gifts. We who have an education have a duty to enlighten, to try to make the world a better place. There are enough forces working to degrade the world without those who should know better offering their support." Anne pulled a handkerchief from her sleeve and pressed it to her eyes. "But Emily does not listen to me anymore. *The twins*, Ellen used to call us. How many years ago is that?" She dabbed at her eyes then rested her hands in her lap. "I love Emily. That is why I confront her but she is so set on this story that she is quite prepared to lose me for it." Anne looked so alone at her end of the seat. There is a force in nature that demands we reach out to tears and I wanted to comfort Anne but of course I could not and so stayed at my end of the seat.

"But *your* book is still going to be published isn't it?"

"Yes, with *hers*." Anne gave a bitter laugh. "Nine months, Newby has been sitting on my manuscript and now he is going to publish it with Emily's abomination."

"Why would he do that?"

"Because novels are published in three volumes and *Agnes Grey* is only long enough for one so he is boxing it up with two volumes of Emily's."

"*Agnes Grey* is your first novel?"

"Yes."

"The one you told me about last year?"

"Yes."

"And what is Emily's novel called?"

"Does it matter?" No, it didn't matter. I was only trying to help Anne talk through her tears to calm her down and she did calm down. She dabbed at her cheeks with her handkerchief.

"The world will know soon enough, I suppose. It's called *Wuthering Heights*." She heaved another sob. She looked heartbroken, and I didn't really see why.

"But your single volume will have your name on it surely, and Emily, her name on hers. Does boxing them together matter that much?"

"Yes," she glared at me, "it does matter *that much*. I have struggled, in *Agnes Grey*, to show that happiness in this world is attainable through virtue while Emily promotes vice, and Newby is boxing us together."

"You make it sound like a boxing match."

"Hasn't God always had to do battle with Satan?"

"Your sister Emily as Satan?" Anne shook her head, still sobbing.

"I know, I know, I shouldn't have said that, I didn't mean that, it's just that ..." I lost patience.

"You live too close," I told her, speaking my mind. "All three of you. Ever since you came back from Thorp Green, you have shut yourself in that dining room with Charlotte and Emily and it's oppressing you. I can see it." She laid her hands in her lap. "Do you remember that morning, here, in this garden, when you were just back from Thorp Green?" She looked along the seat at me.

"I do. It was the first time we talked. You told me about your plans for the chapelry and you've done well."

"And you've done well too. You've achieved your ambition and written your book and now it's going to be published but do you know what I remember most about that morning?" She waited, watching me. "Your spirit of independence." I made her keep watching me. "Do you remember? *I don't need my sisters watching over me*, you told me, *I've been six years in the real world while they've stayed here with their fantasies.* Didn't you say that? Or words like it? But, since then, Charlotte and Emily have dragged you in with them. You've forfeited your independence and burdened yourself with your constant worrying about Emily and Branwell – and you let Charlotte dominate you – and …" I put out my arm to her. "It's just not necessary. Look at yourself: you're an intelligent, accomplished woman in the prime of life with all your best years ahead of you …" The veil came down. She hadn't moved a muscle but I saw it, behind her eyes, she had left me. It was the same every time. Whenever I mentioned the future, Anne withdrew like the soul from the dead. She leaned down to Flossy and he rested his chin on her knee.

"I hear you are going away again," she said, gazing at Flossy, and that was it: the conversation was over. It had reached no conclusion but I was glad I'd spoken my mind because if I didn't show Anne the broader view then who would? I resettled myself at my end of the seat.

"I am, yes," I told her, "things are desperate in Ireland and my aunt thinks I can help." She turned up her face to me.

"A month again? Like last time?"

"I think it might be longer. The only Anglican minister still officiating in Banagher has had to leave to attend to his own family's crisis in Cork. He cannot say how long he will be away and my aunt has offered my services, as a temporary expedient."

"Did she ask you?"

"Oh yes. She asked me first." Anne returned to gazing at Flossy.

"Papa will miss you."

"I wouldn't have considered it before his eye operation but, well, you see how strong he is now. He thinks I should go. I have his blessing." Without loosening her watch of Flossy, Anne then said,

"You might want to stay once you are there." I knew I would not, but she'd begged the question:

"Would you miss me if I stayed?"

"A lot of people would miss you. You've made your mark here."

"And would *you* miss me Anne?" She turned back to me.

"Yes, I would."

"Then I shall not stay in Banagher."

It was just under a year since my last visit to Banagher and conditions had worsened. Nearly half the population had deserted what had once been a prosperous town at the heart of the corn country with breweries and distilleries but now all but one of the distilleries had closed and just one corn-mill was grinding. With its boarded-up shops and empty cottages, the town was a sad sight but when I saw the newly-built church of St Paul's, with its tall spire rising above the rooftops, I set my thoughts on the higher things and determined to do what I could.

Aunt Harriette had organised everything. She had set up meetings with the church wardens and the vestry committee, with the sexton, the organist and the parish clerk. There was so much support, in fact, that I wondered why I was needed but everyone was welcoming and my aunt grateful.

"Thank you for coming, Arthur." We were having a cup of tea at the big, deal-topped table in the cavernous kitchen that had once served the household of the retired Governor of Cuba. "I told them you were the best man for the job."

"There were other candidates then? You told me the diocese was desperate."

"Did the diocese write to you? Or the vestry committee? Did anyone ask for references? No," she answered for me. "These are exceptional times. They left it to me." My aunt settled herself in the housekeeper's chair at the head of the table and watched me over her cup. "I thought it was an opportunity for you."

"An opportunity?"

"Yes. A chance to get the feel of running your own parish in your own country. A chance to come home."

"Well, thank you for the thought aunt, but this arrangement is strictly temporary, I shall be going back to Haworth."

"But you must be thinking about your future, Arthur? About getting your own parish somewhere? For two years, you ran Haworth pretty-well single-handed so you have the experience – and you are twenty-eight."

"Aunt Harriette, please understand, I have no thought of leaving Haworth."

"But why?"

"Because I've just nicely settled in. Haworth is an odd place and the people slow to accept strangers but I am accepted now, I have all the freedom I need from Mr Brontë to do what I want and I am making real progress."

"So, you are content to be an assistant curate for the rest of your life, is that it? You are twenty-eight and you have no ambition."

"I have lots of ambition: for the advancement of the Church, for the school, for pastoral welfare …"

"But none for yourself." I sat back and opened my palms.

"Aunt, I am a minister of religion. Personal ambition should not be part of my creed."

"You are also a man." She shot me a loaded look.

"Meaning?"

"I wondered if it might be one of Mr Brontë's daughters that was keeping you in Haworth."

"Ah." I put down my cup. "You mean Anne." My aunt raised an eyebrow and inclined her head. I sat back and looked up at the row of square windows high in the wall of the basement kitchen. Conversations with my aunt only ever went one way – to the heart of the matter – and I didn't mind that, but what could I say about Anne?

"Anne's complicated," I attempted. "Strong but delicate, generous but principled, and with the purest faith." I looked back at my aunt. "So, if it is what you are asking – yes – I could fall in love with her."

"You *could* fall in love with her? Is there an impediment then?"

"Yes, there is an impediment: I can't get near her." My aunt pulled a face. "Oh, don't look like that, it's nothing like that, she's always perfectly at ease with me, even when we're alone, no, the impediment is mental: whenever I mention the future, she immediately withdraws and won't speak of it. It was like that when I first met her and it hasn't changed."

"Because of her curate?"

"Yes, Weightman." I looked back at my aunt. "I didn't know you knew about him."

"You told me in one of your first letters." I pushed aside my cup and saucer and leaned my arms on the table. "How long is it now since he died?" my aunt asked.

"Five years."

"That's a long time; time enough to grieve. It would be a pity if a man dead five years were to blight both your lives."

"But what can I do?" I asked her. I thought it a hopeless question but it wasn't to my aunt.

"If you say you could fall in love with her, you are probably in love with her already. Have you told her?" I laughed and sat back in my chair.

"No, of course I haven't."

"Then perhaps you should. You might be surprised and, anyway, you cannot go on being lovelorn for ever. Her answer might help you decide your future."

I wrote to Anne a few days later. Not because of anything my aunt had said – I had made up my mind to write to Anne the moment she told me she'd miss me – but I kept it light; nothing too personal. I told her about my aunt and my cousins and my work in the parish. I described to her the severity of the distress in Banagher and how my experience in Haworth had prepared me for the challenge. I confessed too that, despite the crisis, I was enjoying my authority, and I drew parallels between the liberty I was enjoying and the liberty Anne and I had enjoyed together in the parsonage twelve months before. My letter was, I hoped, a commonplace one that one friend might write to another; it required no reply so, when one came, I was surprised.

The Parsonage
Haworth
20th October 1847

Dear Mr Nicholls,
Thank you for your letter. I am pleased to hear how well you are doing for the poor people of Banagher and congratulate you on your achievements but your notion that the liberty you and I enjoyed last year somehow presaged present fulfilment does not, I am afraid, hold for me: what pride I took in finding a publisher last year has proved to be only hubris, and I am reaping my proper reward.

You will remember, from when we talked in the garden, how aggrieved I was that, after nine months of doing nothing with my manuscript, Mr Newby had paired it with Emily's. Three more months have passed since then and still Newby gives no indication of when he will publish but, if *Agnes Grey* has languished for a year, it has not gone unread. Charlotte, with her own novel, *The Professor*, rejected, has taken inspiration from *Agnes Grey* and written her own story akin to it. What is more, Charlotte has found her own publisher (an evidently sharper pin than Newby) who is publishing her story, *Jane Eyre*, this week.

If I am bitter about the ill-usage my novel has suffered it is just punishment for my hubris. I am penitent and I shall not flaunt my pride again but I must, as a Christian, answer blasphemy, and while I wish Charlotte success with *Jane Eyre*, I am redoubling my efforts, in my second book, to answer the immorality of *Wuthering Heights*.

Take pride in your ministry, Mr Nicholls, and hold high the light of Christ, but keep guard against self-pride.

Yours sincerely,
A Brontë

The following day I received a second letter from Anne.

The Parsonage
Haworth
21st October 1847

Dear Mr Nicholls,
I am embarrassed that in my letter I said too much. I am not shy that I shared with you my frustrations over the non-publication of my novel – frustrations have to be aired or they fester – my anxiety is more practical. Charlotte's novel is published under the name of Currer Bell, the *nom de plume* that she used for the collection of poems, and she would be mortified if her anonymity were breached. Anonymity is essential to all three of us, not least for the sake of poor Branwell,

so I am sure that now you are aware, you will keep the confidence.

Yours sincerely,
A Brontë

PS I have just opened a letter from Mr Newby. He tells me that he will publish my novel with Emily's during the first week of December. We shall see.

The Rector of Banagher returned from Cork in December leaving me free to go back to Haworth. I had enjoyed my three months as priest-in-charge but, if my aunt's intention had really been to keep me in Banagher, she had failed: my stay had confirmed that my life was in Haworth, and my connections.

I thought about Anne on the long journey home: her obsession with her sisters and their books, her being chained to her desk, day after day, writing a book to answer a book and would anyone read the books anyway? It was a convoluted means, I thought, of returning Emily to Christ. What was wrong with prayer?

My train rattled on through Wales and it started to rain – big clear drops of rain that slithered across my reflection. I needed to raise Anne's sights but how could I do it? I had tried confronting her. I'd challenged her, face to face, to reassert her independence but the veil had come down and she had, as ever, withdrawn. Weightman ... Emily ... Branwell: when would Anne ever think of herself? Or of those who cared about her? Of me? I looked at my rain-streaked reflection. I would have to be more assertive; my aunt was right about that. I'd stop short of a declaration of love but Anne had told me she'd miss me so on that I could build and on that, I decided, I would build, the minute I got back, but then, when I did get back, the east winds were cutting through Haworth and Anne was in bed with her asthma. Again, I was frustrated and would have to wait but, in the meantime – in those three weeks between getting back and seeing her – I managed to read the sisters' three novels and knew what it was that so troubled her.

I had used my influence as President of the Mechanics Institute to acquire the Bells' novels for the lending library and then borrowed them. *Jane Eyre* had been published in October and quickly become the sensation of the year but I could not agree with Anne that it aped *Agnes Grey*. True, the eponymous heroines are both governesses and, in the earlier chapters, Jane Eyre pretends to the Christian principles personified in Agnes Grey but then she throws herself at her master, a married man, and the tale goes awry. With *Agnes Grey* though, I was more impressed. It tells of a young governess's battle to instil virtue and religion into the feral children of Philistine parents even against their open hostility. She is beset by many setbacks but, through her moral constancy, she triumphs and, at the end of the story, she marries the exemplary young minister, Edward Weston, and they raise a happy family.

The absurdity of putting *Agnes Grey* with Emily's novel is glaring. Where to begin with *Wuthering Heights*? I won't even try. Sufficient to say that it is a saga of depravity the like of which I never thought ever to have to confront. Brutality, petulance and the mocking of religion – enough said! Anne was right to be outraged at the boxing together and as to its author: if I never caught Emily's eye again, I should be content.

When I did meet up with Anne again, it was in church. I had been working in the vestry and when I came out Anne was there, standing on a stool, cleaning the memorial tablets above the parsonage pew. It was a chore she had always taken to herself but, so soon after her illness, I was surprised to see her there.

"Miss Anne," I called out to her, "you are up!" She turned on her stool. She was wearing a winter cloak and scarf and a poke bonnet but, despite the layers of clothing, she looked chilled. "Are you sure you should be doing that? It's bitterly cold in here."

"I had to get out. I've been bed-ridden for a month and who else will clean these tablets?" She gave me a smile. "How are you, Mr Nicholls? Welcome back."

"I'm all the better for seeing you up and about." I offered her my hand to help her down from the stool and she took it. "I've been back three weeks and worrying about you." She stepped down to the floor. "How are you? You look pale."

"Oh, I'm a lot better than I was."

"Still, you must be careful."

"I am being careful." She looked pained, I thought; her eyes dark beneath a frowning brow. The memorials she had just been burnishing were those to her family and Weightman so perhaps that was what saddened her – or was it her present troubles: her asthma, Emily, *Wuthering Heights*?

"I read *Agnes Grey*," I said, hoping to cheer her, "and I thought it quite wonderful: beautifully paced; eloquent on the rewards of the Christian life; I congratulate you."

"Thank you." She cast down her eyes to the duster in her hands.

"Unbelievable that Newby should pair it with *Wuthering Heights*." She looked up again.

"You have read Emily's novel?" I nodded. "And?" I shrugged a speechless shrug and shook my head.

"Unbelievable," I said again, "iniquitous. You have been ill-served by Newby."

"Charlotte thinks we should move to her publisher."

"A bit late for that."

"She means for our next novels."

"Ah! Your answer to *Wuthering Heights*. You were still working on that when I left. How is it coming along?"

"I finished the first draft some months ago and Newby has accepted it but I am still making revisions." Her breath ran short and she coughed, holding her chest.

"While you are still ill?" She paused to regain her breath then, in a thin voice, answered:

"The work needs doing, and I have to do something." There was a click of a latch and the north door creaked open.

"Ah, yer here." It was Mary. She looked at me and then at Anne. "Mornin', Miss Anne." Anne gave her a smile. "Just lookin' to see where you were. Dinner's out in ten minutes."

"Thank you, Mary." Mary gave me an old-fashioned look then closed the door behind her. I turned back to Anne.

"Isn't that what made you ill last year?" I said, my resentment rising. "And why you're ill now?" Anne looked puzzled. "You told me once that this second novel was more important to you than your health and look at you. Where is the sense in that?" Anne lowered herself into a pew.

"Because *Wuthering Heights* has to be answered, and Emily returned to Christ."

"By making yourself ill?" I resented *Wuthering Heights* and I resented Emily. I stepped forward to face Anne. "If you will forgive me saying it, Anne, your constitution is not strong and to put yourself at risk for the sake of a morbid tale that no one will read – and anyway, haven't you already answered *Wuthering Heights*? Agnes Grey is a powerful exemplar of the virtues of the Christian life – and of its rewards. Contrast Agnes's happy ending, with a husband and children, with the desolation at the end of Emily's tale. You have already answered her."

"No, I haven't." Anne shook her head. "*Wuthering Heights* is more complicated than that." I was exasperated. I needed to lift Anne out of her corrosive obsession.

"But look up." I waited until she did. "Look up from your books. You were six years away. You know, better than your sisters, that the world is larger than the parsonage dining room and life much more than a literary contest. You write with such feeling at the end of *Agnes Grey* for your heroine's happiness with her minister husband, Edward Weston," I felt a rush, "surely you must want that for yourself." Anne was not fazed.

"My sisters and I do not expect to marry, Mr Nicholls."

"But why not?"

"Because Papa has trained us for independence. We can make our own way in the world as governesses, or even as writers. We do not need to make a bad marriage and a good marriage, in this part of the world and in our circumstances, well …" her wistful smile returned, "this is not Bath, is it? There are no Mr Darcys in Haworth nor, in the real world, are there any Edward Rochesters for governesses."

"Nor Edward Westons?" I did not return her smile. I had never been more serious. Anne lowered her eyes to the duster in her hands but then, after a moment, she raised them again, away from me to the memorial tablet over the stool – Weightman's tablet. I hesitated, but then I thought, why give the last word to the dead?

"Anne. He's been dead for five years. Your father might not have expected you to marry but he did not forbid it. He will want you to be happy, as any parent would, just as you wanted Agnes Grey to be happy with a husband and children of her own." The focus of Anne's eyes drifted through me. She lowered her eyes to her hands in her lap and said quietly,

"It must be ten minutes by now. It would be a shame to let Mary's dinner spoil."

And so was I dismissed. I felt rejected. Not that I had been rejected. I had not made any proposal that could be rejected, but I had raised the subject of marriage and even at the mere mention, Anne had quietly but firmly closed the door inscribed with the name William Weightman. How could I get through that? I knew what I was dealing with from Mary's encomium: how good-looking he was, how charming and generous to all, what a scholar, what a wit and – as if all that were not enough – how, at the age of twenty-eight, he had martyred himself to cholera while selflessly tending to the sick. How could I compete with a saint? With a man who would never age, make a mistake or disappoint? A man who was only a memory, and in the memory of one who loved him, could only grow sweeter and wittier and more handsome as remembrance beatifies what once was a man? 'Be bolder', Aunt Harriette had told me. How bold would I have to be? Hadn't I just confronted

Anne, telling her that the man was dead and life goes on, but when those eyes glaze over, Anne is impenetrable. I was deeply disheartened – for myself and for Anne because the parsonage dining room was a joyless place and if I couldn't lever her out of it then who else would even try? I could have sunk into despondency myself if I had had the leisure but, after three months away, I did not, there was too much to do: Haworth was in crisis.

The wool textile trade, upon which Haworth depended, had been depressed since before I arrived and, in the spring of '48, James Greenwood failed at Bridgehouse Mill. Bridgehouse had been Haworth's first spinning mill, built by the Greenwoods in the 1770s, so news of its failure came as a great shock. Mr Greenwood blamed the French. French manufacturers had been buying his yarns for years but after that country's latest political upheavals some of Greenwood's biggest customers had defaulted leaving him ruined – and Greenwood was not alone – across the West Riding, mills were closing and hands being laid off. The government blamed the crisis on the political turmoil on the continent but as the continental leaders blamed economic factors for their political ills, exactly which chicken was hatching which egg was hard for a mere curate to know. All I did know was that, two years after the repeal of the Corn Laws, the mills in Haworth were slacker than ever, the hoped-for upturn had not come and there was widespread distress in the village.

We did what we could for those without work but the task was beyond us. I won't say that the plight of the poor was as desperate as I'd seen in Ireland but it bore comparison. There was just no money about, not for the labouring classes anyway, and the increased burden of poor relief on the ratepayers was putting them under strain as well. Any ideas that Mr Brontë and I might have entertained about raising money for improvements to the public health – piped water and sewerage – now had to be shelved; there wasn't the money and there wasn't the will, although one small project managed to squeeze through to completion: I raised the last few pounds I needed for the Stanbury mission school, and my clerical friends at least were pleased for me.

"I congratulate you, Nicholls," Sutcliffe Sowden had told me, "you've done well to raise the money in these difficult times."

"I couldn't have done it now. I've been knocking on doors for three years and, in the end, it was the Committee on Education that topped the fund up."

"Still, credit where it's due. You've done well." We were setting out with Joseph Grant for a day's walking round the Sladen watershed. The sky was grey and raindrops were flicking in the westerly wind but we all had our coats and rain wouldn't dampen a rare day out. We turned north off West Lane down the steep hill to Oldfield Gate where we crossed the beck at the old packhorse bridge. The climb up the north side of the valley is steep and so talk was muted till we reached the top and turned west along Oakworth Moor. The hillside path there is flat and well-trodden, giving lovely views of the valley and the moors beyond and, once we'd recovered our breath, Sowden asked me about Ireland.

"So, how did you enjoy your stint in charge of a parish?"

"I don't know about *enjoy*," I told him. "The famine over there is terrible you know, truly terrible, and though Banagher is not the worst affected place, it puts the West Riding's troubles in proportion."

"Powerless to help then, eh?" Sowden jutted his chin at me.

"No, I wouldn't say that. I think I managed to touch the consciences of one or two with the means to help, and to provide some organisation."

"You'll be looking for your own parish now then," put in Grant, "now you've tasted power."

"Oh, I don't know about that."

"Of course you will," Grant insisted. "A parish, or a chapelry at least. You've as much experience as either of us." He turned and looked at me. "Tell me again you didn't enjoy Banagher." I had to smile. Of course I'd enjoyed being in charge, even among such misery – or because of the misery – the work being so necessary.

"Yes," I told Grant, "I liked being in charge." And we both laughed.

We followed the path for an hour or so, as far as Old Snap, then turned south to climb up Crow Hill. This was the head of the Sladen Valley and, in a hollow beneath the wind, we sat down on some rocks to enjoy the view with our bread and cheese. We had talked all morning, putting the world and the Church to rights, but now, as we ate, Grant returned to the subject of me.

"Have you been looking for a parish," he asked me, "since you got back? You didn't say."

"No, I haven't. It's not in my mind." He leaned forward to catch my eye.

"Really?"

"Yes, really. I like it in Haworth."

"As an assistant?" He remained leaning forward, watching me. "As a Perpetual Assistant Curate?" Grant's eyebrows were raised, expecting an answer. *Perpetual!* There was a word! I couldn't think that far; I couldn't think further than … well, Anne, if I were honest: when she would finish her book, be up and about, feel better, feel happier, be my friend again.

"I haven't thought that far," I told him, hoping to settle the matter, but then Sowden chimed in.

"I have." We looked at him. "I think you should stay in Haworth." He turned to Grant. "Why not? As Nicholls says: he's established here, he likes the place and Brontë is what … seventy?" I nodded. "Then look to the succession. That's what I'd do. If you're happy, sit tight and advancement will come in God's good time."

We tramped off across the wastes of Crow Hill to the south side of the valley where, above Top Withins Farm, our paths parted. We said our goodbyes with promises to meet up again; Sowden taking the path down Dean Stone Edge for his ten mile walk back to Mytholmroyd, Grant heading for Moorside and Marshlands, while I sauntered, pensive, down South Dean to Haworth. Should I be thinking about my future, I wondered, as I walked down off the moor? Everyone else was. Aunt Harriette and Grant thought I should move on and Sowden thought I should stay. What, I wondered, would Anne think? She was so impenetrable. She had told me she would miss me if I stayed in Banagher so that was some answer. But then, what *me* did she think she would miss? Just a neighbour? An extra body in the village with an education? Part of the parsonage furniture – or something more? I really didn't know but, by the time I got back to Haworth, I knew I couldn't leave the place: deep down in my heart, despite Anne's reserve, I sensed a strengthening bond. I would stay and I'd be patient.

And, in the spring, my patience was rewarded.

"You look happy," I had greeted Anne, one morning, as she walked up the lane with a parcel.

"Do I?" she'd smiled, "I'm sorry."

"No, don't be sorry. It's lovely to see you out again." I glanced at the parcel and Anne looked at it too.

"It's my books."

"Your books?"

"The three volumes of my second novel, *The Tenant of Wildfell Hall*. I've just collected them from the post office."

"Aah, no wonder you look happy. Are you pleased with them?"

"I haven't opened them yet but I was happy with the proofs." She dashed a glance at the parsonage. "You do know that …"

"I know. I'm the only man in Haworth who knows Acton Bell and so it will stay. May I read them?"

"I've to give them to Charlotte and Emily first so it might be a while but, yes, when they've finished."

"Don't worry about it," I put up a hand, "I'll get a set for the Institute. What did you say was the title?"

"*The Tenant of Wildfell Hall*."

"I'll order it." I gave her a smile and tipped my hat. "I'm happy for you. Congratulations." Then I went straight down to the Institute to order the books.

I was surprised by Anne's second novel. It wasn't at all what I had expected. As the successor to *Agnes Grey* and 'answer to *Wuthering Heights*' I had expected another tale of high morality but the one work that *The Tenant of Wildfell Hall* resembled more than any was *Wuthering Heights* itself; the same brutality and coarse language, and even the structure – a tale within a tale – was the same as *Wuthering Heights*'. And it was contentious: the secret flight of a mother with her five-year-old son from a dissolute husband. Certainly, the heroine, Helen, maintains a strong moral purpose, even towards her unworthy husband, but the story is so undermined with secrets and misunderstandings that I found it hard to follow and I was left, at the end, with little conviction that the heroine's re-marriage, after her husband's death, would be any happier than her first. I was disappointed after all Anne's hard work; I didn't think *The Tenant of Wildfell Hall* nearly as good as *Agnes Grey* and I struggled to know what I could say to Anne about it.

"It's a powerful piece of writing to be sure," I told her when she asked me. We were walking down the church together. Anne had come to find me after a confirmation class, ostensibly with a message from her father but really, I think, to know what I thought.

"Do I hear a *but*?" she asked, looking up at me.

"Some of the violence is a bit graphic, and some of the language coarse."

"I am only trying to be honest. I have seen brutality, Mr Nicholls, and the language of brutes is coarse."

"But I thought you deprecated violence and coarseness in Emily's novel; and that this book was supposed to counter it." Anne stopped and turned to me.

"Emily's novel is a historical fantasy and its violence is gratuitous. What I have attempted is an exposé of a current social injustice, of which violence is too often a part. Do you not see the purpose of *The Tenant*, Mr Nicholls?"

"Well," I attempted, "your story – like *Agnes Grey* – extols the importance of a religious education and of the religious life being the path to happiness." Anne watched me, wanting more. "You also treat with marital law – with the wife's impotence against a tyrannical husband."

"And the mother's impotence," she added. "The law does not recognise any right of a mother over the lives of the children she bears. That is why Helen and her son had to go into hiding."

"Yes," I nodded, "that was clear." Anne still watched me.

"Then you did not recognise any other purpose?" I thought hard.

"A warning to young men against strong drink?"

"Nothing else?" I had run out of themes, unless dissimulation was a theme. I shrugged and Anne looked disappointed.

"Well, Emily saw it, and so did Charlotte but, for you, it seems, I must spell it out." She gave me a rueful smile. "The clue, Mr Nicholls, is in the title, and in the name of my heroine." Tenant? Wildfell? Helen? I shrugged again. "You have compared *Wildfell Hall* with *Wuthering Heights* when I intended you should contrast them. It's why I wrote the story in the first place – to answer *Wuthering Heights*." She gave me a governess's scowl and clasped her hands in front of her. "Wuthering Heights and Wildfell Hall are both isolated moorland homesteads. The Heights is the redoubt of a tyrant; the Hall, a haven from one. The occupiers of the Heights, Heathcliff, Hindley and Hareton, are brutish and godless; the occupier of the Hall, Helen Huntingdon, is a model of Christian probity. In *Wuthering Heights*, vice and tyranny triumph and all those touched by it either die or are left scarred but, in *Wildfell Hall*, vice and tyranny are defeated, and not by a counter-tyranny but by the constancy of Christian love. Emily knew all along that I deplored *Wuthering Heights* but she refused to amend it. Now I have answered it."

Anne had a spring in her step that summer that I had not seen since *Agnes Grey* was accepted and, with no new novel to keep her at her desk, we saw much more of her. By *we* I mean at Sexton House. 1848 was a fine, dry summer and whenever Anne was in the lane and the Browns or I on the bench, she would join us. Anne was spending much less of her time with her sisters. She would share the morning chores with them and walk the dogs but then she would be off down the village, visiting the old and infirm and running their errands and then, coming back, she would sit with us. It was wonderful to see how much happier Anne was and, sitting beside her on the Sexton House bench, I felt closer to her than I ever had – although I was careful not to mention the future – until she did.

The topic arose up at Stanbury. The builders had just about finished the mission school and, as Anne wanted to see it, we had taken a walk up there with Eliza and Tabitha and the parsonage dogs. The school occupied George Taylor's small paddock in the middle of the village, closing the gap between his barn and a short row of cottages. It was not a large building; just room enough to seat about eighty scholars or worshippers, because I had oriented the building to serve also as a chapel. The entrance, sheltered by a shallow porch, was in the middle of the south front and flanked by symmetrical sets of four-light mullioned windows. On that

September afternoon, the building still looked stark – too yellow and too new – with the builders' rubble still scattered around it but, with the girls and dogs gone off to play, I led Anne across the debris and showed her around.

"It's a little gem," Anne exulted, "very pretty, very pretty indeed." I took her round to the west side of the building to show her the big segmented church window.

"It's designed to double as a chapel-of-ease," I explained, "once the school is established, but one step at a time."

"You've done well." Anne stroked the smooth quoins with her finger tips. "It will make such a difference to the Anglicans here."

"It will. Some of the families on the farms have a three or four mile walk down to Haworth. Once we are established here with a school *and* a chapel, it will give the Church a huge boost."

"I can see that," Anne agreed. "You must feel very proud." She turned and gave me a smile. "Papa was never so well served."

Never so well served! Weighty words: words so loaded with the unspoken name that we continued along the back wall in silence until, at the corner, Anne said:

"Papa would not exchange you now, you know, not even for Mr Weightman." She looked up at me. No veil clouded her violet eyes, no colour warmed her cheeks. Her eyes were so steady, and I, so surprised, that it was I who demurred, casting my eyes to my boots. We turned down the east side of the school and walked back along the front where, quietly, I had to observe,

"If Mr Weightman had lived, I would never have met you or your father." Anne looked up and our eyes met; hers were sad but still unveiled, she had not withdrawn. We continued along towards the porch, sharing the single thought and I asked her: "do you remember telling me once that you never intended to marry?"

"I remember telling you that Papa never *expected* us to marry."

"So, if Mr Weightman had lived, do you think you would have married him?"

"Oh, Mr Nicholls: too many imponderables there."

"Imponderables?" We stopped in front of the porch and Anne gave me a level look.

"Yes. Would Mr Weightman ever have asked Papa; and would Papa ever have accepted him?"

CHAPTER EIGHT

Into the valley

*W*ould Papa ever have accepted him! Anne had said it with such a level look that she could not have been plainer if she had put out her arm and pointed me in the direction of her father's parlour. Of course Anne would direct me to her father. Why had I not seen that for myself? It was obvious from everything I knew about Anne and from the probity of her heroines that such an important step could only be taken in the prescribed manner and engagement begins with the approach to the father. I thought it all through over the next few days. Would Mr Brontë think me suitable for Anne? Well, I calculated, I was an Irish-born minister in the Church of England so he shouldn't find too much fault there. What were my prospects? Weren't they in Mr Brontë's own gift? If he valued me in Haworth, as I believed he did, then I could continue as I was, which suited me, and would surely suit Anne, staying close to her home. Where would we live, and could I afford the expense of running a home? Now that could be a problem. I had no money and no prospects of any beyond my curate's stipend but, there again, couldn't Mr Brontë do something about that? There were funds available for increasing a curate's salary: nationally, there was Queen Anne's Bounty and, locally, George Taylor, my Stanbury benefactor, was a Trustee of the Haworth Church

Lands Trust that found Mr Brontë's stipend so, if Mr Brontë had the will, surely, he could find the way. I pondered these things over the next few days and the auguries all seemed set fair. The mission school was to be dedicated on the following Monday, the 25th September. The bishop would be there, and the vicar and the Anglican clergy from miles around, to celebrate an achievement that was entirely mine. Could there be a better day to ask Mr Brontë for the hand of his daughter? There could not, I decided, but then, on the Sunday, the 24th, the very day before the dedication was to take place, Fate struck a blow that dashed my hopes and all of Mr Brontë's when Branwell died.

I had seen Branwell in the village only three days before. He had looked gaunt and his shoulders were bent around his hollow chest but if Branwell had the look of a dying man it was the look he had worn for a long time so I had felt no particular concern. No more had Dr Wheelhouse who saw Branwell a deal more than I did. He had told Mr Brontë that if Branwell would only drink less and renounce opium then good health would be restored to him but Dr Wheelhouse had not looked beyond the symptoms of delirium and inebriation, he had not noticed the wasting and the coughing and the shortness of breath. If he had, he might have seen that Branwell was dying of consumption.

Branwell had remained in bed on the Friday morning complaining of feeling unwell. This was not in itself unusual but his demeanour was altered. Instead of being irritable he was calm and pleasant with his family. Anne had spent the afternoon with him and he had allowed her to pray with him for the first time in years. On the Saturday, Branwell asked for his father. He wanted him to intercede for him for absolution and, through his father, he became reconciled with Christ Jesus. Early on the Sunday morning Branwell sent for John Brown. He had passed a good night and John found him improved. They had talked for a few minutes but then, at about half past eight, Branwell was suddenly seized by convulsions.

"Oh John!" he'd cried out, "I'm dying! I'm dying!" and he'd writhed on his bed, gasping for air. John had taken alarm at this and run downstairs, bursting into the parlour where the family was at prayer. He'd glared at Mr Brontë.

"Yer'd best get upstairs," he'd told him, and Mr Brontë had run from the room. Branwell was huddled on the bed when his father found him, clutching at his throat for breath. His father plucked him up, as if he weighed no more than the nightshirt that covered him and held him to his breast.

"Oh my son!" he cried, "My son! My son!" and, with the rattle sounding in Branwell's chest, he'd paced the floor crying, "God absolve and take this sinner, God absolve and take this sinner," over and over, for twenty minutes, until, at nine o'clock, 'Amen' sighed out through Branwell's lips and he passed from this world to the next.

All this, I pieced together later. The first I heard directly of Branwell's death was from John himself when he came back to Sexton House. I was up in my parlour, preparing for morning service, when I heard the commotion downstairs. John's voice was raised and agitated and Mary was talking over him. I went down to see what the matter was and found John and Mary embraced in the hall. The girls were fussing around them and I asked to know what was wrong. Mary turned to look at me and John lifted his head from her shoulder.

"I told 'em!" he said with a quivering lip. "I told 'em they'd lose 'im." Tears were standing in his eyes and his body was shaking. "But did any of 'em take any notice of me?" Mary slipped away and took the girls to the kitchen. I asked John again what the matter was and he pointed up to the parsonage.

"Have yer seen them lasses lately?" he asked me. "Aye, well, yer must have done. Yer can't miss 'em, can yer? Proud as Punch, taken up with their books, off in their own little worlds. Didn't they hear their brother coughin'? Didn't they see 'im fallin' as 'e tried to make the stairs? Didn't they see he was dying?" John glared at me ferociously, his grief etched in the lines of his face, and I knew what had happened.

"Oh I don't blame the old man," he went on, swaying behind his front door. "He did his best after his wife died and then, after Maria and Elizabeth, I think 'e were that fearful, 'e kept the rest too close – wouldn't let them out of his sight, kept them to himself and taught them all he knew." John drew his cuff across his cheek. "So what did they expect?" He gave me a sad smile. "Yer teach a lad Latin 'n Greek, yer fill his head from dawn to dusk with music 'n poetry 'n paintin' 'n fancy talk; yer closet him up with lasses who tell 'im he's brightest bobbin since Lord knows who – and there's no one round 'ere to say whether 'e is or 'e isn't – then yer let 'im out into t'world with never a clue as how to go on. Nay," he shook his head at the floor, "what did they expect?"

I gripped John's arms and embraced him then I ran up to the parsonage. Tabby and Martha were out in the lane, standing by the kitchen door in the autumn sunshine, talking to the joiner-cum-coffin-maker, William Wood. I went up to the front door and rang the bell and then, when no one came, I put my face to the glass. The hall was deserted. I waited for a few moments more and was just about to go round to the kitchen when Charlotte appeared on the stairs and came to the door.

"How is your father?" I asked her. Charlotte's cheeks were flushed and her jaw set. She stared up at me from behind her thick lenses but she did not reply. I said, "I see William Wood is here," and Charlotte seemed to grasp that.

"He has come to repair the sash window in Papa's room."

"What? This morning? On a Sunday morning?"

"I think so." Charlotte looked confused. She was holding the door open but she did not invite me in. I had no wish to intrude but I wanted to know.

"Are you all alright?" I asked her. "Is there anything I can do?" Charlotte watched me. I don't think she understood quite why I was there.

"Emily has taken the dogs out. Papa and Anne are with Branwell." I nodded that I understood and then I asked her again:

"Is there anything that you would like me to do?" Charlotte looked beyond me towards the church.

"Shouldn't you be taking matins?" I turned round and looked at the church clock. It was twenty-eight minutes past nine. I turned back to Charlotte and, for the first time, she seemed to recognise me and the depth of my concern. She took off her spectacles. I had never seen her without them before; her eyes were greenish brown and much larger than they appeared behind her lenses. "Please pray for him, Mr Nicholls. Ask everyone to pray for him."

None in the congregation needed to be asked to pray for Branwell; the passage of his soul was the single thought on everyone's mind because, whatever his flaws, Branwell was much loved. I abandoned my sermon, it was not appropriate, and reduced the service to its bare essentials and then, when I walked out into the lane, the realities of the altered world confronted me – not least, the dedication of the Stanbury school, arranged for the following day. I realised at once that it would have to be cancelled. There could be no question of holding any such celebration so soon after Mr Brontë's loss. My first thought was to go to him and gain his consent but then realised it was not the time so I set off for Stanbury to see George Taylor.

"I don't see how we can cancel it," he'd said when I'd told him.

"But we must," I insisted, "as a mark of respect." We were standing to the fire in his Manor House parlour.

"I'm not saying we *shouldn't* cancel it, Mr Nicholls, I'm just saying we *can't*. We've the bishop coming from Ripon and the vicar from Bradford and all the clergy from the Craven Deanery." He pointed out of his window to the village beyond. "The procession, the musicians, the tea …"

"But everyone will understand," I insisted, "in fact, they'll expect it."

"But how?" he asked again. "It's Sunday. There's no post, and we can't send runners to Ripon and Bradford and every parsonage in the Craven Valley, there just isn't time." He was right; it could not be done but, if I am perfectly honest, my own reputation now loomed before me. The mission school, as everyone knew, was my project and its dedication should have been my celebration and the last thing I wanted now was for all Stanbury and the clergy of Craven to think that I was putting my hubris before my senior minister's loss.

"Well, if it cannot be cancelled, it will have to be cut right back and Mr Brontë's loss recognised. No procession, no music, no tea, just the solemn dedication of the school and then prayers for Mr Brontë's family."

And so it was, and a grim affair. The bishop came from Ripon and the Vicars of Bradford and Skipton and a half a dozen other clergymen, but those who had already heard the news stayed away, out of respect, as did most of Stanbury. After twenty minutes of shuffling in and out of the school in our assorted hoods and surplices we repaired to George Taylor's for refreshments and that was my big day done.

Branwell's funeral, the following Thursday, was a much grimmer affair. A blustery westerly was blowing and leaden skies threatened rain. Dr Morgan from Bradford, one of Mr Brontë's oldest friends, conducted the service and I assisted. We stood together outside the north door, holding down our surplices against the wind while the short cortège emerged from the parsonage. William Wood, the coffin-maker, led the procession across the garden and down through the burial ground to the church. The pall-bearers followed him, shouldering the coffin, then Mr Brontë, on his own, then Emily and Anne followed by John and Mary and the girls. There was no Tabby, she was unwell, and no Charlotte. She had taken to her bed with a bilious fever, the day Branwell died, and she stayed there for a week.

Young men – Branwell's friends – came from far and wide to join the local mourners and the church was full. The atmosphere was charged – as it ever is for an untimely death – and Dr Morgan did nothing to mollify it. Any intimacy that his association with the Brontë family might have brought to the proceedings was missing. The Welshman spoke with power but his stern strictures offered no comfort to the bereaved and by the time he'd stepped down from the pulpit the impression he left was that he had not approved of Branwell. I thought it a job ill-done and Mr Brontë ill-served and I felt for him. At the committal, Branwell's remains were placed in the vault beneath the church with his mother, his aunt and his two older sisters. It was the reunion he had been waiting for for the past three years.

Charlotte may have been prostrated by Branwell's death but Anne was joyous.

"Did Papa tell you about his end?" she'd called to me as I passed the dining room door and, seeing her alone, I'd walked in.

"He did and I'm glad – for Branwell and for all of you." She was standing before the fire, her eyes wide and shining.

"I prayed with him just two days before you know. He had asked for me. I think it was because I was there at Thorp Green and he wanted to be reconciled. He really did, Mr Nicholls. It was the true confession for which I had prayed and I witnessed it at the last." Glowing with triumph, she stepped to the window and looked out over the burial ground to the church. "It is the consummation. I know that he is in paradise."

"Consummation to be sure," I agreed. "That is in the end the greater prize than any worldly fulfilment denied your brother." Anne looked back at me.

"Consummation is fulfilment." I smiled and relaxed my weight onto one foot.

"I would not bandy semantics with you, I was merely making the point that we are permitted to fulfil our legitimate desires in this life. It is no sin to aspire to a degree of happiness that eluded your poor brother." Anne frowned, thoughtful, then raised a finger.

"Just a moment." She turned to the bookshelf beside her and took down a pocket edition of the New Testament. She leafed through the familiar pages while I shifted again and held out a hand,

"Can I help you?" but Anne was close to her object. She stroked her finger down a page.

"Here we are. '*Love not the world neither the things that are in the world. If any man love the world, the love of the Father is not in him.*'" She raised her eyebrows at me.

"The First Epistle of Saint John," I said, but then she raised her finger again.

"'*For all that is in the world, the lust of the flesh and the lust of the eyes and the pride of life is not of the Father but is of the world. And the world passeth away and the lust thereof, but he that doeth the will of God abideth forever.*'" Anne laid the silk thread back into the page and returned the book to the shelf. "Chapter two, verses fifteen to seventeen." Anne's eyes were burning with righteous zeal and I found it unnerving.

"I am surprised to hear you recommending the conventual life," I told her, "I do not see withdrawal from the world in the works of Acton Bell."

"No, I do not recommend the conventual life. Christ did not withdraw from the world, he confronted it, but without vanity."

"That's right," I agreed, "he did. Glad as I am for Branwell, the purpose of Christ's teaching is not how to die but how to live – it is there in the commandments and the beatitudes." There was more that I wanted to say to Anne, and at a deeper level than biblical banter. I put out my hands to her. "We are allowed to be happy, you know, Anne. To enjoy, while we are here, the beauties of God's Creation and the pleasures of his gifts."

"But we know neither the day nor the hour, do we, Mr Nicholls? Our life on earth is but a speck in the life of eternity." I was losing her again; but not behind the old Weightman veil – something worse – a hovering distancing, as if she were, herself, preparing to leave.

"*Know not the day*?" I lost patience. "Anne, we are young. You are twenty-eight and at the height of your powers with your best years still to be enjoyed," I threw out my arms, "your career as a writer and as a mother – I know that you want to be a mother – I have seen you with children." I stepped forward. "Your father might have made a wise precaution but he didn't forbid you from marrying." She lowered her eyes but I pressed on. "I am sorry you lost Mr Weightman all those years ago but it *is* years ago and you and I …" she looked up.

"Have you spoken to my father?" Her eyes were like spears. Accusing? Anxious? Expectant?

"Would you like me to go to your father?" I felt that she did. "This is not a good time, so soon after Branwell ..."

"No," she bit her lip, "it isn't."

There was a sharp rap on the door and Martha put round her head.

"Ahh, here you are, Mr Nicholls." She looked quickly at Anne and then back at me. "Mi dad's lookin' all over for yer. Summat about the vault." I looked back at Anne. Our conversation wasn't over but her eyes had returned to the fire so perhaps it was. I turned back to Martha.

"I'll come."

There was more that Anne had wanted to say, I could feel it. That was why she had bitten her lip and turned away. Anne must have thought Martha's entrance extraordinarily timely because, if she had been ready to accept me, what could she have said? She could not have declared affection for me without her father's consent and this was not the time to ask him. No, Anne was right: the best thing for us both was for me to go to her father as soon as the period of mourning had passed. Until then, we must both bite our lips.

If Branwell's death had been to Anne transfiguring and to Charlotte an agony, it was to Emily much like any other. She was a cold character. Death, birth and renewal were as normal to her as the turning of the seasons; she coolly accepted nature's violent laws so, when she became ill herself and faced her own death, she was neither surprised nor fearful and she spurned all help.

Emily had been coughing at Branwell's funeral. It had irritated me and I had wished she would control it but, as the weeks passed and the cough grew persistent, the fear arose that Emily had contracted Branwell's consumption. Anne was desperately worried and tried to keep Emily indoors but Emily would have none of it; she had always taken long walks on the moors and so she would continue. As October ran into November, Emily began to look ill. She grew thinner, her eyes sank and her cheeks hollowed and her tall frame, usually as straight and strong as her father's, bent over her painful chest. Both Anne and Charlotte did everything they could to try to persuade Emily to modify her behaviour, trying to keep her indoors and take over her housework, but Emily would not hear of it. Emily's fixed routines were as much a part of her as her poetic vision or love of nature, and she was not going to change them just because she was dying so, as she struggled to wash, sweep or even climb the stairs, her sisters could only watch and wonder at the power of her will.

I wanted to help but what could I do? I prayed of course. I prayed that Emily would return to Christ, just as her brother had, but there was no room for me to advise Emily Brontë. She had never acknowledged me and in any case, she had, under her roof, a minister far better qualified than me and infinitely more concerned for her. The only help I could offer was to take out the dogs when the weather was bad, which I did.

I was in the parsonage on the day that Emily died. It was Tuesday the 19th December and I had walked the dogs during the morning. There was sleet in the south-east wind and the dogs were muddy so I had wiped them down in the scullery before returning them to the kitchen. Tabby was at the range when I went through, struggling with a heavy kettle, and I helped her bring it to the table in the middle of the room.

"I'm makin' a brew," she said, "do yer want one?" I thanked her and sat down at the table while she brought forward milk and two cups. Tabby was a heavy woman and she rolled precariously when she walked on account of her lame leg. She had been at the parsonage since the children were small and the love that she might have devoted to any children of her own she lavished on Mr Brontë's.

"There's grim comin's 'n' goin's this mornin'," she said gloomily. She passed me a cup of tea and dropped herself onto a chair on the other side of the table. For a moment she said nothing, gazing quietly into her tea, but then, when she looked up, I saw there were tears in her eyes. "She's sent for Dr Wheelhouse." She said, setting her jaw. "So that's it."

"Who has sent for Dr Wheelhouse? Charlotte?"

"No, not Charlotte! Emily's sent for him. He's up there with her now."

"Well, that's good news," I said. "And none too soon."

"*None too soon.*" Tabby chided. "*None too late* yer mean. She knows he can't do nowt for her. That's only reason she's let him in." Tabby looked away, through the kitchen window. "So that's it then. She knows it's her time." And she gazed forlornly out towards the moors.

"We shall have to wait and see what Dr Wheelhouse says," I said, hoping to cheer her, but she did not answer; she just stared out of the window till her thoughts had settled then she took up her tea.

"I don't suppose yer know Emily right well, do yer, Mr Nicholls?" I shifted in my chair.

"She's never been very forthcoming, I have to say. I don't think she likes me very much." Tabby huffed a little laugh.

"No, yer wrong there. Emily doesn't bother with likin' an' dislikin'. She doesn't judge. She just looks an' listens an' takes it all in, but she doesn't judge."

"She does take it all in," I agreed, "I've read her poems. They're very perceptive."

"'Her poems, aye, and her book."

"Her book? You would compare the brutality of *Wuthering Heights* with the beauty of her poems?"

"Of course. She only ever writes about one thing." Tabby took a drink of her tea. "Life."

"Life! *Wuthering Heights!*"

"*Wuthering Heights* is a simple enough tale. A chap fightin' to get food in his belly an' a roof over his head; fightin' to get a wife an' some security an' to get on top of his enemy. Isn't that just life?"

"Life no better than the animals'."

"No better. No worse." Tabby gave me a sharp look. "Do yer think Heathcliff an' Cathy an' the rest of 'em are any different to all them self-seekin' beggars yer've to deal with in t'village? An' are they any different to foxes killin' for food or weasels protectin' their young or rooks fightin' over nests? Emily Brontë doesn't think so."

"But what of morality?"

"*Morality!*" Tabby scoffed. "There yer go again. Morality and judgements."

"But Tabby, we have to have a moral compass." She gave me a sideways smile.

"Aye, well, it's work for you an' the Master."

"Tabby, that's outrageous."

"There yer go again! Another judgement!" Tabby sat back in her chair. "New Testament lays down laws; before that, Old Testament laid down laws and before that – before there were any testaments at all – there was the law of nature, an' if that isn't the law of God, I don't know what is. Emily was just remind us."

I heard Dr Wheelhouse coming down the stone stairs and went out into the hall to meet him. He told me that the case was hopeless and that Emily's time was near, then he went into Mr Brontë. I stood, all alone, in the hall, listening to the low murmur of their voices beyond the door. The clock in the stairs struck eleven, and then the church clock too. I let myself out and went to the church to pray.

Emily died three hours later. Her father and her two surviving sisters were with her. There was no admission of sin, no last-minute atonement, no intoned 'Amen'. 'Amen' had been implicit in Emily's life, she had lived in the conviction that God's purpose was unassailable and that was how she died.

Mr Brontë sent word of Emily's death to Dr Morgan but like many in Bradford and Haworth that miserable winter he was indisposed and so it fell to me, two days before Christmas, to conduct Emily's funeral. It was one of the hardest tasks I have ever been asked to perform. Bad enough to commit the virgin body of my employer's beloved daughter; tragic, for all who love letters, that a poet so peculiarly affecting should die with her work unfinished, but what was I to say over the body of one who had shunned the Saviour and his Mother Church? For '*whosoever denieth the Son, the same hath not the Father*'.

It was three months since Branwell's funeral and it felt like three days. Again, a cold westerly was blowing off the moors and black clouds threatened but, thankfully, the rain held off. Again, I stood at the church porch, watching the procession make its way towards me, only this time Mr Brontë did not walk alone, he had Keeper beside him and, throughout the service, Emily's mastiff lay at Mr Brontë's feet, with Charlotte and Anne on one side, and Martha and Tabby on the other.

I have only a hazy recollection of my address at Emily's funeral and my notes are long since lost but I remember that I quoted Emily's own lines in evidence of her intense spirituality, and I reminded the congregation that if Emily's faith were unorthodox, then God alone would judge.

Yes I could swear that glorious wind
Has swept the world aside
Has dashed its memory from thy mind
Like foam-bells from the tide –

And thou art now a spirit pouring
Thy presence into all –
The essence of the Tempest's roaring
And of the Tempests' fall –

A universal influence
From Thine own influence free –
A principle of life intense
Lost to mortality –

Thus truly when that breast is cold
Thy prisoned soul shall rise
The dungeon mingle with the mould –
The captive with the skies.

CHAPTER NINE

The Deluge

Anne, Charlotte and their father were now all coughing. The turn of the year can be bitter in Haworth and the easterlies cut through the parsonage like knives. With Anne prey to asthma and Mr Brontë to bronchitis, these winter coughs were common enough but consumption is infectious and the trauma of losing Emily so soon after Branwell had weakened the resistance of them all. By the first week in January, Mr Brontë and Anne were confined to their beds and Charlotte had sent to Leeds for a lung specialist.

I sensed a crisis but what could I do? Ellen Nussey arrived to help Charlotte defend what was left of her family against intruders which, for Charlotte, included me. I was completely debarred from seeing Anne or Mr Brontë – 'wait,' I was told, 'till they've seen Dr Teale.'

I saw Teale arrive from my parlour window. I had been working at my desk and I watched as he paid off the carrier and walked up the parsonage path. I saw Martha admit him and I put down my pen. I hurried downstairs, donning my coat as I went, and ran to the parsonage back door where Tabby let me into the kitchen. She poured us both tea and we exchanged faux assurances that Teale was only a precaution then Tabby took up some mending.

Teale had gone into the dining room first, to examine Charlotte. Miss Nussey was with her and Martha, in the hall, listening at the door. After a few minutes, she brought us the news.

"He says it's a head cold and exhaustion," she told us, leaning in through the doorway, "he's told her to rest." Martha rolled her eyes at that – she knew what Charlotte's resting would mean for her – then she ducked out and ran off upstairs.

"There y'are," Tabby gave me a firm nod, "what did I tell yer?" I leaned forward and picked up my tea. It wasn't Charlotte I was worried about.

Charlotte and Miss Nussey took Dr Teale upstairs and, again, we waited: Tabby, absorbed with her mending and I, staring at the fire, trying to think about nothing. Ten long minutes passed before we next heard footfalls on the stairs and this time they were Martha's. She elbowed open the door carrying a tray with the remains of two dinners.

"Well," I asked her, rising from my chair, "what has he said?" Martha bustled on through to the scullery.

"Master 'asn't got bronchitis; he's got flu."

"What did I tell yer?" Tabby slapped her knee and nodded again. "Head cold and flu; nothing to worry about."

"And what about Anne?" I followed Martha through to the scullery. "What did Dr Teale say about Anne?"

"Dunno." She set down her tray. "They sent me out." She moved to the back door. "Master wants his fire lit." Then she went out to fetch peat and kindling.

Another fifteen minutes passed before we next heard feet on the stairs. I leaned over and opened the door an inch, so I could see. Mr Brontë was in his dressing gown with Dr Teale and Miss Nussey and Charlotte were behind them. None of them was speaking until they reached the front door where Charlotte quietly thanked Dr Teale and let him out.

"Now, are you sure …" Charlotte began, but her father checked her.

"Yes, don't worry. Martha has lighted a fire. I just need some time in my parlour."

"Well, if you're sure. We are just across the hall." Charlotte went up on her toes and kissed her father's cheek, then he retired to his parlour and she and Miss Nussey to the dining room. I looked across at Tabby.

"Well?" I asked her. "What do you think?" She straightened out her mending over her knee.

"They were quiet."

"That's what I thought," I looked again through the crack of the door, "too quiet."

I needed to know what Teale had said about Anne. Martha wouldn't know, she'd not been back upstairs, and there was no point asking Charlotte so I had only one option.

"I'm going to ask Mr Brontë." Tabby raised an eyebrow.

"Do yer think yer should? I dare say we'll be told soon enough." I got up from my chair.

"I'm sorry, Tabby. Soon enough isn't soon enough." Then I went out and tapped on his door.

Mr Brontë was standing before the banked-up fire with his back to me. He was in his long woollen dressing gown with socks and pattens on his feet to keep them off the flags. He was leaning on his stick, examining the engraving that hung on the chimney breast: John Martin's *The Deluge.*

"Tell me what you think, Mr Nicholls," he said, as I clicked the door closed, "does Mr Martin have the truth of it in his composition? Do all of these teeming bodies have souls? Or are they just shoals of fishes washed away on the waves of God's will?" Mr Brontë remained with his back to me, looking at the picture. "I don't think Mr Martin holds humanity in very high regard, do you, Mr Nicholls?" Mr Brontë's question wrong-footed me. I was seized by a much more pressing question than art criticism and I didn't quite know how to answer. Was he asking my opinion of the worth of human kind in general? Or my assessment of John Martin's opinion of it?

"Sir, Noah lived before Christ," I offered. "The rock of His Church was not yet there to be clung to." Mr Brontë moved over to the window and looked out across the burial ground to his church. "Mr Brontë, Sir…" I stepped towards him, ready to ask about Anne but he interrupted me.

"You read the newspapers, Mr Nicholls. What think you of the news from the Continent?" Mr Brontë still did not look at me, but continued looking out of the window. "Habsburgs unthroned in Vienna, Bourbons in Naples and a Bonaparte restored to the Elysée in Paris. Lawful rulers and the rule of law are everywhere upturned. In German states, in Poland and in Spain, from the Baltic to the Balkans, constitutions are trampled and the mobs rule. Even here," he tapped his stick on the flag floor, "the Chartists stir the sediment rising with their rallies and riots and their Great Petition." Then he turned from the window and looked at me. He leaned both hands heavily on his stick and, whether from fever or passion, his body shook and there was fire in his eyes.

"In Ireland," he rolled the name round his mouth, "the famine is unabated. Three years now and the blight is still in the crop. A million of our countrymen dead and still there is no end." He looked again over to the picture above the mantelpiece. "Pestilence," he hissed, then he looked back at me. "How many died in London last year of The Great Stink, Mr Nicholls?"

"Of the cholera morbus, Sir?"

"Yes. Of the cholera morbus. How many do you think died in London?"

"More than fourteen thousand I have read, Sir."

"Fourteen thousand souls," he repeated, still leaning on his stick, "and from the same disease in Bradford not ten miles away? How many have perished there?" I shook my head.

"I cannot say, Sir. The figure is still rising. Many hundreds at least."

"Many hundreds in Bradford," Mr Brontë affirmed. "Fourteen thousand in London. A million in Ireland and millions more on the Continent – War!" He banged his stick hard on the flags. "Pestilence!" He banged his stick again. "Disease!" Again his stick. "And Death!" He glared furiously across the room at me, his tall skeletal frame shaking involuntarily over his stick and then the tears welled, quenching the fires in his old man's eyes. "How many of my own shall die?" his voice was breaking, "when the great day of his wrath is come? Who shall stand then, Mr Nicholls? Who shall be able to stand?" He glared at me accusingly through tear-filled eyes and I knew he'd been told Anne would die. My heart dropped to my stomach and my legs went weak. Mr Brontë was staring at me, demanding that I answer him but I could not speak. I wanted to know but I could not ask. I felt hot in front of the fire and then as I watched, Mr Brontë swayed dangerously and I thought he would fall. I rushed across the room and, taking hold of him, lowered him carefully into the chair at his back and, as he sank into the cushions, his tears spilled.

I went out into the hall and called for Charlotte. She came quickly with Miss Nussey and I took them in to Mr Brontë. I stood back and watched as they took charge of him then I left them and went to find Anne.

I had never been upstairs in the parsonage before and I found myself on a small open landing with five doors. I opened the door on my right. It was the servants' bedroom. I opened the door next to it and inside there was Anne. At first, I did not see her. She was on the far side of the further bed, bending down to something (the pot?) and when she heard the door, she looked up. She was surprised to see me, but not alarmed, and she rose unsteadily to her feet. She was wearing an over-sized night gown and a lace-fringed cap. She looked pale and stooped.

"Mr Nicholls!" she said. "Is something the matter?" I remained in the doorway.

"What did Dr Teale say?" She lowered her eyes and put a hand on the bedpost.

"He said that Papa has influenza and Charlotte a head cold."

"Yes, I know that, but what about you? What did he say about you?" Painfully, Anne straightened her shoulders and looked at me.

"That I have consumption in both lungs; that it is advanced and I should prepare for the worst." My head swam and my belly dropped. I gripped the door knob.

"But you mustn't," I told her, "you must hope for the best. We must pray for the best, believe in the best, not the worst." Anne half turned and sat down on the bed. I reached out to her. "Your life is ahead of you Anne: marriage, children and grandchildren, and you will write more books. You will not die. This isn't the end." She looked over to me and smiled.

"But then death isn't the end, is it? There is Paradise, and reunions." *Reunion*s! So, that was it!

"You mean Weightman." She shook her head.

"No, I wasn't thinking of Mr Weightman. You were always too possessed of him, no, I was thinking more of Emily. I am anxious to know ..." she frowned and bit her lip, "in spite of all, I am hopeful that she will be there." I exploded.

"Anne, will you listen to yourself? You are ill but you are not on your way to Paradise."

"But if it is God's will; I must be ready for whatever He intends."

"But we don't know what He intends!" I let go the doorknob and stepped towards her. "You still have your free will, and a strong will can move mountains. Look at Agnes Grey: she didn't submit to misfortune, nor did Helen Huntingdon and nor will you, you don't believe in predestination." She raised a wry eyebrow.

"Do we really choose what we believe in, Mr Nicholls?"

Now what did that mean? Anne seemed already to be casting off this world but I wasn't ready to let her.

"We have *self*-belief," I told her, "you know the power of that – and you still have obligations – Charlotte needs you, your father needs you ..." then I added, "and *I* need you." She met my eyes and, for the first time in three and a half years, I believe, she saw me: the man who cared about her, understood her, was ready to sacrifice and support her and make her happy – the man who loved her. She looked down at her hands.

"Dr Teale has recommended some treatments," she said, attempting to appease, "blistering, hot compresses, cod liver oil." Footsteps clicked on the stairs.

"Did he suggest a change of air?" I asked. "Haworth is so damp. I have heard that Penzance is a good place for consumption. It's warmer there, and drier."

"Aunt Branwell was from Penzance. She said they have palm trees there, but it is a long way." She gave me a brave smiled. "Scarborough would be nice." I sensed a presence.

"What yer doin' here?" It was Martha. She took hold of my sleeve. "Yer can't be up here." She looked in to Anne. "Can he Miss Anne?" Anne was looking down into her hands and I knew that I must leave. I said,

"You will get better, Anne. For me, for Martha, for your father … We just need you to believe," but she did not answer. Martha pulled me from the doorway then led me downstairs and out of the house.

Consumption had taken Branwell because no one had noticed the symptoms; Emily's diagnosis had been clear but she had refused medical help but Anne was offered the best medical help, and at an early stage, so all that she needed to recover was her own self-belief and if she lacked that through timidity or providential determinism then I would buttress it. I decided I'd talk to Mr Brontë again. I wouldn't be asking for Anne's hand, that would, in present circumstances, be crass, but I would be positive with him: I would encourage him to believe in Anne and believe that, with the best medical help and a move to better air, she could be made well again and if my concern should demonstrate to Mr Brontë my fitness for Anne, then that too would be to the good.

Mr Brontë was up and dressed when I called but, though he claimed he felt better, he was skeletally thin and I thought he'd have been better in bed. We sat up to the fire discussing chapelry business for a while and then, when I thought the time right, I asked him about Anne. He had sighed.

"Mr Teale's prognosis was the worst possible I'm afraid." He cut me a warning glance. "Consumption – like all my others – in both lungs." He inhaled deeply. "We must prepare for the worst."

"But, with respect, Sir," I leaned forward, clasping my hands over my knees, "in your long experience, you will have seen cases where the most desperately ill have, through the power of their will, triumphed over illness and recovered – because I know that, even in my short time, I have."

"Yes," he agreed, stroking his temples with his fingers, "miracles do happen and I have been privileged to witness one or two but, in this case, Dr Teale is adamant: Anne's lungs are already too damaged. False hopes will help no one, Mr Nicholls, our wisest course is to prepare ourselves and pray that Anne's piety will serve her."

"And a change of air?" I suggested, sitting back in my chair. "Everything one reads about consumption says that sea air can be beneficial."

"But in Anne's case ..." he began again but I stopped him.

"But if Anne wanted it; if she asked to be taken to Scarborough for instance, you would not forbid it."

"If it were also the medical advice." He opened his palms. "I will be guided by Dr Teale." I sensed movement. His total despair had now softened to taking advice and I needed to weaken that further.

"Do you think, Sir, that I might see Anne?" I knew this was bold, but I thought it essential if I were to keep her buoyed.

"Anne is confined to her bed."

"Yes, I know, and she is likely to remain there for some time. I just thought that her days must seem long and she might welcome a visit from someone beyond her own family."

"Yes," he said, a slight smile in his eye, "I dare say she would." He rang the bell for Martha. "Let us see if she is prepared."

I stood behind Martha while she tapped on Anne's door and it was Charlotte who answered. She shot me a glance and stepped out onto the landing, closing the door behind her.

"Yes, Martha?"

"Mr Nicholls, Miss Charlotte, come up to see Miss Anne." Martha shot off downstairs and Charlotte rushed to the bannister.

"No Martha! Martha!"

"Mr Brontë says!" Martha called back, then she disappeared round the corner into the kitchen, leaving Charlotte staring helplessly after her. A strong winter light was flooding the landing from the tall staircase window. It exposed the craqueleur in Charlotte's dry face and the halo of hairs escaped from her chignon. She looked desiccated in that hard light and much older than her thirty-two years.

"Your father has asked me to call on Miss Anne," I told her and she looked up at me.

"The time is not appropriate," she snapped, "I am sorry if you have been inconvenienced."

"I am not inconvenienced," I answered her. "Your father thought a change of company might cheer Anne." Then I gave her a level look. "I am sure that, when you ask her, she will see me. I hear she is improved." Charlotte held my level look.

"Not so improved as to be receiving strangers." The blood rushed to my head. That was bitterly unfair, and rude.

"Are you refusing to admit me?" My throat was dry and I struggled to contain myself but Charlotte stood firm. "Are you defying your father? I am here at his specific request, you know." She moved back to Anne's door and stood against it.

"Good day, Mr Nicholls." It was outrageous. I was there with Mr Brontë's blessing but what could I do? I could not throw Charlotte aside, nor could I run downstairs and complain to her father like some mewling schoolboy. I felt utterly humiliated and through clenched teeth I told Charlotte,

"Tell Anne that I was here, that I agree with her about Scarborough and that I am at her disposal at any time." I stayed glaring at Charlotte. I was not going to leave without an answer and, eventually, I got one.

"I shall," she said quietly, and so I left her barring the door and went down to let myself out.

I was furious with Charlotte but what could I do? As long as Anne was confined to her room Charlotte could debar me. I could go back to Mr Brontë but any hint of my fermenting a family dispute over what, to them, in present circumstances, was a triviality, would be both thoughtless and counterproductive. I needed to feed some hope into Anne, but how? I thought of Miss Nussey.

Miss Nussey had always struck me as a sensible woman and, what was more to my purpose, she was friendly with Anne. I made tentative enquiries of Martha, the following day, to find out how I might see Miss Nussey alone but Martha had told me she'd already left. She had taken the carrier's dogcart down to Keighley, just half an hour before, to catch the train to Leeds and I decided, there and then, I'd catch up with her. I calculated that she'd be catching the 4-45 train so I still had time if I walked quickly. It occurred to me that, actually, this was a perfect opportunity: the railway is a public place and neither Charlotte nor the servants would be there to disturb us.

I was down at the station in seventy minutes. It was getting dark when I arrived and a porter was lighting the lamps in the new ticket hall. I bought my ticket and walked down onto the Leeds-bound platform. There was a handful of commercial gentlemen and others already waiting beneath the yellow gas lights and, through the windows of the ladies waiting room, I saw Miss Nussey, cloaked and bonneted, sitting by the fire. When the train arrived and Miss Nussey came out, I affected surprise. I invented some plausible reason for my travelling to Leeds – I forget now what – and Miss Nussey agreed we should sit together. We climbed into the second class carriage and settled down for the seventy minute journey.

I did not want Miss Nussey, as Charlotte's confidante, to guess at the depth of my feelings for Anne so I approached the subject obliquely through more general talk of Emily and Branwell and the effects of their passing. The train was halfway to Leeds before any specific talk of Anne's condition were possible and Miss Nussey's opinion was fixed.

"I know few people better prepared than Anne Brontë," she affirmed. "I have known her since she was fourteen and I can tell you with perfect confidence, Mr Nicholls, that you will go a long way to find a more pious woman."

"Oh I agree with you," I told her. We were shoulder to shoulder: Miss Nussey beside the window that reflected, from the darkness, the interior of the carriage. "That is not my concern. My concern is that she should live." Miss Nussey gave me a look from inside her bonnet, a simple look that said, more eloquently than words, that God's will is inscrutable and where now were Branwell and Emily? "I mean only to say that there is great power in the human will and, if Anne is encouraged to believe she will recover, there is a better chance that she will. That is all." Miss Nussey smiled sadly.

"Dr Teale is the most successful lung specialist in the West Riding. He would not have told Anne to prepare for the worst unless he were sure. He too prefers that his patients live, you know."

"Yes, I understand that too, but we should not take even the most eminent physician's opinion to be the will of God. I just want those around Anne to encourage her, to take a positive attitude with her." I looked down at my hat on my knees. "And to pray as hard for her life as they do for her soul." Miss Nussey was peering out of the window, looking through our reflections for the rows of factory lights that would signal the beginnings of Leeds.

"You are a very diligent minister, Mr Nicholls," she said, still looking out, "you will wear yourself out if you worry this much about all your flock." There was an insinuation in Miss Nussey's tone that I did not like and I wondered what Charlotte had told her about me. I decided to ignore it.

"Anne believes that the sea air at Scarborough would do her good and I think she is right. There is plenty of evidence in the literature …" Miss Nussey turned to me.

"That is out of the question."

"But why?"

"Because it is too far and the weather too cold."

"Not far these days," I replied, turning to face her, "the railway extends to Scarborough now." Miss Nussey seemed about to speak but then changed her mind. "It's Charlotte who objects isn't it?" Red and orange lights were flicking past the window. We were approaching Leeds. Miss Nussey rested her head against the bulkhead at the back of our seat.

"You must bear in mind, Mr Nicholls, that Charlotte has suffered terrible loss in the last months." She rolled her head to face me. "If you had known this family as I did when they were young, when they were thrown together by the loss of their mother and their two older sisters, you would understand just how grievous is Charlotte's loss. Charlotte does not want Anne to die, Mr Nicholls, however well. She would sooner die herself than lose Anne after Branwell and Emily. That is why she protects her. Charlotte will not risk the journey to Scarborough, not until the spring."

We alighted at Leeds. I conducted Miss Nussey to her connection for Batley and then caught the next train back to Keighley. As I walked back up the Worth Valley to Haworth, it started to snow and by the time I was standing outside

Sexton House it was already three inches deep. I looked up at the shuttered windows of the parsonage: to the room where the last two siblings, beds together, were huddled against Fate and now the snow. No one was going to travel to Scarborough in this.

Charlotte nursed Anne through that long winter, attending to her every need. Miss Nussey had been right: Charlotte guarded Anne with the intense jealousy of a mother clutching the last of her brood. Caring nothing for herself and looking no further than Anne's immediate needs, Charlotte's commitment was total but what, I wondered, did Anne think? Charlotte was not Anne's mother and Anne not Charlotte's child. She was an independent woman made dependent only by a fate whose fickleness could so easily have reversed their roles and who then would have played the mother?

I do not know whether Charlotte passed on my message to Anne – that I was at her disposal at any time – but no invitation came and I was powerless to impose. I heard from Martha that Anne continued to ask to be taken to Scarborough but Dr Teale was doubtful and Charlotte adamant, throwing up objections about the snow and the cold and the battering that the east coast towns suffer from the North Sea gales. Unable to speak to Anne or Charlotte, I put it to Mr Brontë that Scarborough was imperative. I offered to take Anne myself but the idea worried him, everything about Anne worried him, I think he was by then frozen by a conviction that Anne was lost and all decisions about her he now left to Charlotte. And so we waited. I think Charlotte feared that, once Anne had left home, she would never come back but, by early April, Dr Teale was coming to the view that, with the warmer weather, Scarborough might indeed do Anne some good. Charlotte continued to resist but in May the grounds of Charlotte's objections melted with the snow and arrangements were finally made: Charlotte and Miss Nussey would accompany Anne to Scarborough and my offer to chaperone and shoulder the administrative load was declined.

It was Thursday, around noon, on the 24th May when I heard the carriage and horses in the lane. I had been in church, praying. I got up from my knees and went to the north door to watch. The carriage, Michael Pickles' closed landau, had turned round in the drying field and was drawn up at the parsonage gate. The morning was mild, but even so, when the three figures emerged from the parsonage, they were all wearing heavy travelling capes and bonnets and even inside those clothes the figure that Charlotte and Miss Nussey supported between them seemed little burden.

John Brown and Michael Pickles loaded boxes onto the back of the carriage and Martha held open the door while Keeper and Flossy sniffed around the axles trying to make sense of the altered routine. Only when all was stowed and Pickles was up on his box did Mr Brontë come out. He neither waved nor smiled but stood on his front step and watched as the last of his family was taken from him. I looked into the carriage as they passed but saw only shapes. Keeper and Flossy were trotting behind. I called them back and took them for a walk on the moors.

Anne died in Scarborough on the following Monday, at two o'clock in the afternoon. Charlotte and Miss Nussey were at her side and, according to their accounts, Anne passed away peacefully and in full confidence. At least she had died in Scarborough, and in the same Woods' Lodgings where she had holidayed with the Robinson girls and been happy. Anne left us some last words and they are characteristically selfless: 'Take courage, Charlotte, take courage.'

Had Anne thought anything about me at the end? I don't know. I wasn't allowed to see her for the last months of her life, let alone be with her at Scarborough. My last sight of Anne, and my abiding memory, is of her in her bedroom. She was sitting, small and stooped, on the edge of her bed in an over-sized night shirt and cap. She was smiling at me: a calm, confident smile of reassurance. Had she been reassuring me of her confidence in the hereafter? Or reassuring me of her confidence in me? If she had lived, could Anne Brontë have loved me as I had loved her? I shall always believe so.

CHAPTER TEN

Charlotte alone and exposed

It had been Charlotte's decision to leave Anne at Scarborough. She had written to her father the day following Anne's death and even while he was giving the sad news to Tabby and Martha in the parsonage kitchen, Anne's body was being lowered into its grave. I was dismayed. I had never heard any suggestion that Anne would lie anywhere but with the rest of her family in the vault beneath St Michael's Church but the deed was done, *fait accompli*. Charlotte should not have left Anne all alone ninety miles away. She belonged with her family and besides, where now could her father mourn her, or Tabby or the Browns or I – for I too grieved and needed Anne near.

The parsonage fell silent. The busy household of three strong-minded women and the flamboyant brother had, by successive scythe cuts, shrunk. During that terrible harvest, the energy of the house had been sustained by the bustle and worry of caring for the sick but now that they were all gone, there was nothing. The silence was profound and, though the servants and Mary and John and I all nursed our private griefs, we all knew who it was that grieved most.

I found it hard to face Mr Brontë. His loss was so overwhelming that I could not imagine how he must feel, especially as he had taken it so calmly. Perhaps he already knew that he wouldn't see Anne again. Perhaps he had drained his cup of grief six days earlier when he'd watched the closed landau roll down the lane, or perhaps the repeated hammer blows of loss had reforged his spirit into some new and harder stuff. I didn't know, but he did not falter; he remained straight and stoic and carried on with the business of his calling. I was in awe of him and, at the same time, disappointed. After all he had suffered with his wife and two oldest, to lose, within the span of a single pregnancy, three more children, was the stuff of Job and yet he still stood. He must have been anguished but he would not show it. I wished that he would. I wanted to see him grieve and share it with him because I had loved Anne too and she deserved our tears but he would not share it, not even with Charlotte. Replying to her letter that had brought the sad news, he had asked that she remain on the coast with Miss Nussey to give herself time, as he put it, to 'restore her spirits' and, in deference to him, she did. She left us in our mournful silence for a month.

When Charlotte did finally come home, on the 21st June, the parsonage fell under her rule. Suddenly, everything was about her: Charlotte's grief, Charlotte's headaches and Charlotte's outpourings of concern for her father who had, just the day before, as it happened, taken to his bed with bronchitis. Martha, who was an experienced nurse by then and used to Mr Brontë's ways, was set aside. I, his assistant, was set aside too. It was her possession of Anne all over again. Charlotte had clung to Anne as the last of her siblings and now that the tide of loss had risen even higher she clung to the last of her entire family. It was a moving display of filial devotion and I hope I behaved well towards her but in my heart I was bitter that she'd kept me from Anne, vetoed for too long the journey to Scarborough and then, when all was arranged, refused my help. Nothing rankles like injustice. It seemed to me that after four years in Haworth I was still to Charlotte nothing more than her father's latest curate whose feelings need not be considered but then, one day, following her father's recovery, she came to the door with me.

"Papa does appreciate your support, Mr Nicholls." She was holding open the door for me. "Your presence is a great comfort to him. He has told me as much." The civility was so unexpected, I didn't know what to say. Charlotte rarely said anything to me; I was frankly suspicious; I expected a *but*, but when none came I answered her as best I could.

"I have worked with your father these past four years," I told her, "and I must tell you that whatever value he puts on me is as nothing compared to the profit I take daily from his example." Charlotte squinted up at me through her spectacles, her russet face glowing in the sunlight streaming in through the door.

"That is not what I meant." She lowered her eyes to the flags but then, when she looked up, I saw there were tears in them. "My father has suff … *we* … have suffered terrible loss." She was watching me now, defying me to notice her tears. "If I feel the loss then how much more must my father? I know that you were attentive to him when I was away and I believe that your continued attention fills some part of what he has lost. I thank you for it." Charlotte then handed me my hat from the hall table and turned back into the house.

Mr Brontë continued to fulfil his duties throughout those terrible months – and more than his duties – even at such a time, he revived his campaign for the public health. Shocked by the cholera epidemic of the year before, the government had rushed into legislation with its Public Health Act. The measure established a General Board of Health to which communities could petition for a free survey of their sanitation provision and recommendations for improvements. It was just the legislation for which Mr Brontë had, for years, been campaigning and he formed a committee comprising myself, Dr Wheelhouse and the Dissenting ministers under the chairmanship of Joseph Greenwood — Branwell's 'Five Bob Joe'. Our first task was to garner the signatures of ten percent of the affected population which, after a slow start, we managed to do and the petition was dispatched at the end of October.

Mr Brontë was magnificent in those months following Anne's death. He'd grasped at the petition for the good of the village and also, I am sure, for his own sake too, as an engine of hope that might drag him, if not out of grief, then at least out of morbid self-pity but I found it hard. I felt disorientated. I don't think I'd realised, until Anne fell ill, just how much my hopes had rested with her. I felt lost. I continued to go through the motions of doing what the chapelry expected of me but my heart wasn't in it, it was ninety miles away, lying in a grave on the Yorkshire coast. Faith, Hope and Charity are the Christian virtues. The Church has much to say about Faith and Charity but Hope also matters and Anne, even the wistful Anne, had been my hope for the future.

I saw little of Charlotte that summer: like her father, she had thrown herself into work which, for her, meant finishing her next novel. It suited me well enough not to see her although, to be fair, her manner had changed. Ever since the day she saw me to the door and thanked me for my care of her father, she had continued to be civil and, while it was years by then since I could be hurt by her coldness, the thaw was welcome. Had the hammer blows of loss that had toughened the father had the reverse effect on the sister? It appeared so.

Charlotte's third novel was published in the October and to lukewarm notices. The successor to *Jane Eyre* had been keenly anticipated and so was widely reviewed but, with only the odd exception, the critics were disappointed with *Shirley*: it was 'a feeble effort' … 'at once the most high-flown and the stalest of fictions.' Critics will find interest where they can however and they were triumphant that, if they did not know the true identity of Currer Bell, they had at least discovered her gender: 'the hand of a woman is unmistakably impressed on the present production'.

I read *Shirley* but I didn't enjoy it. It argues too many contradictory points of view and I couldn't see its purpose. It is the story of two parallel love affairs, and a secondary plot concerns the conflict between master and men in a textile mill. There are also conflicts between the Church and Dissenters and the narrator delights in mocking the clergy; I found the whole thing disjointed and unsatisfactory. *Jane Eyre*, for all its faults, is a book that insists on being read; *Shirley*, I struggled to finish.

Residents of Haworth who read *Shirley* claimed to recognise in its pages portraits of some of their neighbours and Miss Nussey identified others of Charlotte's acquaintance from Birstall. Of the Haworth portraits, I shall mention just two: the first caricatures one of our best-loved and most dedicated clerics as a conceited bigot called Donne; the second is an equally exaggerated portrait of a Reverend Mr

Macarthey – 'a decent, decorous and conscientious curate who laboured faithfully in the parish and who was sane and rational, diligent and charitable'. The first was said to be Charlotte's impression of Joseph Grant, and the second, her impression of me.

* * *

Charlotte had been in Birstall when *Shirley* was published, visiting Miss Nussey, and it was from there that her authorship was exposed. It could not have been otherwise; so many of the book's characters were based on Charlotte's Birstall acquaintances. Did Charlotte's concern for anonymity loosen with the deaths of her sisters? Both Emily and Anne had been jealous of it. Or did she really think that her portraits would go unrecognised? Whichever it was, it was only a matter of weeks after *Shirley* was published before Charlotte had to acknowledge that she was indeed the celebrated author, Currer Bell.

Word of Charlotte's exposure passed from Birstall to the Bradford wool market where Michael Merrall picked it up and brought it back to Haworth. Currer Bell, the author of *Jane Eyre*, was a celebrated name among the borrowers of contemporary fiction and the news that she was in fact Charlotte, the daughter of our own Anglican minister, created a local sensation and unprecedented demands on the institute library. The news spread also to London where the barrier erected by Charlotte's publisher was finally breached. Currer Bell's admirers started writing to Charlotte at the parsonage. Aspiring novelists sought her advice and established writers, such as Mrs Gaskell and Miss Martineau, congratulated her. The Secretary to the Board of Education,

Sir James Kay-Shuttleworth, wrote admiringly to Charlotte as did the celebrated astronomer, Sir John Herschel. Almost overnight, the salons of literary London were thrown open to Charlotte and her publisher, George Smith, exhorted her to enter. At first, Charlotte hesitated, aware that to step across that threshold might change her life for ever but then, having temporized, she accepted Smith's invitation and in November she left us to spend two weeks with his family in Paddington.

George Smith was only twenty-six at the time and still lived at home with his widowed mother, a younger brother and three grown-up sisters. It was another family of educated women such as Charlotte could not have expected to find and, knowing her story, the Smiths took Charlotte to their bosom. Smith was a gentleman and a businessman and while, as a gentleman, he was careful of Charlotte's sensibilities, he was not, as a businessman, going to squander the opportunity to promote his most profitable author. He took Charlotte to the theatre, to galleries and to the new Houses of Parliament. He took her to salons and soirées, introducing her to the famous and fashionable and, on the final evening of the visit, he hosted a dinner for Charlotte at which the principal guest was none other than Charlotte's paragon of fictive truth, W M Thackeray.

That London visit, at the end of '49, had been sandwiched between Charlotte's sojourn at Birstall in the October and Miss Nussey's return visit to the parsonage over the New Year. This round of visiting suited Charlotte. In London, she had been accepted into England's leading literary coterie while at home she had fallen into the arms of her oldest friend. These new alliances were a balm, an opiate to

Charlotte's crippling sense of loss and she resorted to their efficacy with increasing frequency. She stayed with Miss Nussey again the following April and with the Smiths in London for the four weeks of June. Nor was Charlotte's taste for visiting confined to Birstall and London. She accepted invitations to Mrs Gaskell's home in Manchester and to Sir James and Lady Kay-Shuttleworth's establishments at Padiham and on Lake Windermere. Her attentive, half-Scot publisher, George Smith, took her to Edinburgh where he showed Charlotte the sights of that ancient capital as assiduously as he had shown her London and after both her Edinburgh and London trips, Charlotte returned first to Birstall before coming home. Neither distance nor time were a barrier to Charlotte nor, evidently, was expense. She was now a woman of independent means, she could come and go as she pleased and she did.

Charlotte's circumstances had changed so much since the publication of *Shirley*. With her anonymity torn from her, she was exposed to the public gaze. Wherever she went, her movements were reported in the newspapers, strange faces appeared in church and uninvited visitors came knocking at the parsonage door. Two such were Lord John Manners and Richard Monckton Milnes, and while Mr Brontë delighted in receiving these High Tory literati, Charlotte avoided any visitor if she possibly could. Charlotte was ambivalent about her fame. She disliked the social snobbery of literary London but she endured it for the access it gave her to those she had always considered her equals and, in the company of a Thackeray, a Matthew Arnold or a Harriette Martineau, she could discuss her craft with her peers.

An encounter that particularly impressed Mr Brontë was Charlotte's brush with the Duke of Wellington. During the June visit to London, Smith had taken Charlotte to the Chapel Royal in Saint James's Palace. The chapel was the Duke's place of worship and, after the service, Smith had contrived to twice meet the great man on his way back to Apsley House. Wellington was to Mr Brontë and Charlotte the very soul of England, the hero who could do no wrong, it was something that father and daughter had always had in common and that Charlotte should actually meet the Duke was the stuff of Mr Brontë's dreams.

"I am blessed, am I not, Mr Nicholls?" Mr Brontë had confided to me one day. "All the promise of my brilliant son is fulfilled in my daughter. All his life, Branwell had but one over-riding ambition, to be a successful author, to inhabit the milieu of intellectuals and to banter with the makers of fashion. He never visited London you know, but he was so fascinated with the metropolis that he knew every street and building of it, he knew every picture in the National Collection and he knew which oratorios were playing to what notices in what theatres. I am sorry that my son did not achieve his ambition," Mr Brontë mused, "but I thank God he was spared the sight of his sister achieving it for him."

Poor Mr Brontë. He was so proud of Charlotte and he enjoyed her success but after the decimation of his household he would have enjoyed her company more. During the winter and spring of 1850, Charlotte was absent more than she was at home. Her continuous round of visiting was her way of filling her void of grief, I understood that, but then, if Charlotte was bereft, how much more was her father? I felt for him. He was a stoical man – the most stoical I ever met – but I could see he was anguished: it was there in the set of his jaw, in the sag of his shoulders and in the far-distant gaze of his mis-matched eyes when he thought he was not being observed. During that first year after Anne's death I spent more time with Mr Brontë than I ever had before. Alone for weeks in that empty house, he needed my company and I needed his. He was Anne's father. The least I could do for her was look after him.

In the summer of '48, just before the deluge broke, my Oxenhope friend, Joseph Grant, had married and, at the beginning of 1850, his wife Sarah was delivered of a son. They had called the boy Charles and, on a sunny afternoon in May, I accepted an invitation to meet him. I should have been glad, walking beneath the elms on the way to visit friends with the scent of fresh growth and birdsong filling the air, but my heart was not glad, it was heavy, and I knew why: we were three days away from the anniversary of Anne's death. Her own words will speak for me:

> Brightly the sun of summer shone,
> Green fields and waving woods upon,
> And soft winds wandered by;
> Above, a sky of purest blue,
> Around, bright flowers of loveliest hue,
> Allured the gazer's eye.
>
> But what were all these charms to me,
> When one sweet breath of memory
> Came gently wafting by?

I closed my eyes against the day,
And called my willing soul away,
From earth, and air, and sky.

I heard Charles' bawling before I got to Marshlands and when I turned in through the garden gate, Sarah was bent over his crib.

"Is he hungry?" I asked, by way of greeting, and Sarah looked round.

"Mr Nicholls!" She gave me a sunny smile. "You look hot."

"I am hot." I went and peered in the crib beside her. Charles was four months old by then and a grand fat fellow with a big pair of lungs. "What a terrible noise!" I picked him up and held him out in front of me. "He doesn't look hungry."

"He isn't. He's just been fed. I hope it's not colic." I put him over my shoulder.

"He's getting a bit old for colic. It's probably just wind." I jiggled him lightly on my shoulder, rubbing his back and walking up and down the path until the wind came and he quietened.

"You're a wonder." Sarah held out her arms and I passed Charles back to her.

"Brothers and sisters and lots of cousins," I told her, "I've had plenty of practice."

Sarah was tall and slim with heavy auburn hair that she let fall, when at home, down her back. I liked her. She was positive and cheerful and, as a rector's daughter, the model of a clerical wife.

"Joseph is in the parlour if you want to go in. I'll give Charles to Susie and bring us some drinks."

I found Grant in his armchair sitting beside a grate filled with May blossom. He'd been reading a book and, when I walked in, he held it aloft to show me the spine. It was *Shirley*.

"Aah," I said, "how much have you read?"

"I didn't have to read very far," he smiled, "I'm libelled in the first chapter. She doesn't care who she offends, your Miss Charlotte, does she? Although, I see you get off pretty lightly; she obviously likes *you*!" Sarah came in with three tumblers of barley water and I brought up a side chair to sit with them. Sarah sank into her armchair, glowing after her exertions in the garden.

"Tea in five minutes. Just time to cool off." She took a long draught of the cordial and relaxed into her chair. "I wish I could take Charlotte's lampoon as lightly as Joseph," she said, "but I'm afraid I can't." She looked at me. "If she had traduced just one local clergyman, people might at least have been left in some doubt as to who her victim might be but when she caricatures three close colleagues, anyone who knows them – and, mark me, everybody will read this book – anyone who knows them is bound to recognise them. It is so cruel. So gratuitous. What harm did Joseph do to Charlotte Brontë that she pillories him? Or James Smith? Or James Bradley? And how does that silly tea party advance her plot anyway? You are a friend of Charlotte's, Mr Nicholls. Can you tell me why she has to be so cruel?" Sarah was pretending to be playful but I could see she was annoyed and I didn't blame her.

"I wouldn't say I was a friend of Charlotte's."

"Well, she clearly thinks well of you, *Mr Macarthey*! Yours is an altogether different portrait." I shifted uncomfortably and crossed my legs.

"Writing novels is Charlotte's career," I attempted, "she observes people." Sarah drained her cordial and rested her arms along the arms of the chair.

"If she knew people better she wouldn't need to *observe* them. Charlotte is far too close, so was Emily. If Charlotte would only mix and talk with people as her sister Anne did then she could furnish her books with real characters instead of these distortions fashioned from prejudice."

"Anne was a good woman," Grant agreed, "quiet, but an asset to her father in the village." He looked at me. "Brontë will miss that one." I said nothing. I was not going to enter into a conversation about Anne as the dutiful pastoral visitor. There was an awkward silence, but then Sarah slapped her hands on the arms of her chair.

"There we are then," she said brightly, "I've got Charlotte Brontë off my chest. Shall we go through?"

Tea was, as always at Sarah's, excellent. There was pink ham and parsley and a fresh cob of bread, preserves and cakes and cracknel biscuits for cheese, it looked splendid but I didn't have the appetite. Grant rendered thanks and we sat down then he asked me about the parsonage.

"I hear the parsonage is to be pulled apart this summer," he said, buttering bread, but my mind had been elsewhere.

"Pulled apart?"

"I ran into William Wood. He told me he'd had you up on the roof about turning the slates."

"Yes, I went up with him but I don't think it needs turning. I think we can patch it. That's what I've told Mr Brontë anyway. It's up to him and the trustees."

"Then why do you have to go up onto the roof?" Sarah asked me.

"Well, there was water getting in last winter and Mr Brontë is not really up to climbing roofs."

"But the parsonage is not your responsibility," Sarah bridled, and she looked at Grant. "Mr Nicholls should not be looking after the parsonage roof should he Joseph?" Grant could not answer; his mouth was full of food. "You already do too much for Mr Brontë, what with the sanitation committee and the Haworth and Stanbury schools. I hope he appreciates it."

"Mrs Grant, please," I reminded her, "you know what Mr Brontë has been through and he cannot leave building works to Tabby and Martha."

"There's Charlotte. Charlotte is perfectly capable." Grant had emptied his mouth.

"Charlotte's paying for it. That's what Wood told me." I was surprised.

"I'm sure that's not necessary," I said. "The Church Lands Trust is responsible for the building."

"Ah," Grant pointed his knife at me, "but while the roof is being done, Charlotte is taking the opportunity to move some internal walls. She has asked Wood for drawings and costings for enlarging the dining room and her bedroom above it – and she's ordered new furniture. Major works."

"I don't know anything about that," I told him. "I thought it was just the roof."

"Well," Sarah said, "if Charlotte wants to spend her new-found wealth on remodelling the parsonage, she must manage the work herself." She looked to me to agree but I hedged.

"Charlotte will be in London this summer."

"And last month she was in Birstall. I am sorry, Mr Nicholls, but, on top of everything else, you should not be left managing Charlotte's extravagancies." Susie came in with the tea pot and Sarah stood up to pour.

"If something were to happen to Mr Brontë," she continued, "would you stay on in Haworth?"

"Oh dear!" I sat back in my chair. "That's a big question."

"You would not stay on as somebody else's assistant, surely?" Grant added. "You would go for the living yourself, wouldn't you? Or go for another parish?"

"I really cannot answer this," I told them, embarrassed. "God willing, that is all a long way off."

"As you point out though," Grant persisted, "Brontë is not what he was and you are a capable priest. Many men with less experience than you have their own parishes."

"Men with wives, though," Sarah added. "Vestry committees like their incumbents to be married, don't they Joseph?"

"That's right. You must marry, Nicholls. Get yourself a wife and children and a parish of your own." My hosts exchanged self-satisfied smiles and then Sarah asked me:

"Have you never thought of marrying, Mr Nicholls?"

I had been a poor guest at the Grants' that day but our friendship could stand it. The truth was that I was absorbed with the approaching anniversary. All through May, I had been inexorably drawn towards the day and on the day I went to Scarborough. Nobody knew I had gone. It was another low time in the parsonage and I don't think I was missed.

I walked from the railway station to Castle Road, then up the hill across the back of the harbour to St Mary's church and the headland crowned by the castle's walls. St Mary's burial ground lies between the church and the castle, on the sloping headland that looks out over South Bay and the cold grey mass of the North Sea beyond. Anne is buried in an exposed position at the highest margin of the ground and the clean new headstone was not hard to find. It had a draped urn engraved on it and the text beneath it read:

Here
Lie the remains of
Anne Brontë
Daughter of the
Rev.d P Brontë
Incumbent of Haworth Yorkshire
She died, Aged 28
May 28th 1849

The age at death was incorrect and there were other errors of careless execution. No *author*, no *poet*, no *sister and friend* – no apposite scriptural text. I stood at the foot of the shallow mound where a few sparse grasses were struggling to establish themselves. There she was, in that desolate spot. I felt cold to the bone and I wept.

CHAPTER ELEVEN

Of men and heroes

It was in the spring of 1850 that the Board of Health's Superintendent Inspector, Mr Benjamin Herschel Babbage, came to make his inspection. Forearmed with maps and statistics, he visited every corner of the district – and not just the stinking yards – he walked the moors as well, to view areas of water catchment, and along the valley seeking sites for outflows: he was thorough, professional and systematic, and when his report arrived at the parsonage, Mr Brontë was elated.

"This is first class," he told me as I entered the parlour one morning, "meticulous statistical analysis and all to the very heart of the matter." Mr Brontë was standing at the window, bending the report to the light. He indicated one of the chairs beside him and I sat down. "'Seventy-three midden-steads and manure heaps each capable of inducing fever and disease,'" he read triumphantly. "Did you know there is only one privy in Gauger's Croft? Over a hundred people live there, and it is as bad at the bottom of Kirkgate. You just cannot know these things until they are properly surveyed." And he read out to me some of the more ghastly examples of our putrid wells and seeping soil heaps that the inspector had detailed in his report. "Now this is what we needed to know." He waved the report at me. "Here, at last, we have evidence on which we can act. 'Haworth …'" he turned again to the light and leafed through the report. "Here we are … 'the village of Haworth has a mortality rate and a rate of sickness relief that is 44% higher than its neighbours in Stanbury and Oxenhope.' What do you think is the average life expectancy in the village, Mr Nicholls?" I thought for a moment but it was an impossible question.

"I don't know, Sir."

"You must have an idea. What do you think?" I was obliged to hazard a guess.

"Forty?"

"*Forty*!" Mr Brontë chided. "It is twenty-five! Twenty-five years and ten months! And nearly a quarter of all our children back in the bosom of the Lord before they see six months. This is the mortality rate of Whitechapel in the heart of the Great Wen, and we here surrounded by the good air and clear streams of the virgin moors. Well …" Mr Brontë, clutching his report, put his hands behind his back and paced the floor. "There are now things that we can do about it." He pointed the rolled paper at me. "Water catchment areas, piping, drainage, flow rates, costings, rateable charges – it is all here." He removed his spectacles and looked out of the window to the church. "Mr Babbage believes that if we implement his recommendations then twenty people every year that, under present conditions, die, will be spared to remain among us – twenty every year!" Then he smiled down at me in the chair beside him. "How many pennies on the rate is that worth, Mr Nicholls?"

"Amen," I agreed, and I returned his smile.

Mr Brontë had invested a deal of time and energy in securing the Board's report and its recommendations had exceeded his highest hopes. To Mr Brontë, the report brought Haworth into the modern world, connecting the village with the larger England as surely as if a railway had been pushed up the Worth Valley. The highest professional standards of the capital's civil administration had been applied to Haworth and comparisons drawn with communities as diverse as Castleford, Whitechapel and Manchester. Haworth had, for the first time, been measured by the national standard. It was no longer admissible to declare that such is the way that we do things here and so it always shall be, or accept as normal that in Haworth we live in our own filth and die before our time, for the report showed us that our ways of life and death are not normal; we had been put to the national measure and we had failed.

Mr Brontë called a public meeting to present Mr Babbage's report and, while initial reaction was positive, factional interests inevitably emerged. The occupiers of outlying farms, who were the backbone of the rate-paying body, objected to paying for pipes in the village that they would not use, and the Merrall family petitioned for exemption for all their properties. Mrs Ferrand, the absentee Lord of the Manor of Haworth, and her influential heir, William, did the same, a move that doubtless weighed with the socially aspiring Joseph Greenwood – the committee's chairman – who turned his coat too. Mr Brontë was furious. It was a critical moment. It was the moment when Mr Richard Butterfield, the new owner of Bridgehouse Mill, recently come up from Keighley, chose to organise his own petition alleging malpractice in the whole process.

The majority of the village thought it outrageous that a newcomer, who had barely unpacked his boxes, should mount such an aggressive move but, with the Ferrands, the Merralls and Joseph Greenwood assuring him of the signatures of their tenants and employees, Butterfield's petition went forward and Mr Brontë's campaign was stopped. Mr Brontë challenged Butterfield as to the real purpose of his petition but, as a Whig and a Methodist with no loyalty to the village, Butterfield would not answer to the ageing Tory parson; it was a conversation of the deaf, a dishonourable business, and Mr Brontë was brought low by it.

At seventy-four and unused to defeat, Mr Brontë succumbed to a bout of chronic dyspepsia and the doctor ordered rest. His spirits sank and, though his dyspepsia improved, he remained morose. I did what I could to interest him in the affairs of the chapelry and the wider world but he remained abstracted, it was not like him and it saddened me. Charlotte, who was away at the time and hearing only by letter, would not credit Butterfield with the power to bring her father down, but I did. I had always believed that the passion Mr Brontë expended on bringing Babbage to Haworth had been a displacement of his grief. I wondered now if the depth of his resentment of Butterfield was the displacement of his resentment of Providence herself.

A cheerful event that punctuated the gloom of the summer of 1850 was the arrival, at the end of July, of two pictures from London. One was a portrait of Charlotte that her publisher, George Smith, had commissioned as a present for Mr Brontë, and the other an engraving of the Duke of Wellington, also from Smith, as a memento of Charlotte's encounter with him. Charlotte happened to be at home when the pictures arrived and she invited me up to view them. It was a courtesy that would have been unthinkable only twelve months before but one that was in line with her growing acceptance of me and of my closeness to her father.

It was a hot afternoon of high summer, the first dry day after many of rain and, the front door being open, I called a 'Hello' and walked in. The remodelled hallway was narrower since Charlotte's alterations, not much more than a passage, but the dining room was larger and really quite grand. There was a new fireplace, new rugs and curtains and a beautiful mahogany dining suite with console tables to match. As I walked in, the family was already examining the portraits propped on the back of the sofa.

"Urgh!" Tabby groaned, peering at Richmond's portrait of Charlotte, "It makes yer look old before yer time." And then, moving to the engraving, "good one o' the Master though." Mr Brontë and Charlotte both laughed.

"It's not the Master yer doilem!" said Martha, "that's Duke o' Wellin'ton!" and Martha too shook her head and laughed.

"Well," said Tabby, setting her jaw, "it looks like Master to me. Now get me up. I've some scones in." And Martha helped Tabby to her feet and took her through to the kitchen.

"I think Tabby is right," Mr Brontë agreed as the servants left, "Richmond does have you older than your years, Charlotte, and the features are imperfect, but the expression is wonderfully good, wonderfully life-like." He examined the watercolour more closely. "No," he decided, "he may not have your exact physiognomy but he has achieved a true representation of your mind. There is life and speech and motion in this portrait. I do believe he has captured the genius of the author of *Jane Eyre* and *Shirley*." He nodded in agreement with himself. "It is a skilful execution. We shall hang it on the chimney breast." Mr Brontë then moved to the engraving of Wellington. He picked it up and carried it across the room to compare it with an earlier present from Smith: an engraving of Thackeray.

"Shall we hang the Iron Duke beside Mr Thackeray, Charlotte?" He held the one beside the other on the wall. "They are of a similar colour and size. They will make the beginnings of a gallery of your heroes."

"Mr Thackeray a hero?" I asked Charlotte. "Would you agree with that?"

"She dedicated *Jane Eyre* to him," Mr Brontë replied, propping Wellington against the wall on the floor.

"Only the second edition," Charlotte corrected him, and Mr Brontë tipped me a wink.

"I do not receive a letter from my daughter in London but it carries the name Thackeray a dozen times." Charlotte's face flushed.

"Mr Thackeray is a prodigious talent with an unerring nose for truth," she told her father, "but my dedication was a mistake for a number of reasons. I did not know Mr Thackeray then as I know him now."

"Perhaps it is unwise for us to meet our heroes," I suggested.

"She has met Wellington," Mr Brontë now put in, moving towards the door, "I don't think the experience diminished her regard for him."

"I did not *meet* Wellington," Charlotte insisted, following her father out, "we saw him in the street and Mr Smith merely bid him a good day." But Mr Brontë had closed his parlour door, leaving Charlotte all alone in the hall. I too was left all alone, in the dining room. Charlotte turned and looked back at me. I don't think she wanted to re-join me, but nor could she decently leave me.

"Shall we go into the garden?" she suggested, for want of an alternative, and we went out into the sunshine and sat down together on the rustic seat. The intimacy felt strange and not entirely comfortable. I returned to the subject of Wellington.

"Perhaps if you had met Wellington properly," I suggested, squinting back at the house against the sun, "you might have found failings in him, as you found in Thackeray."

"I think the man who saved the world for civilisation might be permitted some foibles," Charlotte answered. "I cannot conceive of a more heroic figure than the Duke of Wellington. He is the very model of a man."

"The very model of a military man I will concede, but the emancipation of the Catholics has not been an unalloyed success, nor is his family life untouched by scandal." Charlotte shot me a look.

"We need heroes, Mr Nicholls. Without our exemplars, the rest of us would have no higher measure to aspire to than our own poor selves and then how far would our civilisation advance?" and she added: "Can you tell me that you never had a hero?"

"Once," I told her, "but he was human and he betrayed me." I raised an eyebrow at her. "There is one infallible hero though isn't there? I think you will find that it was Christ Jesus who saved the world for civilisation." Charlotte's eyes softened.

"Politics and religion."

"I beg your pardon?"

"People talk of 'politics *and* religion' because they are separate."

"I don't think your father would agree with you there. He is equally evangelical about both."

"Ah," Charlotte now smiled, "but Papa is the exception that proves the rule."

"He is," I agreed, "and a hero who would never betray you."

"Unless you betrayed him." Charlotte's smile turned wistful. "Papa too is human."

The sun had gone off the front of the house but every other part of the garden baked. Insects buzzed intermittently but no birds sang and the only other sound was the steady 'chip – chip' of John Brown's engraving chisel in the barn across the lane. I thought about Mr Brontë in his parlour, standing erect in his iron faith, and I wondered if he looked out on his daughter and his curate sitting together on his garden seat. I wondered, if he did, what he thought, and what he might have thought if he had been looking out on that other summer's day when I had sat on the same seat with Anne, and I wondered what he might have thought if …

"You are quiet, Mr Nicholls." Charlotte had been watching me. She had removed her spectacles and, without them, her green-brown eyes were large and clear.

"I was just thinking about such a day as this, some years ago, when we sat here with Miss Nussey," I confessed. "How is Miss Nussey by the way? It's a long time since I've seen her in Haworth."

"She has been unwell but she is better now, thank you." Charlotte put her hands under her thighs and swung her short legs like a child. "The care of her mother and her sister Mercy keeps her at home, and since her sister Ann got married last year and brought home her husband, there is much to keep Ellen occupied."

"Her sister Ann was married last year? I don't believe I heard about that. How old is her sister?"

"Ann?"

"Yes."

"Fifty-four."

"Fifty-four!" I was amazed. "She is twenty years older than Miss Ellen and she has only just married?"

"Twenty-one years older. They are the oldest and the youngest of twelve." I thought about Ellen Nussey: how pretty she was, how cheerful and always so beautifully dressed.

"Does Miss Ellen never think of marrying?"

"She has had her suitors, but no, Ellen will not marry. Those of us who have the care of a parent are not free to give ourselves to another." I had to smile. All those weeks and months that Charlotte had been away. Charlotte did not see me smile. She was watching her feet swinging over the grass.

"You are fortunate in your friendship with Miss Nussey." Charlotte looked up at me.

"Yes I am. Ellen and I have been friends from childhood. I lost my mother, Ellen lost her father; I was brought up by a maiden aunt, she by a bachelor uncle; we have both lost sisters and troubled brothers." Charlotte half closed one eye against the sun. "I love Ellen, Mr Nicholls. There is no one in the world now who means as much to me." Charlotte gave me a smile which I returned. I was glad for her.

"Your sister believed that you and Miss Nussey might be happiest if you could be together always."

"My sister Anne?" Charlotte looked amused. "Anne said that to you?" She looked at me curiously, but the idea did not seem entirely foolish to her. "But we both have commitments. Ellen in Birstall and I in Haworth."

"And if you did not?" She did not blench.

"You have seen who my heroes are, Mr Nicholls. If I ever make such a commitment, it will not be to a woman."

That sunny afternoon at the parsonage was a pleasant interlude in an otherwise wet and miserable summer during which Charlotte was frequently ill. It was part of a developing pattern: sojourns away followed by homecomings followed by sickness. Within days of her return from Birstall or London Charlotte would have pains in her shoulders, pains in her sides and head, and all this on top of the bilious fevers to which she was monthly martyred. Going visiting may have been a palliative to Charlotte's loneliness but reaction followed as soon as she returned and I wondered if the remedy was worth the reaction. I also wondered if the company Charlotte was keeping was really good for her. Charlotte was herself openly critical of the worldly cynicism of Thackeray and others of Smith's London circle, but the pack that she ran with in Westmoreland seemed to me just as dubious: John Ruskin, the self-proclaimed arbiter of all taste and radical social reformer; Miss Harriette Martineau, novelist, social economist and proselytising atheist; Francis Newman, the 'freethinking' brother of the apostate John Henry, and Mrs Elizabeth Gaskell, the Condition of England novelist wife of a Unitarian minister. But of all the fashionable people that Charlotte associated with when she was away, the largest presence among them was that of her publisher,

George Smith, and I wondered whether his influence was any better than the rest.

Smith had paid Charlotte £500 for the rights to *Jane Eyre* and it had been the publishing triumph of the year. The further £500 that he paid for *Shirley* had also repaid him handsomely and, having purchased from Newby the rights to Anne's and Emily's novels, he was doubtless profiting from those works too, but the firm Smith inherited from his father had debts and he was a long way from being free of them. Smith needed Charlotte to stay with Smith Elder & Co and he needed her to write more novels but, since *Shirley*, Charlotte had found it hard. The loss of her sisters had not only drained Charlotte emotionally, it had deprived her of the critical questioning that had been central to her creative method. Charlotte did not know how she was going to write again, there was no subject that inspired her and her spirits were so low that she could not rise to the task. Smith understood that. It was why he entertained her so assiduously in London and exposed her to stimulating company. I think he believed that if Charlotte were to find her creative drive again, she would need to be taken out of herself and out of Haworth. When he went to Edinburgh to bring home his younger brother from school, Smith took Charlotte with him and showed her the sights and he would have taken her further, on a tour of the wild highlands, if Charlotte had allowed him. Smith even tried to persuade Charlotte to holiday with him on the Rhine. He was an unmarried man; Charlotte, an unmarried woman, seven years his senior. His attentions at once stimulated, flattered and confused Charlotte. The invitation to Germany had put her in a fever and she returned from the Edinburgh trip suffering from nervous exhaustion.

Miss Nussey was very uneasy about George Smith, as she told me herself during her visit in the spring of '51. She and I were on amicable terms by then and, as I came out of Mr Brontë's parlour one morning, she'd called to me from the dining room where she was sitting on her own by the fire. She invited me to join her for a few minutes and I pulled up a chair and sat with her. We talked about Charlotte – her poor health and low spirits, their cause and possible remedies. Miss Nussey was sceptical about Charlotte's London connections.

"George Smith has fixed intentions upon Charlotte," Miss Nussey had declared, "only I don't know what they are."

"I don't follow you," I said. "Do you mean there is something improper in his manner towards Charlotte?"

"I don't know. I've never met him. But Charlotte shows me his letters and there is a definite undercurrent of feeling in them and it is turning Charlotte's head." Miss Nussey was rocking vigorously in the small rocker in short, sharp strokes.

"When you say that Mr Smith has 'intentions' Miss Nussey, do you mean intentions as in marriage?"

"Who can say with a rising man like George Smith. All I am saying is that he dogs her like a collie and Charlotte is charmed by it."

"You sound as if you disapprove."

"I disapprove if it ends in tears," she flashed me an anxious look, "they usually do."

"You talk as if Charlotte's life were littered with failed suitors. She must be very discreet. In six years, I've never seen one."

"Charlotte's life is not littered with failed suitors, it is littered with failed heroes. She *will* set a man on a pedestal. It is her one great fault."

"Does she set her publisher on a pedestal?"

"She is piling the blocks up daily. It is what comes of having an overwrought imagination." Miss Nussey was still rocking. "When Charlotte admires a man, she weaves a heroic mantle in her imagination and lays it across his shoulders. The poor fellow is, of course, unaware of his new, invisible garment and so goes on behaving as the ordinary mortal he is and Charlotte is disappointed. She did it to Branwell. She did it to her teacher in Brussels. She did it to Mr Thackeray and now she is doing it to George Smith whose intentions are very far from clear. I am afraid, Mr Nicholls, that it will end in tears."

Charlotte went off to London for the month of June in '51, again staying with the Smiths. She wrote assiduously to her father when she was away and Mr Brontë passed on to me her more interesting news but, from her letters that summer, he also passed on her good wishes: Charlotte 'hoped I continued well'; she offered me her 'kind regards', her 'best regards' and Mr Brontë had to 'remember me kindly to Mr Nicholls'. On Charlotte's return from London, Miss Nussey came to us again, this time for three weeks. Throughout her stay, she and Charlotte extended to me invitations to tea or country walks but as I was leaving for Ireland at the end of the month and Mr Brontë was preoccupied with the Board of Health enquiry, I simply did not have the time. It was not until Miss Nussey had left that I could accept an invitation from Charlotte and that was on the eve of my own departure.

The tea was not a cheerful one. I was about to go on leave and I knew that Mr Brontë would miss me while Charlotte, after two months of constant visiting, faced a summer at home alone with him. It would be the first time, since the holocaust, that father and daughter had been left alone without me and the atmosphere was strained. I left for Ireland the following morning. I was tired, I missed Anne and I was wary of Charlotte's changed manner. I was glad to be getting away.

CHAPTER TWELVE

A universal remedy

My brother Alan met me off the Holyhead packet. I had not seen him in three years and he was as pleased to see me as I him. Alan had left Trinity after his first year and gone into commerce as an agent for the Grand Canal Company and, from all I could see, he had prospered. He took me in a hansom to his four-storeyed town house on Sir John Rogerson Quay at Ringsend. It was one of only a handful of houses among the rows of warehouses that served the wharves of the Liffey at the front and the Grand Canal Basin at the back, and Alan used it as his home and his office. Ringside was a bustling district and what it lacked in the picturesque it gained in the ever-changing scenes of movement and endeavour, loading and unloading, boats, barges and ocean-going clippers and, most interesting of all to me, the movement of people: stevedores, sailors, merchants and chandlers and the silent lines of the pitiable poor preparing to leave Ireland for ever.

Alan had married since we last met and he and his wife, Caroline, had a six month old daughter called Ellen. Caroline was trim and orderly and clearly in her element managing a busy household and, with family roots embedded in Dublin's commercial establishment, she brought Alan the connections to which he aspired. Caroline welcomed me very civilly and provided for my every need but I was tired after my journey; tiredness that no doubt magnified my compassion for the families at Alan's front door. Over dinner, I asked him how things now stood.

"Things are on the up, Arthur," he told me, pushing away his empty plate and dabbing his lips with his napkin. "The canal and the docks are busy. I am not complacent but I think our prospects are good." I was surprised. It was not what I had expected to hear.

"But what about the emigration? There must have been five hundred people on the quayside this afternoon and they were pitiable. Most of them looked incapable of surviving the voyage let alone building a new life in an untamed land." Alan pushed back his chair and crossed his legs.

"Not so many last year. Around a hundred thousand."

"And still it goes on? After six years? What is happening, Alan? It cannot just be the potatoes." Caroline, leaving much of her meat on the side of her plate, laid down her knife and fork.

"These are extraordinary times to be sure," she averred. "A great purpose is unfolding and, God willing, we shall see it to its end."

"A great purpose?" I was astonished at my sister-in-law. "A million starved and diseased to early deaths and a million more fled abroad? You think this is God's purpose?" Caroline raised her eyebrows and settled her hands in her lap. Alan shot her a look.

"Well, I don't think a fair-minded observer would blame the government. Goods are pouring into the docks and fuel and foods coming down the canal."

"Yes, for export. Food is being exported while the people starve."

"And also being imported." Alan raised a finger at me. "The situation will not be helped by interfering with the natural flow of commerce. The government understands that."

"But the food that is coming in isn't commercial though is it, Alan? It is charity shipments from the Continent, from Canada, from Englishmen with bad consciences. I am not a man of trade but I would have thought that the importation of free food would only worsen the agricultural economy. No!" I shook my head. "The ports should be closed."

"Oh thank you, brother!" Alan laughed. "You would throw me out of work as well would you?" And then Caroline said it:

"You close the ports and the Catholics won't be able to leave."

I was sorry that Alan and I had set off with a disagreement. I will not blame Caroline entirely, I was tired and it is not wise to discuss politics in unfamiliar company. I avoided contentious issues for the rest of my visit but I had started out on the wrong foot and we did not manage to get back in step. Even when our conversation turned to the personal I seemed to disappoint my brother. 'Why,' he asked me, 'at the age of thirty-three was I still in my first cure? Was I applying for parishes? Why not? Had I thought of a military chaplaincy? Or a prison? Did I intend to remain single? Did I appreciate how fulfilling it was to have children of one's own?' Alan was only concerned for me, I knew that. He wanted to succeed in his career and he wanted me to succeed in mine. He wanted to be head of a large respectable family and he wanted that for me too. Alan loved me but he did not know me. I wished we could have started again.

I found myself under similar pressure when I arrived in Banagher. My welcome was warm enough. Four of my cousins were at home: the boys, James and William, and the girls, Mary and Harriette who, at twenty-one and eighteen, were now quite grown up. Aunt Harriette greeted me with her full maternal concern, concern that was, like Alan's, well-meant, but it was nonetheless oppressive when all I wanted was a few weeks peace. All my cousins, it seemed, were doing wonderfully well: Arthur was in England training to become an army surgeon, Alan was a missionary in Cape Colony, Joseph was wining prizes at Trinity and James was now Master of the Royal Free School. My career, by comparison, seemed hopelessly becalmed. Aunt Harriette did not criticise me but her questions, like Alan's, were pointed – about my career and my personal life.

"I was sorry to hear about Anne Brontë." We were out in the garden. We'd been weeding the borders and were taking a few minutes out on a stone seat. I clasped my hands together over my knees and looked down at my boots on the grass.

"That was a cruel waste."

"I know that you loved her." I did not want to hear that from my aunt. She hadn't known Anne. There was nothing useful she could say. I watched a beetle struggling through the grass between my boots and said nothing, but my aunt went on. "I am going to tell you something now that you might not want to hear but I shall say it and you do not need to answer." I could see her from the tail of my eye; sitting poker-straight with her hands in her lap. "You are listless Arthur and at a time in your life when you should be in control of it. Whether it is that you need a change of situation or to settle down with a wife and family I do not know, perhaps it is both, but I know which it is that matters most." I was hearing every word that she said but from a distance far greater than the two feet between us. "You have suffered a loss," she continued, "and you have every right to grieve, but it is more than two years now; you are a strong, handsome fellow in the prime of his life and if you think you will never love again you must bear in mind that there are other good reasons to marry: companionship, convenience, connections. They are often the better reasons to marry too, and if you have heard that said before it is only because it is true." She rested a hand on my sleeve. "I say this only because I love you, Arthur. I want you to be happy, but to be that, you must regain control of your life."

Aunt Harriette's advice had irritated me because it was intrusive and because it was true. I *was* unhappy, but Anne was gone. Over the next few days, I did make the effort to take control of myself, to rationalize my emotional malaise and in that muddled, struggling state I did something that seemed supremely right at the time but which I immediately regretted and, to this day, blush to think of: I proposed to my cousins. I proposed to Mary first and then, when she refused me, I asked Harriette if she would marry me and she refused me too. It was such a crass thing to do. I suppose I was taking my aunt literally – *companionship, convenience, connections* – didn't they all apply to my cousins? I think I tried to appear light-hearted when I asked them but my heart was not light, as they must have seen, the whole thing was a ghastly embarrassment and a further weakening of my self-esteem.

I thought about myself on the way back to Haworth. My career and my personal circumstances had been of such interest to my relatives that I felt I should be interested too. Their concerns were, after all, only echoes of those articulated by Joseph and Sarah Grant but, though I examined myself at my travelling leisure, I could not share their concern for my career. I did not want to be a prison or an army chaplain, nor did I want to move to a strange parish for the sake of the title of Vicar because the title and the stipend would be all I should gain. I already served as a vicar. Haworth was only a chapelry but it was larger than most parishes and, in the prevailing circumstances, I fulfilled most of the offices of a vicar and enjoyed a degree of the attached respect. Rough and frustrating as Haworth was, I knew the place, I knew the people and they had accepted me. I am not an ambitious man. Lack of ambition may not be in the spirit of the age but it is surely not a sin. I should be quite happy to make my home in Haworth – but there it is, the conditional 'should' – the conditional that bears on that other concern of my Irish relatives – marriage: I shall not have a home until I have a wife, and as I thought about myself on my journey back to Haworth, I had to accept that yes, I was lonely.

I still missed Anne. I missed her presence and I missed the hopes that I'd had for our future together but Aunt Harriette was right; it had been two years and there is nothing to be wrung from regrets but resentment. It was time to move on, but to where and with whom? Models of family happiness besieged me. I envied Joseph Grant his Sarah and Charles, and the Browns their swarm of happy girls. I loved the Browns but, though I lived in their house, my position as a priest and a lodger set me apart from them and when one of the girls brought my dinner to my room and then left, closing the door behind her, then I felt the pang of my loneliness, and each year I was feeling it more.

I arrived back in Haworth at the beginning of September and, after dispiriting times in Ireland, I was glad to be back. Mr Brontë was pleased to see me, and so was Charlotte.

"Welcome back." She was coming down the lane returning from a walk with the dogs. I hadn't seen them since I got back and they greeted me with much snuffling and whining and wagging of tails. I bent down to give them some fuss and Charlotte smiled down at me. "I trust you enjoyed your holiday?"

"Thank you. Yes," I told her. "But I'm glad to be back." I looked up at her. "I hope you've kept well."

"I have, tolerably." Charlotte was twisting two lengths of twine in her hands. "It has been quiet." I gave the dogs a final pat and stood up.

"Has Miss Nussey not been up to see you?"

"Ellen's mother has been poorly while you were away. Ellen has been confined to Birstall looking after her."

"And is she now better?"

"Improving." Charlotte continued fiddling with the twine in her fingers. I was not used to exchanging small talk with her and I felt at a loss.

"Well, I am sorry your summer has been quiet."

"Oh don't be sorry," she insisted, "I am writing again."

"Ah, good." I nodded approvingly. "Another novel?"

"Yes, another novel. I have been planning it for some time and now I have begun to write."

"This is good news. You will not want for company while you are exercising your imagination." I dart of pain shot through her eyes. I had raised the spectre of her missing sisters: the three of them together, in the dining room, conjuring their fictive worlds, but then the moment passed.

"No indeed," she said, giving me a brave smile, then she took the dogs back to the parsonage.

I saw little of Charlotte for the rest of the month, she was busy at her desk, but at the end of September she had a house guest, Miss Wooler, and for ten days she put down her pen. Miss Wooler had been Charlotte's teacher at the school where she first met Miss Nussey. She was something of a mentor to Charlotte and, as Mr Brontë also enjoyed her company, the ten days passed pleasantly for all but, as soon as Miss Wooler was gone, Charlotte succumbed to the familiar reaction of depression and neuralgic headaches. It was the same after any visit. Through the summer, Charlotte had conquered her ennui by throwing herself into her work and I put it to Mr Brontë that she could do the same again but he would not agree; this time, he insisted, she was ill.

Charlotte was hypochondriacal, there is no doubt about that, but then who would not be when five of her siblings had died of a disease from who's symptoms she persistently suffered? Charlotte worried about herself and she worried about her father who, in his turn, worried about Charlotte. Father and daughter were like the two last pins standing together at the end of a skittle alley waiting to see where Fate's next ball would strike. They had a bond of mutual dependence that was so strong that as soon as one fell ill the other soon followed and as Charlotte went down with her headaches, Mr Brontë caught a cold that settled on his chest. It was the beginning of a fearful run of illness.

At the beginning of November, Tabby caught influenza. She passed it on to Martha who then developed quinsy. Poor Martha could not speak and she could only swallow liquids with difficulty. Mary went up to the parsonage to nurse her and prepare meals and another daughter, Eliza, took on the fires and cleaning and then, on the 1st December, we suffered a death. Poor Keeper, Emily's big mastiff-cross, died peacefully in his sleep after just one day's discomfort. It was a good end for an old dog who had enjoyed his food and his walks to the last. It upset us all to lose him, none more so than Flossy, whose spirits sank to the level of the rest of the household. John and I buried Keeper in Emily's garden and I recommended him to his maker.

By the middle of December, Mr Brontë was up and about but Charlotte was no better, in fact she was worse. To headaches, pains in her sides and indigestion she now added toothache. Mr Brontë sent to Keighley for a doctor new to the district, a Dr Ruddock who, as a member of the Royal College of Surgeons and a Licentiate of the Society of Apothecaries, came well recommended. I think Charlotte's fame must have preceded her because Ruddock was uncommonly attentive and after much prodding and poking at the seat of her pains, he diagnosed an inflamed liver. He told Mr Brontë it was a condition that he could cure and he left him with a course of blue pills.

Charlotte took the pills as Ruddock prescribed and in a day or two felt better – just as Miss Nussey was arriving. I was frankly sceptical at this turn of events, even more so when, on Miss Nussey's departure, a week later, Charlotte relapsed. She returned to her bed with a fresh set of symptoms that included mouth ulcers, painful, loosening teeth and a swollen tongue. Swallowing became difficult for her and when vomiting and purging were added to her misfortunes, I was bound to accept that Charlotte's sickness was not of the mind.

Charlotte was worried, her father was worried, we were all worried that Mr Brontë's worst nightmare might be realised. Mr Brontë combed through his copy of Graham's *Modern Domestic Medicine* searching for the cause of Charlotte's extraordinary set of symptoms and he alighted, in the end, on mercury poisoning. Straight away, he dispatched a rider to Keighley to fetch Dr Ruddock. It was a wild night and I waited with Mr Brontë in his parlour. We sat together at his peat fire and I read him a story from *Blackwood's Magazine* but I knew he wasn't listening; he was waiting for the sound of hooves and, when they came, he strode out to the hall and threw open the door. Ruddock was coming up the path.

"Dr Ruddock," Mr Brontë called to him before he had even reached the steps. "My daughter is exhibiting symptoms of mercury poisoning." Mr Brontë stood on his threshold while Dr Ruddock, who might have expected a warmer welcome on such a night, remained at the foot of the steps.

"You should not be out," Ruddock told him. "You will not conquer bronchitis by standing before a night like this."

"Dr Ruddock," Mr Brontë repeated. "If my daughter has been poisoned with mercury, she may well die. I shall be obliged if you can tell me how she might have ingested the metal." I was standing in the hall at Mr Brontë's back. Rainwater was dripping from Ruddock's riding coat; the weight of his bag in one hand and his sodden hat in the other were dragging at his shoulders and he looked tired but he knew his business.

"There is a small dose of mercury in the pills that I left with Miss Brontë," he told us, "it is an active ingredient of that particular preparation. It has proved very effective in reducing liver inflammations in the past. I have used it many times." Mr Brontë looked down at Dr Ruddock but, despite the wildness of the night, he made no move to invite him in.

"Would you say that inflammation of the tongue, loosening of the teeth and a narrowing of the throat were symptoms of mercury poisoning, Dr Ruddock?"

"They could be among the symptoms, yes," Ruddock agreed, "but mercury poisoning does not show itself overnight, it would take weeks or months to become evident. There will be some other explanation for Miss Brontë's symptoms. If you will allow me to examine her …" Ruddock moved forward but Mr Brontë stopped him.

"She is sleeping. Can you confirm for me, from your professional training, that the damage caused by mercury to the internal organs can be permanent? Including, in womankind, to those of procreation?"

"Yes, Sir, in a large dose that might be a possible consequence, but I can assure you that in the very small dose contained …" Mr Brontë's long, haggard face drained of its colour, his body shook and, with a breaking voice, he shouted at Dr Ruddock:

"Good night, Sir!" and slammed the door on him.

Although none dared say it, we all thought we should lose Charlotte that winter. To what extent Ruddock's pills were responsible for Charlotte's sharp decline, I cannot say, but the fact is that as soon as she stopped taking them she began to recover. Charlotte had taken to her bed just after Christmas but, though she improved in the New Year, she remained there. Martha, who was herself still not fully recovered from the quinsy, wanted her out.

"It's alright 'er lyin' there," she complained to me one morning, "but I've enough to do without fetchin' and carryin' for 'er. I've told 'er: 'Yer need to be up and movin', 'you'll go backwards laid there doin' nowt'."

Charlotte would see no one but her father and those visits she kept brief. She neither read nor wrote nor entertained any stimulation. I had seen this behaviour before, in those who can afford to stop in bed, and Martha was right, it leads to depression, so I was pleased when, towards the end of January, Charlotte finally came down to the dining room.

Mr Brontë asked me if I would talk to her. Having failed himself to gain any response, he must have thought that a fresh face might stimulate her. I was not optimistic but I wanted to help and so I called on Charlotte one afternoon after tea. The shutters were already closed against the descending darkness and the rushes were lit. Charlotte was sitting alone, close up to the fire and, though she was wrapped in a heavy blanket, I could see how thin she was. All the weight she had gained in the summer was gone and a few pounds besides. Without saying a word, Charlotte turned her face to me and I saw that she had lost teeth, her hair was dry and lifeless and the lines on her pale face aged her beyond her years.

The visit was not a success. I sat at the fire with Charlotte and told her how pleased I was to see her up again. I gave her such news of the chapelry as I thought might interest her but, although she was not impolite, I don't think she returned half a dozen words and, after ten minutes, I left her as I'd found her.

It had saddened me to see so fierce a spirit as Charlotte's brought low. She and I had never got on particularly well but out of common humanity I wanted to see her strong again, both for her own sake and for her father's. On my way back to Sexton House I decided I would do what I could for Charlotte to bring the colour back to her cheeks and the fire to her eyes. I decided I would visit her every day but, the following day, she left for Miss Nussey's. I was disappointed.

Charlotte missed a visitor while she was in Birstall: her publisher, George Smith. He was breaking a journey to Scotland and he had decided 'on the spur of the moment' as he told Mr Brontë, to 'look in on Haworth'. Smith was sorry to have missed Charlotte of course but Mr Brontë was pleased to receive him, the young man, so important to his daughter, of whom he had heard so much. I met Smith briefly. He was much as I had imagined him: tall and good-looking, beautifully tailored and groomed but, for one so young, there was a world-weariness about his shoulders and eyes and his smooth black hair was already turning grey. Like the rest of us, Smith was worried about Charlotte. He asked after her illness, its cause and likely duration and whether we expected any permanent harm. He asked if she were writing and if she had mentioned any plans for another novel and all the time that he talked he looked about him: at Mr Brontë's books and out through the windows to the church and the burial ground in its winter mantle of mist and moss.

"Sorry as I am to have missed Charlotte," he said, when he had seen and heard enough, "I am glad she is up to visiting again. Charlotte talks warmly of Miss Nussey and I am sure a spell at Birstall will do her the world of good." Then as he stood up to take his leave he added, "I shall invite Charlotte to London. I shall write to her this evening."

Charlotte declined that particular invitation for, although she returned from Miss Nussey's looking better, she was too frail for a London trip, but Smith was tenacious, and if he could not coax Charlotte from Yorkshire, he was not going to leave her there idle. Over the next few weeks he wrote incessantly to her and whatever it was that he wrote, by March he had achieved his purpose because, after four barren months, and two and a half years since *Shirley,* Charlotte was back at her desk.

I was pleased to see Charlotte working again. I am a great believer in the efficacy of work for taking us out of ourselves but as the weeks passed I could see that Charlotte did not thrive. I wondered if it were the weather. When I got back from Ireland in September, Charlotte had been enjoying her work, but then the weather was warm and now it was cold and the end of winter can be a dispiriting time. I had an idea, in April, that I thought might cheer her. The fourth annual meeting of the Mechanics Institute was to be held on Easter Monday in the National School and in my capacity as President, I invited Charlotte, in her capacity as celebrated novelist, to be our guest speaker. I thought the event might demonstrate the affection that Charlotte's neighbours felt for her and perhaps take her out of herself but Charlotte declined. The following week was Charlotte's thirty-sixth birthday, her father wanted to celebrate that but Charlotte declined and when she also declined an invitation from Miss Nussey to go with her on an extended visit to friends in Sussex, it seemed clear that the reason she gave for all these refusals – her need to get on with her novel – must indeed be the true one, so what were we to make of her removal to Scarborough?

Charlotte left for the coast the day after Miss Nussey left for Sussex. She didn't tell Miss Nussey she was going, she simply slipped away on her own and if Mr Brontë did not guess why, I know I did. Charlotte left us on the 27th May. She would be in Scarborough on the 28th, the third anniversary of Anne's death. It was an anniversary that drew me as inexorably as a lunar tide and when I met Charlotte's eyes, as she mounted the carrier's dogcart, I saw that that same tide pulled her. Did she see that in me? Did she know that my heart travelled with her? She never, in three years, gave any indication that she knew how I grieved for Anne but, that morning in the lane, I felt an empathy with Charlotte and, in a letter to her father a week later, Charlotte revealed her own empathy with me.

Charlotte described, in her letter, her amusement at a service she had attended in a tiny country chapel down the coast from Scarborough. The chapel was so small that the choir was forced to turn away from the congregation and the congregation away from the preacher. The rustic antics had tickled Charlotte and she told her father that she had wished I could have been there to share them. I smiled when Mr Brontë told me this because I recognized Charlotte's reference: I had encountered a similar fiasco once when taking service for James Bradley at his remote chapel-of-ease attached to a farmhouse at Newsholme Dean. I had told Charlotte about it when I got back and we had laughed about it together. Again, in her letter, Charlotte asked that her father pass on her good wishes to me.

Charlotte stayed at the coast, on her own, for a month, and I was not surprised that she came back suffering headaches. She would have done better going south with Miss Nussey or even staying at home. Mr Brontë said nothing to me but I knew that he felt the same. He worried about Charlotte when she was away, and he worried about her depressions when she got back. I felt sorry for Charlotte and I felt sorry for Mr Brontë. He was ageing and it was beginning to show. Only days after Charlotte's return, Butterfield's petition to the Board of Health was to be investigated. It was a cause for which Mr Brontë had, after his initial despondency, exerted himself strenuously – too strenuously – because, on the eve of the inspector's arrival, he had a seizure leaving him partially paralysed down one side. Charlotte was beside herself with worry, worry and guilt that her father's seizure might have been caused by his worry about her. After a few days, Mr Brontë recovered most of his feeling but the seizure had weakened him and he was unable to present his case to the inspector. Butterfield won the day and it would be years before another attempt could be made to improve conditions in Haworth. It was a bitter blow to an old man's self-esteem.

A man who raises six healthy children through infancy has a right to expect support in his old age. Five of Mr Brontë's children and the mother who bore them were gone and all the comfort that Mr Brontë could look forward to rested with Charlotte. As for Charlotte, she cleaved to her father and mourned the rest while she struggled on alone in the dining room trying to finish her novel. For how much longer could she do that? Mr Brontë was seventy-five and Haworth Parsonage was not his, it belonged to the Church Lands Trust and, when he passed on, where then would Charlotte be? Where then would I be? I already had the management of the chapelry, in all practical terms, and of the parsonage too. As Mr Brontë grew older, and passed on to me more and more of his responsibilities, even Martha was coming to me for domestic decisions that should not have been any of my business. I had been drawn beyond the threshold that separates the lives of curates from their senior priests, it was an unconventional relationship, and it did me no credit for a future career.

'It's time you moved on,' Joseph Grant told me. 'Seven years. It's too long. The Church will take the view that you do not want preferment – have no ambition. You will be overlooked. If you are going to make a move, you have to make it now.' It was only as much as my aunt and my brother had told me, but move where? I could not leave Mr Brontë, I loved the man. He was more of a father to me than my own father who had passed me on to his brother-in-law, and more to me than my uncle who'd paid no more attention to me than to any other boy at the Royal Free School. If looking after Mr Brontë would impede my career then what value should I put on a career? And then there was Charlotte. Charlotte did not need me as her father did, I knew that. She supped at many wells for her sustenance: at her father's, at Miss Nussey's, at George Smith's and at those of her fellow authors up and down the land, but though she supped so widely, she did not thrive. Charlotte had realised her life's ambition to a degree that she could never have imagined. She exercised her talent as a free woman and she was applauded for it by her peers and the public alike. She was financially independent and beholden to no man – a state she had championed for all womankind in her novels – and although she had suffered the loss of her family, she had the consolation of old and trusted friends and yet she did not thrive. I felt for her. I knew that she could be acerbic, that was because she was shy; I knew that she could be argumentative, that was because she was principled, and I knew that she could be passionate, that was the expression of a brave heart. I wanted to breathe vitality back into that brittle, desiccated, little frame and to renew Charlotte's faith in her future. Anne would want me to do that and besides, it was what I wanted myself.

I was lonely and I had a man's needs, not least to cherish, shelter and protect. My aunt had maintained that there are other good reasons to marry besides love and she had instanced companionship, convenience and connections. Was it not convenient that I was drawn to cherish a woman so demonstrably in need of cherishing? If I did not love Charlotte, were not our seven years of companionship and my intimacy with her sisters and brother a basis of common sympathy? And as to connections? Charlotte's father. If I married Charlotte and moved into the parsonage, I would be in a position to support Mr Brontë's tenure against all eventualities, I would without doubt succeed him on his demise and so then provide for Charlotte the secure occupancy of her home for the rest of my life.

But perhaps Charlotte looked elsewhere for a husband. Perhaps she hoped that her urbane young publisher might one day propose to her. It was impossible for me to tell where her hopes for affection lay but I had met George Smith and I did not believe that his dalliances with Charlotte would ever stray far beyond the interests of his business and if Charlotte had been led to believe otherwise, then I believe she had been misled. I could not read Charlotte's mind and nor did I need to because my immediate duty was clear: I must make my feelings known to Charlotte, after that, she would speak for herself.

CHAPTER THIRTEEN

Rejection

I had wanted to put my proposal to Charlotte straight away, at the end of August, but then Tabby went down with bilious diarrhoea and the parsonage was thrown into confusion. Then, while Tabby was still ill, we got the news that the Duke of Wellington had died. That cast a pall of mourning over the household. Then the week after that, we had the anniversary of Branwell's death and, through all this, Charlotte struggled doggedly on trying to finish her novel. The times were just not conducive to a radical proposal. Then, at the beginning of October, Miss Nussey finally returned home after her four months in Sussex. She wanted to come up to Haworth to see Charlotte but Charlotte and her father both had heavy colds and so Charlotte put her off until the middle of the month when Miss Nussey spent a week with us. Obviously, that was not an appropriate time but then, when Miss Nussey left, Charlotte declared that she would brook no further interruptions until she had finished her novel. 'That will be the appropriate time then', I told myself, 'when she has finished her novel' but then when she did finish it, in late November, she removed herself to Birstall for two weeks to recuperate with Miss Nussey. I hardly knew what to do with myself. I was bursting to propose to Charlotte and the constant delays were harassing me. I had headaches, my limbs ached and my normally good appetite disappeared but there was nothing I could do, I just had to bide my time. Charlotte came back late on Wednesday the 8th December. Our paths crossed in the hall on the Friday. Her two weeks in Birstall had done her good, she looked well and more cheerful than I had seen her for months. On the Monday, I would be having a working tea with her father. I decided I would see Charlotte then.

I had rehearsed what I would say for months and I had a sleepless night on the Sunday with the words tumbling round in my head. I woke tired and thick-headed and went up onto the moors for some air. It was still dark when I set off, and cold, but though I walked for an hour and my lungs and limbs chilled, still my head did not clear. I returned to Sexton House. I washed and shaved and prayed for composure but I could not eat breakfast – my belly was too knotted – and my arms still ached. I was glad when it was nine o'clock and time to go out on my rounds.

My arms and shoulders still ached at dinner time. I was not hungry but Mary insisted I eat something and when she brought me mutton broth and bread I managed about half of it. I took Flossy for a long walk in the afternoon, up to Stanbury and across to Withins Heights returning via Cold Harbour and Marsh. After dropping Flossy off, I went back to my room and tried to relax for an hour but nothing I did – exercise, resting, eating or fasting – did anything to unfog my mind or loosen the knot in my belly.

At half past four I went up to the parsonage for my working tea with Mr Brontë. Charlotte was at her desk in the dining room and would not be joining us, for which I was glad; I would see her later on her own. I don't remember now what Mr Brontë and I talked about over our tea but it was chapelry business and when we had risen and given thanks I left him, closing the door behind me.

The hall was dark but for the glow under the dining room door. She was still in there then. I stood and listened in the dark to the quiet. The ticks of the clock struck the flags like icicles and I froze, pinioned by the aches in my arms, but was it the aches in my arms or was it reluctance? My mind was still fogged and I couldn't think. I needed to get a grip and remember why I was there. My future security and that of Charlotte and her father all depended on the simple proposition that Charlotte and I marry, I knew that, I had known it for months, but how could Charlotte know it if I didn't tell her? Why was I holding back? Because my arms ached? Because of nerves? Was it base cowardice then that kept me from knocking on the door? If I walked away and came back tomorrow, would I feel any better then? Or the day after that? The anniversary of Emily's death would be upon us in ten days' time and then it would be Christmas. There was no possibility of delay and no reason for it but cowardice. I tapped on the dining room door.

The next few minutes were the strangest of my entire life. I heard Charlotte's voice call 'come in' and then, the moment I opened the door, my perceptions left me and rose to the ceiling. I looked down on Charlotte at her desk. She looked plump from up there and I looked black – black hair, black coat, black boots. I heard myself speak. It was a low rumble, not at all the voice that I knew, and nor was my address the one I'd prepared. Instead of talking about our mutual happiness, I talked of my difficulty expressing it and I employed old-fashioned terms that I never use – *I crave your leave for some hope*, was one such I remember. I looked down at myself and saw I was shaking and, despite the cold, sweat was glistening on my brow.

"Have you spoken to Papa?" Charlotte asked me when I had finished and I told her I had not. She rose from her chair and walked round the table. I watched myself watching her, wondering what she would do, but she walked past me and opened the door. "You shall have my distinct reply in the morning," she said, and I left.

I had a second sleepless night after that. I had made an embarrassing spectacle of myself but, as I argued through the long watch of night, Charlotte knew me, she had known me for seven and a half years and her impression of me as a prospective husband would not be changed by a two minutes speech, however mangled. All I had had to do in the dining room was deliver my message. I had done that and, in the morning, I would receive her reply.

I was on tenterhooks next morning, waiting for Charlotte's answer, but none came. At dinnertime, as I came out of the schoolroom, I saw Martha, walking up the lane. I felt sure she'd be carrying the message and called out to her but she ignored me and continued on up to the parsonage. In Sexton House, there was a subdued atmosphere. I asked if there had been any messages left but there hadn't and I went up to my room. Mary followed me with my dinner, beef pudding and potatoes, which she put down in silence.

"Is everything alright with you, Mary?" I asked her.

"Nothing wrong with me, Mr Nicholls," she said, pointedly, then she went back downstairs.

I felt sick and ate little, although I did sleep afterwards, for which I was glad. As soon as I woke, I hurried back downstairs, but still there was no message, nor was there for the rest of the day and I went to bed that night with the darkest forebodings. It was only on the second morning that the letter came. It was propped up on the hall shelf, bearing my name in Charlotte's hand.

"When did this letter arrive?" I called down the stairs to the kitchen, and it was John who called back.

"Master sent it with Martha first thing." Then he added. "You'd best take it upstairs." I took the letter up to my room, breaking the seal as I went. It contained two notes, one from Charlotte and another from her father. I relit the lamp on my desk by the window and brought Charlotte's note to it.

Dear Mr Nicholls,
Having read Papa's reply to your proposal of Monday evening, I wish you to know that I disclaim participation in the sentiments calculated to give you pain. Papa has assumed a hardness against your proposal that is not to be bent, and his present constitution may not withstand contradiction. I must ask you therefore never to expect me to reciprocate the feelings you have expressed, but I do exhort you to maintain your courage and spirits.

C. Brontë.

I put Charlotte's note down and opened the one from her father.

To A B Nicholls, Curate.
I learn from another that you would take Charlotte from me: that you would use the celebrated author

of *Jane Eyre* and *Shirley* as if she were the wilting daughter of a country parson, fit only to be married to his curate. Nor do I doubt that Charlotte's treasure lustres her attraction for you; treasure that might furnish a fine vicarage or pleasant rectory, from which you might exercise such accomplishments as you have gleaned from the Old Man of Haworth.

You have betrayed me, Sir, when there are few left in whom I can trust, and you would have betrayed Charlotte also. You would not face me in a proper manner to ask for Charlotte's hand because you know what marriage holds for a woman of Charlotte's age and delicacy. Charlotte will not abandon the little that remains of her family – or the name that has made her famous – to cast herself upon you: Charlotte and I are agreed on that. You will not enter my house again unless I particularly send for you.

P Brontë, Incumbent.

I read and reread Mr Brontë's note in a haze of disbelief. It had never entered my mind to abandon him and remove his daughter from Haworth, I had never given a thought to her money and, as to the effects of marriage on a woman of Charlotte's age and delicacy: if, by that, he meant the dangers of child-bearing then, in my experience, pregnancy would be an extremely unlikely miracle for a woman of Charlotte's years. '… not enter my house again.' How could that be? How could we fulfil our offices if we did not meet? Was he dismissing me? I was not permitted to ask.

I reread Charlotte's note. Her meaning was not so candid as her father's. I detected an ember between its lines and I took warmth from it. Charlotte disclaimed participation in her father's hardness and feared for his health. Obviously, if I had put Mr Brontë in a fever then Charlotte must look after him, even if that meant standing against me, but then she exhorted me to maintain my courage and spirits. She told me never to expect her to reciprocate my feelings but that is not a complete refusal, she probably felt that my feelings, as so badly expressed on Monday evening, were extravagant, of a different order to some more common feelings of affection that she might otherwise harbour for me. I found Charlotte's note impossible to interpret but I did take warmth from it.

I heard the front door being opened downstairs then John's cough as the cold hit his lungs. *I* needed cold air in my lungs; I needed to stretch my legs and clear my head. I folded the notes into my pocket and set off downstairs.

The lane was still dark and the moon was casting shadows.

"Well?" John's voice called, from behind the school porch.

"I'm sorry John. I didn't see you there. Good morning to you."

"Never mind 'Good Mornin'!" He moved out of the shadows. "What yer gonna do now then?"

"I'm going for a walk." He came towards me.

"What yer gonna do," he repeated, "to clean up this mess yer've dumped on t'parsonage?" The blood rushed to my head.

"John!" I exploded. "That is none of your business."

"Oh, but I think it is." He squared up to me. "Puttin' the master into a rage when he's still gettin' over a seizure. If he doesn't have another, it'll be no thanks to thee."

"John," I tried to gather myself, "I have done nothing – I have said nothing – that should in any way anger Mr Brontë."

"Yer call it *nothin'*? When yer go round his back to ask Charlotte to marry yer? A poor old chap with one daughter left for his old age, and yer want to take her off 'im?" I despaired.

"I have no wish to take Charlotte *off him*. Quite the opposite. It was my intention – it *is* my intention – to keep father and daughter together and secure the parsonage for Charlotte once her father's passed on."

"Aah!" John feigned enlightenment. "So yer weren't plannin' on takin' her away; yer were plannin' on movin' in and takin' over. Is that it?"

"Yes, but not taking over."

"No? Then how *did* yer think the old man would see it? He's been master of that house for nigh on thirty-five years. He lost his wife there and five of his children, Charlotte's all he's got left and yer think he wants you shovin' in?" John looked me up and down. "Yer can't have been thinkin' at all."

I looked away down the lane, to where a pale yellow glow was crowning Black Moor, and I thought about what John had said.

"But Mr Brontë and I are close. He appreciates everything I do. He's always telling me."

"He needs a curate. Course he does. But he doesn't need one in his house. He's got Charlotte and Martha and Tabby for that – and our Mary and me when needs be. He doesn't need you up there and he doesn't want yer." John stepped back. "Now get off on yer walk and think about what yer've to do."

The air was cold and the ground frozen and, in the rising light, I saw what I must do. If Mr Brontë had closed his door to me I could not do my work and so must resign. If my presence in Parsonage Lane was so irritating to Mr Brontë that he was in danger of suffering another seizure, then I must leave; and if Charlotte's proper concern for her father caused her to stand by him who stood against me, then there was no hope for me in that quarter and it would be kinder to Charlotte if I went away. All this was clear to me by the time I'd climbed Penistone Hill. It was a glorious morning with a hoar frost sparkling the heather in the sun but I could not stay to enjoy it. I hurried back down to Sexton House where, in the hall, Mary was waiting for me.

"You've been a long time," she said, looking worried, "now get yerself upstairs and I'll fetch yer some breakfast."

"I'm sorry Mary." I walked past her to the stairs. "I haven't time now."

"Well have a mug of tea and some bread an' butter at least. Yer'll make yerself ill not eating."

I went up to my room and quickly penned my resignation. I sealed it in an envelope, addressed it to Mr Brontë and went back downstairs. Mary was still demanding I eat.

"At dinner time," I said, striding past her, "I promise you." And I hurried up the lane to the parsonage.

The church clock was chiming the half – half eight – I was supposed to be in school. I pulled on the door bell and Martha came. She was alarmed to see me.

"Yer can't come in here," she whispered urgently, "I've been told yer haven't to come here anymore."

"I want you to give this note to Mr Brontë, Martha. It's very important."

"I can't. Yer not supposed to be here."

"Martha, just give this to Mr Brontë. It's very important." I pressed the note firmly into her hand and ran back down to the school to take my Bible class.

I did eat something that dinnertime – not very much – I found it hard to swallow – but enough, I hoped, to appease Mary. I felt very uneasy about Charlotte. I reread her note a score of times trying to gauge from it her real feelings. It was not a reply to my proposal of marriage, it was a covering note to her father's immediate reaction to my proposal and in it she dissociated herself from his anger. Clearly my proposal had affected Mr Brontë severely and Charlotte's immediate priority had been to safeguard his health but she had exhorted me to maintain my courage and spirits. To maintain them for what? So that I might be constant in my regard for her until the immediate crisis was past and she might express herself freely? Certainly, as long as her father was in this passion there was no possibility of her answering me directly, unless to reject me, which she had not done. The more I reread Charlotte's note, the more hope I drew from it. If Charlotte was minded to accept me, then I must be on hand for her whenever she judged the hour. I decided that I had been too hasty in tendering my resignation and I must withdraw it.

I went straight back up to the parsonage and peered in through one of the glazed panels in the front door. Tabby was running a duster over the hall table and she saw me. She looked at me for a moment and then ambled away down the hall to the kitchen. I continued peering in through the glass, not daring to knock or pull on the bell. After a few moments Martha came out of the kitchen drying her hands on a tea towel. She came quickly to the door and opened it a few inches.

"Go away," she hissed. "He's in yer know. Yer'll get me t'sack."

"I want to withdraw the note I gave you this morning," I whispered.

"Withdraw it? What do yer mean *withdraw it*?"

"I want to take it back before Mr Brontë sees it."

"He's already seen it. I gave 'im it this mornin'. If yer think I'm goin' in there after it, yer've another think comin'."

"No, no, of course…" My mind was racing and I hardly knew what I was saying. "Then can you just tell Mr Brontë?"

"He'd skin me, mood he's in. Now get off. Write another note if yer've owt to say to him – only don't come back here with it – I'll pick it up myself from home." Then she clicked shut the door on me.

I went back to Sexton House and drafted a note as Martha had suggested. I couched it in terms recognising the folly of haste and the needs of the chapelry and I apologised for any distress I might have caused, but the note only needed to be brief and so I kept it. Martha collected it during the evening and I suffered a fourth night of broken sleep.

Mr Brontë's reply – that Martha brought down the next day – showed no cooling of his resentment of me. He would ignore my resignation provided that I promised, in writing, never again to broach to him, or to Charlotte, the 'obnoxious subject' that had precipitated it. I did not have to think long before I decided it was an impossible condition. What if Mr Brontë should die tomorrow, or ten years hence, and Charlotte turn to me? If I accepted Mr Brontë's embargo, I would debar myself from ever being able to give her her home. I felt tired. I had not thought clearly for days and after Mr Brontë's latest injunction, I felt more bewildered than ever. I had two sermons to preach on Sunday and I'd prepared neither of them. Recent events would ensure a full attendance and any diffidence in my delivery would be taken as a sign of weakness, too much confidence, as a sign of arrogance. I needed to get away from Haworth, to view my predicament in a larger landscape. I asked Joseph Grant if he would take my Sunday services but Sarah's parents had just arrived for Christmas and he was fully committed. After some hasty messaging up and down the valley, Mr Mayne from Ingrow agreed to cover for me and, on the Friday, I set off over Cockhill Moor for some sound sense and solace from Sutcliffe Sowden.

Sowden had moved since I last saw him. He had been made Vicar of Hebden Bridge, a town two miles from Mytholmroyd and, though Christmas was only days away, he gave me his time and, on the Saturday morning, took me out for a walk. We climbed up to the Peace Monument, five hundred feet above Stoodley. The monument commemorated the lifting of the Orders in Council in 1814 and, when we attained its base, we climbed the 156 steps to the viewing room. The room was round and empty with four wide apertures that looked out to the points of the compass and through them, on that crisp December morning, we had clear views of open moorland for as far as the eye could see.

I had told Sowden about my proposal debacle the evening before. He had listened without much comment at the time but now, as we leaned on the sill together, looking out over Withins High Moor, he returned to the subject.

"It is a common enough thing for a curate to seek the hand of his superior's daughter," he said casually. "One might almost say it's expected." I knew Sutcliffe Sowden. He had brought me up to the monument with its panoramic views of Creation to make my own woes seem small.

"Charlotte Brontë is no common clergyman's daughter," I told him.

"No. I am sure she is not. Her father is a most singular priest, and I can see it must be fascinating to be on terms with such a celebrity as Currer Bell." I stepped aside to face Sowden.

"Charlotte's celebrity is not fascinating, it is an affliction, it takes her away from those she loves and into some very doubtful company that invariably leaves her unhappy."

"Those she loves?" Sowden turned to face me. "Does that include you?" I hesitated.

"I think I can say we're now friends, which we never were before."

"Friends enough for her to want to marry you?" He watched me keenly from under his bushy red eyebrows.

"I don't know. I don't think she feels free to say."

"Then she has said nothing at all to you?"

"No, not directly, but she exhorted me to maintain my courage and spirits. I am not dismissed." I turned from Sowden, back to the view, but he took me by the arm.

"I too exhort you to maintain your courage and spirits, Arthur. It takes courage and spirit to face the truth, to acknowledge the truth, and then live with the world as it is rather than a world you'd prefer. I am sure that, after all you have done for her father, Charlotte wishes you well, but she did tell you that you should never expect her to reciprocate your feelings, didn't she?" He tightened his grip on my arm. "Didn't she, Arthur?" I had come to Sowden for common sense and here I was getting it.

"Her letter was not easy to interpret."

I felt limp. I no longer knew what I was doing on top of a tower in the middle of nowhere, nor what I was supposed to think. Sowden took my other arm and turned me to face him.

"You still have your ministry." He gave me a muscular smile. "You are still a priest. You do no service to Charlotte Brontë by waiting around where you will not be called, no service to yourself and none to God. You are a priest Arthur and you have pledged your service to all men. Do not squander it on one who may never need it when there are countless millions that do."

"Here speaks the confirmed bachelor," I told him, attempting a laugh, "with the Romanist's argument for a celibate priesthood."

"Not at all. I am fully aware that marriage is the basis of a fulfilling life for most men, lay and clergy. All I am pointing out is that, as Charlotte has told you that she will not reciprocate your feelings, it is a folly to wait upon a faint hope when there are so many other worthwhile things you could be doing."

"By which you mean?"

"Your ministry." He threw out his arms. "You know, Arthur, there are ministries in the Church that are better suited to bachelors than to married men – the overseas missions for instance – you could go to India or Africa, America, Australia. You are young, strong and experienced, with your best years ahead of you. Arm yourself with the

Holy Spirit, shoulder the shield of Faith and take the Word out into the world."

My few days away produced no softening of Mr Brontë's attitude. His insistence that I abandon all hope of marrying Charlotte had remained firm and so my resignation had to stand. A full week had passed and I still felt stunned. My whole world was upturned. My relationship with Mr Brontë was in shreds, that with Charlotte, suspended, and those with everyone else in Parsonage Lane – except Mary, who alone stood firm – were also exploded. I have to say that I found Mr Brontë's harshness unfathomable. I had seen him this angry before, with Branwell, but what crime against morality had I committed? What disgrace had I brought to his name? I didn't understand it, or what it was in me that he feared.

He never did send for me. Such information as he thought I needed he sent in curt messages via Martha and the only times we met were across the pews. I tried to fulfil my duties as best I could but it became increasingly difficult. None but the Browns knew the true cause of the rift between us but everyone could see that there was a rift – how could they not when he so publicly snubbed me – and people take sides. I could not defend myself against malicious rumours and even if I could, I was not going to stand publicly opposed to the man I had always admired above all others and to whom I owed so much. A mood of mistrust developed towards me in the village; the duties that I could successfully fulfil became fewer, and for quite long periods, I retreated to my rooms.

I never saw Charlotte. She had left for London by the time I got back from Hebden Bridge. Her latest novel, *Villette*, was published while she was there, and to favourable reviews, so doubtless she was again being lionised. When she came back to us, four weeks later, she had Miss Nussey with her who, for two more weeks, chaperoned Charlotte wherever she went. Two whole months had now passed since my fateful proposal and Sowden's remark that I served no one waiting where I would not be called was beginning to ring true. Charlotte had had plenty of opportunity to indicate something to me, if she had wanted to, but she had chosen not to, and her father was all the time being more difficult. I decided that I had now no alternative; I must look to pastures new. I wrote to Mr Brontë resigning again and applied to the Society for the Propagation of the Gospel for a mission to the Australian Colonies.

Mr Brontë answered my second offer of resignation with a note telling me that it would not be convenient before the end of May, so I gave that date to the Society. Australia had appealed to me because so many of my countrymen had sought refuge there and I felt I could be more use in a culture that I understood than in an alien one and besides, Australia's being at the other end of the earth lent force to my idea of a new beginning. Having made up my mind to leave Haworth, it became even harder to linger but there were those who stood by me, and to them I shall always be grateful. Mary Brown was one such – defending me even against the denunciations of John. Joseph and Sarah Grant and Sutcliffe Sowden were also steadfast, and there were others, but most in the chapelry believed that if I had displeased their venerable pastor then the fault must be mine and they turned from me.

One memorable gesture of support came from an unexpected quarter. Our diocesan bishop, Dr Longley, paid a rare visit to the chapelry in early March, shortly after Miss Nussey had returned home to Birstall. The occasion was an afternoon tea for the deanery clergy. It would be the first time I had entered the parsonage since the 13th December and, while I dreaded the prospect of encountering Charlotte in the company of her father, the bishop's invitation could not be declined.

I remember the day was cold and wet. I remember because I had been up at Stanbury that afternoon in my heavy coat and other layers of clothing and I had to hurry to the parsonage to get there in time. I had handed my coat to Martha when I arrived and then stepped into the dining room. A dozen clergy were standing at their places around Charlotte's new dining table leaving just one place for me, on the far side, in front of the banked-up fire. I had to squeeze between Mr Brontë and the sofa to get to it, I felt large and conspicuous in my heavy clothes and, even before we had returned thanks, I felt uncomfortably hot.

During tea, conversations gravitated around Mr Brontë at the bottom end of the table and the bishop at the top and, as I had appetite for neither conversation nor tea, I was content to be in the middle next to the visiting schools inspector. We had met in the morning and he harassed me with more questions about the schools than I cared to answer and, as I wilted before the fire in that overcrowded room, I withdrew by degrees from the conversation leaving the inspector to talk to himself.

When Martha came in with the teapot my spirits rose. Charlotte generally hosted these clerical teas and I dared hope that she too preferred we did not meet. Martha took the teapot to the top of the table and began filling cups beside the bishop. Hot and faint though I was, I began to feel that I might relax if Charlotte was not going to appear but then she came in carrying a second teapot. I watched her take it to her father at the bottom end of the table. Her face was fuller than I remembered and her cheeks rosy. She looked well, I was glad, but her expression was grave and her eyes downcast. She must have known I was there but she didn't look at me. Old friends and familiar faces attempted to greet Charlotte but she kept her eyes down, concentrating on the filling of cups, one of which was passed round to me. She knew I was there, I could feel it, but she would not look at me. I had been dreading this moment for weeks but, seeing her there in the life, I now needed her eyes. Her brief note of three months ago, though I had read it a hundred times, was indecipherable and her silence since, inscrutable. If our eyes met, if only for a moment, I knew I would see the truth of her feelings and so know what it was I must do but she kept them averted. She finished filling her half dozen cups and then, acknowledging none in the room but her father, she left and I still did not know.

The tea and chatter continued interminably. I felt hot and faint and wanted to leave but I was hemmed in and so had to stay until the bishop was ready to rise. When finally he did, I had to queue in the hall to take his leave, but at least the front door was open and, by the time my turn came, I felt fresher. Dr Longley was a tall, martial figure with a strong jaw and, as he took my hand in both of his, he drew me out onto the step.

"The diocese is sorry to be losing you, Mr Nicholls," he said, watching me. "Your record in Haworth has been exemplary, especially in the schools. You were marked for advancement if you had wanted it." I did not know what to say. I mumbled some general words of gratitude I think and then he said. "I know why you are leaving, and I pray for a happy resolution, but you must not run away. You cannot run away from your heart any more than you can from your soul. I thought you would have known that." Then he smiled. "Besides, we need you here in Yorkshire." He let go my hand. "Reconsider," was his final word, then I mumbled some more words of thanks and hurried off back to my rooms.

I was invited over to tea at Marshlands a few days after Dr Longley's visit and Grant was impatient to know what the bishop had said. I teased him that the bishop had drawn me out onto the step because his message was private and there was an end of it but Grant wouldn't have that.

"He wants you to stay in the diocese doesn't he?"

"You have some wondrous good ears."

"No. But I keep them close to the ground. I told you before that you were ready for advancement. You've been noticed. You think that because you spend all your time in Haworth no one knows about you. Well, the clergy is a small world and I tell you again, your talents have been recognised. Say to me now that Dr Longley did not ask you to stay."

We were sitting by the fireside in the parlour while Sarah and Susie prepared tea in the dining room. I didn't like Grant's questioning. I had put Dr Longley's appeal to reconsider out of mind even before I had left the parsonage garden and I did not want to discuss it with Grant. I leaned forward to him.

"My dear Grant," I said, suppressing my impatience. "You do not know all the circumstances. If you did you would know that it is impossible for me to remain in Haworth."

"I do know the circumstances. You proposed marriage to Charlotte without asking Brontë. He took exception, Charlotte refused you, and as long as you promise not to do it again, Brontë is prepared to let you stay on." I shook my head and sat back.

"It is not nearly so simple as that and really you do not help me by pretending it is." Sarah walked in. I stood up and offered her my chair but she bid me sit down and drew up a side chair.

"I hope Joseph is minding his manners, Mr Nicholls." She flashed me a smile. "You mustn't let him pry."

"Of course I shall pry," Grant answered, "I would not be his friend otherwise. I was just telling Nicholls how well-regarded he is and what a waste it would be if he threw everything up and ran off to the antipodes." He turned then to me. "Let novices learn the ways of the new territories and minister to the migrants. You have spent years mastering the crotchety ways of the Yorkshireman and master them you have! You can't just walk away from all that experience and disappear off the end of the world. It would be a criminal waste."

"But I cannot stay in Haworth." I told him again.

"Then at least stay nearby," Sarah said. "Stay in the West Riding. You don't have to go to Australia."

"You'd probably die on the voyage anyway," Grant added, "thousands do." Then he leaned to me. "I received a letter from the Society for the Propagation of the Gospel this week, asking me to give you a character reference." I nodded. Joseph's had been one of the six names I had given the Society. "I don't want to do it. I don't want to tell them what a splendid fellow you are so they can take you away and we shall never see you again. In twelve months' time you could have your own living here in the diocese – I have no doubt of it – if you will let me take the appropriate soundings."

"In twelve months' time you could have made new connections," Sarah chimed in, "met someone new." And Grant added:

"Someone younger who could give you a family." It was an intrusion too far. I sprang to my feet.

"It is not for me to tell you how to respond to the Gospel Society," I told him, and then, to Sarah, "the kettle must have boiled by now." And I led the way through to the dining room.

I had not been eating properly since December. I could feel myself shrinking inside my clothes and, had it not been for the constant coaxings of Mary Brown, I might have given up with meals altogether. I had no appetite for food; swallowing was an effort and the list of foods that made me feel sick grew longer. Of course, it is unwise to fast in winter and my health suffered. I seemed always to have a cold, my arm and knee joints ached, I was tired and I struggled to find energy for anything. The idea of migrating to Australia seemed increasingly a barren one. Australia was so far, so unfamiliar and so final. Fired with any degree of enthusiasm for the enterprise, I would have been proud to face a time of trial alone in a strange land, as Jesus had at the beginning of his ministry, but I could not raise the enthusiasm, I did not have the strength. I had continued to correspond with the Society for the Propagation of the Gospel, to supply referees, answer their questions and fill in their forms but I had put off attending for interview in London already on two occasions and I could not put it off for a third. At the beginning of April, I withdrew my application. I cited my rheumatic pains as the reason but I knew they were not the reason; they were just another symptom.

I still had to leave Haworth in less than two months whether I had somewhere to go to or not. Mr Brontë had advertised my position and was considering applicants so there really was no question. It had been easy, in February, to apply for an unknown position, six months hence, on the other side of the world, but it was another matter finding a real vacancy in a real English parish in a few short weeks. I accepted Grant's offer to make his enquiries.

During my final weeks in Haworth, I had to endure an interminable round of farewell functions. Each class of the two schools put on a show of appreciation of me, as did the Mechanics Institute and other bodies with which I was involved. These events culminated, two days before my final departure, in a ceremony at the National School attended by the Church Trustees and clerical colleagues at which I was eulogised by Mr Michael Merrall and presented with an inscribed gold watch. In the circumstances there was a deal more formality than sincerity in these proceedings and speculation, I dare say, about Mr Brontë's absence.

Charlotte went away to friends again at the end of April, which was a relief – I wouldn't be bumping into her and suffering the humiliation of her averted eyes. Our eyes hadn't met since the 13th December and when next they did, it upset us both.

It was on Whitsunday, the 15th May. I was taking my final communion service and these two factors together ensured a larger than usual congregation. The Whit Communion is a long service with many collects and quotations from the apostles and the celebrant must stand before the congregation a full half-hour before he administers the sacrament. Being under some strain in those last few weeks, I knew that that final communion would be testing, so I had prepared myself with prayer and a determined concentration on the meaning of the festival. I had not, for a moment, expected Charlotte to be there so when she came in and sat in the parsonage pew, my resilience faltered.

I maintained my command quite well through the first part of the service and when it was over, I turned from the congregation and went up to our little rustic altar to consecrate the bread and wine.

"*Hear us, Oh merciful Father, we most humbly beseech thee*", I intoned, "*and grant that we receive these thy creatures of bread and wine according to thy Son and our Saviour Jesus Christ's holy institution in remembrance of his death and passion.*" At this point I turned back to the congregation where the first row of communicants was already at the rail. Joseph Redman, the chapelry clerk, was the first, and kneeling beside him was Charlotte. "*…may be partakers of his most blessed Body and Blood …*" and she was looking at me. While all other eyes were lowered, Charlotte was looking up, straight at me, her eyes full of appeal. Appeal for what? To go to her? To try again? To forgive her? To do what? For a moment I froze. Charlotte had not looked at me in months. I was leaving. It was irrevocable. I looked down into my prayer book, I felt weak and dizzy but I continued as best I could. "… *who in the night that he was betrayed took bread and when he had given thanks he broke it and gave it to his disciples saying, take, eat, this is my body which is given for you, do this in remembrance of me…*" then my voice broke and I fell silent. My head was spinning. I looked out over the congregation and now everyone was watching me. I felt about to faint but Joseph Redman got up from the rail and came to me.

"Are you alright?" he whispered, taking my arm. He produced a glass of water from somewhere and I drank. "*Likewise after supper he took the cup…*" he prompted me and, feeling steadier, I continued.

"*Likewise after supper he took the cup…*" and I went on to finish the prayer as I moved to the rail. Redman had resumed his place, by now, as first recipient, and I gave him the sacrament. I blessed him with the sign of the cross then moved on to Charlotte beside him. Her head stayed bowed as I placed the bread on her palm but then, to take the chalice, she had to look up and her cheeks were streaked with tears.

My replacement, a Mr De Renzy, was to take over from me on the last Sunday in May and so I had made arrangements to leave on the Friday morning. By the Thursday evening, with my farewells made and my things packed, I had only one final duty to perform; the handing over to Mr Brontë of the deeds to the Stanbury Mission School – the one concrete memorial of my time in the chapelry.

It was a sunny spring evening when I walked up the parsonage path for what I assumed must be the last time. The air was filled with the cheerful calls of songbirds competing for their mates and territories but my heart was heavy because still I did not want to go. There were so many things that I could have said to Mr Brontë. In spite of the events of the past five months, my overriding sentiment towards him was that of gratitude: gratitude for the model of dauntless faith that he had held up to me, and also for the trust that he had always placed in me. There were many things that I would have liked to thank Mr Brontë for but I knew that it would be impossible. I didn't know if I would see Charlotte. I hoped not. I knew that she was at home, but the time when anything could have been gained by our talking was, by then, long past. The front door was open and Martha was there, standing in the dining room doorway. The room was in turmoil and she was in her brown apron, brandishing a broom.

"Just spring cleanin', Mr Nicholls," she said cheerfully, "gettin' all the winter muck out." She brought her broom to attention under her chin and gripped the top with both hands. "Are you about ready for off then?"

"Yes. About ready." I looked past her into the dining room. "Miss Charlotte not in?" Martha nodded towards the stairs.

"In her bedroom. Havin' a lie down." I looked across the hall to the parlour. "Master's in," Martha offered, and I went and tapped on his door.

My interview with Mr Brontë was too brief and too formal. He stood before his empty grate, tall, spare and straight as ever but his eyesight was deteriorating again and he looked down his nose at me through blue-tinted spectacles. He accepted from me the deeds to the school but he did not invite me to sit. He expressed his satisfaction with my professional conduct and wished me well in my future career and then we shook hands but I dared not look at him. My heart was too full. This stern formality was no way to part from the man who had taught me the imperatives of faith and charity, who had borne up so magnificently against the assaults of Fate and I did not, at that moment, blame him if his need to cling to the last of his family prevented him from seeing charity in me.

I left the house and, by the time I had reached the path, my eyes were too misted to see. At the steps to the lane, I sat down and let go my tears but I was not left alone there for long. I heard light footfalls tripping down the path. I wanted to hide but there was nowhere to go so I looked up and I saw it was Charlotte. She was standing on the path looking down on me and her eyes too were filled with tears.

"Oh, Mr Nicholls," she twisted her hands at her waist, "I am sorry." Her lips were parted to say more but she seemed powerless. She hesitated for a moment and then she turned away and hurried back up the path.

"I only wanted your happiness," I called after her. "I wanted to protect you both." But she did not turn back. She continued up the path and disappeared into the house.

I left Haworth at six o'clock the following morning, still with no position to go to. Sarah Grant's parents, the Turners, had invited me to go to them in Essex but at the last minute I could not face the politeness and the pleasantries and so I took myself off back to Ireland.

CHAPTER FOURTEEN

Exile

I did not call on my brother. I had no wish to tell Alan that my attempt at finding a wife had been a disaster and my career was in ruins. Added to which, Charlotte's new novel was the talk of salon society and I did not want Alan's wife claiming me as her connection to its celebrated author. I wanted only to see my Aunt Harriette and so I bypassed Sir John Rogerson Quay and went straight on to Banagher.

I had given Aunt Harriette only the barest outline of what had passed since December and when she saw me she was shocked. I hadn't shaved since I left Haworth and the accumulated strains of the last seven months had left me two stones lighter. I was tired and did not try to hide it. I collapsed on my aunt like the prodigal returned from the distant land.

Cuba House was quiet, which suited me. Only three of my cousins were at home: James, now ordained, was busy running the school, and William was in school, which left only Mary with time for me. The last time I'd seen Mary, I had blundered a proposal of marriage at her so I was a little wary, especially after my latest rejection, but she didn't allude to it. If I had embarrassed her, I must have been forgiven because her welcome was as warm as Aunt Harriette's. I liked Mary. She was my favourite of all my Bell cousins. She was eleven years my junior, so a child when we were young, but she was intelligent, with a profound self-confidence that few of her brothers recognised, but I saw it, and I admired her for it. We went out for walks in the park together and along the meanders of the Shannon. Mary was now twenty-four and a grown woman but she had not changed: she still had those profound reserves and that quality so matched to my mood: a contentment with silence.

Towards the end of the second week, I received a letter from Grant.

Marshlands
11th June 1853

My Dear Nicholls,

I trust that your journey to King's County was not too strenuous and that your family is plying you with much love and balm after hard times in Haworth.

I have important news for you. The Revd Thomas Cator, the Rector of Saint Mary's, Kirk Smeaton, is in urgent need of a curate as his present one is leaving at the end of this month. I know Thomas Cator and he is a good man. He and his family own a deal of land in that part of Yorkshire and he has family and social responsibilities beyond his clerical ones so he relies pretty heavily on his curate – which will be nothing new to you! That said, Kirk Smeaton, which is in the Deanery of Doncaster, is only a small parish and I am sure that you would enjoy a good deal more leisure there, and in more congenial surroundings, than you were ever used to in Haworth. The stipend, I believe, is close to £140 per annum.

When I mentioned your name to Cator, he told me that he already knew of you from Dr Longley and that he would consider himself fortunate indeed if you were to join him at Kirk Smeaton. There you are! I told you that you had been noticed!

The cure is yours if you want it but please let me know one way or the other by return.

Sarah and Charles send their best wishes, as does Susie, and for my part, I hope that the above is of interest to you for we do want you back among us.

Sincerely yours,
Joseph Grant

It was too soon. I had only been gone two weeks, I needed rest, and besides, I was growing my beard. I slept on Grant's offer and then talked it over with my aunt and my cousins. James was scathing. He said the cure was beneath me and I should be more ambitious. Aunt Harriette and Mary both wanted me to apply for something in Ireland, but I could not raise the enthusiasm for applying for anything in England or Ireland so, if Kirk Smeaton was there on a plate, I thought I might as well take it – but not yet. I thanked Grant for his efforts and told him I would accept Cator's offer if he could wait until August. I posted my letter and retired to an arbour with *Villette*. It was not an easy read.

I found the book difficult. I had to keep rereading sections in order to make sense of them. There is no plot to absorb the reader and carry him forward. Events occur at random. Whole episodes are repeated and characters who were introduced to us in one place and one guise, reappear in another place and another guise and going by different names. The characters all seem strangely isolated from one another and to misconstrue each other's motives. I found it very unsettling.

Certainly *Villette* is another love story like Charlotte's earlier books but it is a wholly one-sided love story and its heroine is far too self-absorbed. Perhaps the book is about isolation, about loneliness, because, like Jane Eyre and Shirley Keeldar, the heroine, Lucy Snowe, is an orphan with no clear past. *Villette* is a strange achievement: after reading six hundred pages of her soliloquising, I knew no more about the heroine at the end of the book than I did at the beginning.

I did not enjoy *Villette*. I found it depressing. Certainly, the must of loneliness hangs about the stories of *Jane Eyre* and *Shirley* but its scent does not suffuse them as completely as it does *Villette*. Jane Eyre is another self-absorbed heroine, but there is the air of brisk optimism about her that is completely lacking in Lucy Snowe. The reader of *Jane Eyre* can feel that, whatever vicissitudes the heroine suffers, the strength of her moral conviction will enable her to withstand them. In *Shirley* too, Shirley Keeldar's sense of righteousness triumphs in the end but *Villette* gives us no such confidence in Lucy Snowe. When Jane Eyre and Shirley Keeldar suffer knocks, we know that they will heal; when Lucy Snowe suffers knocks, she becomes scarred. It is as though, when faced with life's buffeting storms, Charlotte's earlier heroines struggle to raise themselves above the blasts while Lucy Snowe curls up and submits.

I thought about Charlotte and her latest heroine. I knew that Charlotte was lonely but Lucy's isolation lay far deeper. To read *Villette* is to look into the heart of a woman detached from all humankind and if Lucy represented her creator's inner self, then Charlotte was more lonely than I'd ever imagined. I sat in the arbour with *Villette* in my lap and thought about Charlotte. Would she have accepted me, I wondered, if it hadn't been for her father? But then, I thought, if it hadn't been for her father, would I have even proposed? Troubling thoughts, for which, the next morning, I received my rebuke.

The Vicarage,
Hebden Road,
Oxenhope.
29th June 1853

My Dear Nicholls,
Kirk Smeaton is yours – although Cator was not pleased to wait until August. He has had to rearrange long standing engagements to cover parish duties until then, but he evidently thinks you are worth it – though he does insist that you start the first week.
Cator is not the only parson with curate trouble at the moment. Mr Brontë is having a difficult time with your successor, De Renzy. He is not the putty in Brontë's hands that you used to be. Perhaps he is made of drier stuff – or Mr Brontë is losing his grip – or both. Anyway, De Renzy seems in no hurry to take up his responsibilities – many of which he thinks beneath him – and poor Brontë has again found himself having to go out and do everything himself

in order to show his truculent underling what is what, and the agitation of it all, coming so close on the heels of his anxiety over you, has fairly knocked him up, and a fortnight ago he had another seizure. For some days he was stone blind – unable to tell night from day. His sight has improved since then, but it is not what it was and I am afraid he is again quite debilitated. Needless to say, the Revds Mayne, Cartman and I are rallying round to keep things going – I never realised that you did so much!

Cator asks that you send him a formal acceptance of the cure to his home, Skelbrooke Park, Skelbrooke, Near Doncaster – and note that Sarah and I have finally moved into the new vicarage.

Sincerely yours,
Joseph Grant

My blood ran cold and John Brown's words rang in my ears: 'If he doesn't have another seizure, it'll be no thanks to thee.' I had broken a good man. The pain I had inflicted on Mr Brontë in December was now compounded by this seizure brought on in consequence. I had not wanted this and the thought of Charlotte and her father huddled in mutual support against the cause of their troubles made my exile feel distant indeed.

I did nothing for the next few days, but words and phrases of explanation to Charlotte flitted through my mind, the phrases became sentences and the sentences paragraphs until the power of the flood overwhelmed me and I had no choice but to take up my pen. It would be the first time I had addressed Charlotte since the 13th December and I sent off my letter during the first week of July.

Cuba House,
Banagher,
King's County.
4th July 1853

Dear Miss Brontë,

I write to express my shock and very deep regret that your father has suffered this latest seizure. I had the news from Joseph Grant and I understand that again Mr Brontë's sight has been affected. If God wills it, normal vision can be restored in such circumstances, and I pray daily that in your father's case it will. If there is anything that I can possibly do to ameliorate your father's suffering, I will travel any distance and brook any obstacle to do it, for to the great weight of respect, gratitude and affection that I bear your father is now added the burden of guilt that I am the cause of his suffering.

I know that I annoyed your father last December, and that my refusal to abandon all hope of winning you precipitated my departure and the subsequent troubles that he now endures. God knows that I never foresaw such an outcome as this. I hoped that your father would welcome me, that he would understand my commitment to his welfare, to the chapelry, and to the prospect of your retaining your family home. I never foresaw this unhappiness.

I hope you will forgive my intruding like this but I have been in such a position for the past eight years that it would have been impossible for me not to be affected by you and your family. Curates are not obliged to take an interest in their employers' families, nor are they invited to, but for eight years I lodged with your father's sexton, not a hundred yards from your home, Martha lives in with you, and for increasingly long periods in latter years, I too have spent much of my time in the parsonage. Sextons, curates and servants are necessarily embarked in the same vessel as their masters and when the boat rocks, masters and servants are buffeted alike: I witnessed the years of your brother's decline, I counselled Anne, and I buried Emily.

I became involved with many families during my time in Haworth – it was the greater part of my duty as curate – but because I was the curate, I came to know your family better than any other and, had your family been no more interesting than the next, I should still, perforce, have been affected by you. But then your family is not as ordinary as the next, it is not uninteresting. In Paradise, the dead will live for ever, and we shall join them there in God's good time, but until that time comes they survive on earth only in the memories of those that remember them and if those that remember them are left with no one with whom they can share their memories, then remembrance is sad indeed.

Perhaps your father was right and I aspired too high when I wanted to be a member of your family. I have neither the spirit nor the ingenuity of a Brontë but, in the days when I harboured hope, I fancied that we were not so different, you and I; we both know what it is to lose a mother and be raised by an aunt; we have both lost loved ones and we know the isolation of living in a community where education sets us apart – we know what it is to be lonely.

I did not want to hurt your father nor to embarrass you or disarrange the life that you have. I believed that I could make both of your lives happier and I deeply regret that I have made matters worse. I take up a new position as curate to the Rector of Kirk Smeaton at the end of this month. I look forward to applying myself to new challenges there with new people and in new surroundings, and I hope that, in time, the distress that I brought to you and your father might be assuaged by the service I can render in Kirk Smeaton. Some memories of Haworth, of course, I shall cherish forever, and I thank Providence that she permitted me to know you and your exceptional family. Please, at some moment when you think your father might welcome them, pass on to him my warm regards, and be assured that I pray for his speedy recovery.

I remain your obedient servant.
A.B. Nicholls.

Charlotte did not reply to my letter, but then, why would she? What could she say? She had said she was sorry at the garden gate then returned to her father and closed the door. I had to accept that my time in Haworth was over but still I chafed with regrets. To be the cause of a seizure and then shunned was not the memorial that Mr Brontë or I deserved of each other. I felt wretched but, if my mind languished in Haworth, my body could not. After eight weeks of pampering, with a full girth and full beard, I was released into my new unknown world.

* * *

Kirk Smeaton is a village forty miles southeast of Haworth. It was, in many ways, the tranquil English parish of my student dreams, very different from rugged Haworth. Where Haworth clings to a steep hillside surrounded by untamed moors, Kirk Smeaton looks out over the fertile Plane of York and the Wolds and every acre is under the plough. Where the view from Haworth is of piled banks of hills, that from Kirk Smeaton is piled only with banks of cumulus which, on the day that I arrived, were passing timelessly over an endless carpet of ripening corn. In Haworth, the people live by the wool industry where the mills and the land change hands as frequently as the cycles of that volatile trade but, in Kirk Smeaton, the cycle of nature determines the villagers' lives, its two mills grind only corn, and much of the land that grows it has been in the same hands for centuries.

Kirk Smeaton's rector, the Reverend Thomas Cator, was a landowner. He was also the Vicar of Womersley, just north of Kirk Smeaton and, until recently, the Vicar of Woodbastwick in Norfolk where his eldest brother held a large estate and was the patron of the living. Thomas Cator was the youngest of three brothers and the middle one,

Charles, had preceded him at Kirk Smeaton before moving to the more lucrative living of Stokesley in the far north of Yorkshire. The Cator family had estates in Kent as well as Norfolk and Yorkshire and they owned much of the land round Kirk Smeaton. My rector was a wealthy and a busy man.

I was collected from Wakefield station and driven to Mr Cator's seat, Skelbrooke Park, two miles south of Kirk Smeaton. I was numb from my long journey and I sat in the back of the cart surrounded by boxes and parcels. I might have been one of those parcels – a note book perhaps, on its way to being delivered to a new owner who would write in its pages the next chapter of my life. We drove through the deer park that beset the great house. Skelbrooke was an imposing mansion of three stories and seven bays with a central front door that opened as the dogcart drew up. I was taken inside by a liveried footman who, once I had brushed myself off, conducted me into a room with a high ceiling and two walls of tall windows. The room was full of chairs, sofas and consoles, all gilded; the Italian landscapes on the walls had gilded frames and the frieze and covings were also picked out in gold. If this was where Mr Cator conducted his business it was like no office I had ever seen and the only clue to its function was the presence of a secretary seated quietly at a table in the corner. Mr Cator was with him, scowling at a document over his shoulder and, when he saw me, he stood up and strode over.

"The Reverend Mr Nicholls." He gave me a broad smile. "At last. I am very pleased to meet you." Mr Cator was tall and lean and very straight for a man of sixty-three. He had sandy hair and ginger sideburns and I noted he was in tweeds, not clericals. He shook my hand and led me to a pair of chairs overlooking the park but, even as we sat down, he twisted to look at the clock.

"You have chosen a bad time to arrive, Mr Nicholls. You find me with more demands on my morning than there is time to deal with them so forgive me if we are brief." I gave him my attention. "First. Have you got your accommodation sorted out?"

"I have come directly from the railway station," I told him. "So no …" Mr Cator looked to his secretary.

"The Old Rectory," the secretary murmured over his ledger.

"The Old Rectory," Mr Cator repeated, and he turned back to me. "It hasn't been the rectory for a good few years but your predecessor had no complaints about it. It's in the middle of the village. The carrier will take you." Mr Cator stretched out his long legs and crossed them at the ankles. "You come recommended by some very senior churchmen, Mr Nicholls." He clasped his hands together over his belt and raised his eyebrows at me. "Reliable, efficient, High Church. This is what I'm told," he looked at me for confirmation, "and this is what I want." I nodded that I understood. "If you are half the man I am told you are," he went on, "you will have no difficulty at Kirk Smeaton. Three hundred and sixty parishioners, that's all, mainly in the village, and the tenants generally keep on top of any trouble." He raised a finger. "Key men, the tenants. You'll have to talk to them and talk to the churchwardens. They will tell you who the troublemakers are. You mark them and let them know that you've marked them. Show them a firm purpose from the outset and you won't go far wrong." Mr Cator drew in his legs and put his hands on the arms of his chair. He seemed to be about to rise but then he looked again to his secretary.

"Gleaning," said the secretary and, without letting go of the chair arms, Mr Cator turned to me,

"Where do you stand on gleaning?"

"Gleaning, Mr Cator? I'm afraid I don't know what you mean."

"Gleaning," he repeated. "You know what gleaning is. What do you think about people gleaning fields that don't belong to them?"

"I'm afraid I have no experience of the practice. Not coming from a part where…"

"Well, it's a problem here. It has been ever since the enclosure. Some folk can't get it into their heads that there's no such thing as common land anymore and no such thing as common rights." Mr Cator pushed himself up from his chair and I followed him. "Harvest is nearly upon us. You had better get prepared for it. We owe it to the tenants to keep on top of it." Mr Cator held out his hand and I took it. "Any questions?" He gave me another broad smile and I scratched at my beard. "You will have! Jennings here will tell you anything you need to know." Mr Cator then put his arm across my shoulder and conducted me to the door. "You were with Brontë weren't you? Wasn't it his son that caused all that hoo-ha over at Thorp Green? Pants down? That sort of thing? They say that's what did for poor Robinson." It was an extraordinarily tasteless remark from a churchman. I was shocked and Mr Cator saw it. I removed myself from his clasp.

"And for Mr Brontë's son," I told him, and I bid him a good day.

Kirk Smeaton Old Rectory was a rambling old place with many alterations and additions and passages that no longer led anywhere. Though right in the heart of the village, it had evidently been a farmhouse at one time because farm cottages and buildings still attached to its back. The tenants of the farm were the Lamplugh family who seemed, over the years, to have encroached by degrees into the house until it was now hard to tell where the cottages ended and the house began. Being on my own, I was indifferent to these encroachments; it was enough for me that I had a bedroom twice the size of my room at Sexton House and a parlour downstairs even larger than that. Besides, Mrs Lamplugh was retained as my cook and housekeeper so the ill-defined boundaries of the properties kept her close at hand, which suited us both, and the ancient rickety place with its ancient rickety furniture served me very well.

On the evening of that first day, I walked out of the village to look for some open country where I might stretch my legs and fill my lungs with fresh air but I soon found that there is no open country round Kirk Smeaton; all the land is enclosed and the only feature that breaks the monotony of the corn is the occasional coppice, and that maintained for the hunt. I returned to the village and the little parish church of Saint Mary Magdalene that overlooks the shallow valley of the Went. It is an ancient church – Norman, perhaps even Saxon – and the oak rood screen, the pew boxes and the little minstrels' gallery were all splitting with the weight of their age. I liked the old church. Its age and neglect had fashioned it into a hallowed place with a strong sense of God's presence. I knelt down and prayed for His help in this unpromising land.

God was my sole support and companion during those first weeks at Kirk Smeaton. Mr Cator had been taking the services in the five weeks since his last curate had left and now that relief had arrived he was pleased to return to his familiar practice of delegation. I do not mean to suggest that Mr Cator was neglectful. On the contrary, he devoted his life to doing everything that the world expected of him. He had inherited extensive properties and responsibilities and his life was sewn with the thread of his lineage into the tapestry of families that controlled the county. He was the grandson of a peer and his wife the daughter of another. He would do what was expected of him and be what he was expected to be and when his father had asked his two younger sons to take holy orders and fill some of the benefices within his patronage, Thomas and Charles accepted their responsibilities as they had so many others and then, as with those others, delegated them. If Mr Cator had a fault, it was that he had allowed his sense of duty to suppress his sense of curiosity; if he had woken one morning in the last century he would not have been a whit disturbed.

I found Kirk Smeaton a lonelier place than Haworth had ever been. In Haworth, from the outset, Mr Brontë had been my mentor, my working colleague and my near neighbour with an ever-open door. Added to that, there was a tradition of mutual support among the clergy of the Pennine valleys, support through which I had made lasting friendships. I found no such support in the neighbourhood of Kirk Smeaton, no cards were presented at the Old Rectory and I received no invitations to vicarage teas.

The laity, of course, was ever present but the arrival of a newcomer to their settled community excited no curiosity in them. Perhaps it was because it was harvest time. The days were long for farmers and labourers alike, fourteen or sixteen hours, and the work monotonous and hard. Free beer was laid on, as much as they could drink, so perhaps that, on top of their physical exhaustion, dulled the villagers' curiosity. Or perhaps it was that curates came and went with the seasons and the people saw no more point in talking to me than they would to the leaves on the trees, but there was an air of dullness about them. When an Irishman meets a stranger, he asks him straight out who he is and what is his business and he will talk to him for half the day in a spirit of genuine interest. In Haworth, the stranger must speak first, and though the native will be guarded about his own business, he will have discovered all that needs knowing about the stranger before he lets him go. But in Kirk Smeaton, the stranger excites no interest in the native. Perhaps they are a dull breed. Perhaps they fear change that the outsider represents or perhaps it is that in Ireland and the Pennine hills, the native has a say in the direction of his life, and so will be interested in anyone that might affect it, whereas in Kirk Smeaton, where the native has no power over his life, curiosity has no purpose.

I came across none of the 'trouble' that Mr Cator had been so concerned about. The people were so cowed that they had no spirit for trouble. Perhaps the habit of close control was part of Mr Cator's inherited code of management and he felt it had to be maintained whether circumstances warranted it or not. For my part, I could have wished for a little more spirit in the villagers because producing any spark of Christian joy among them was heavy work and after a couple of weeks I could feel their apathy seeping into me and that pulled me up with a start. I prayed for God's guidance and he answered me with a question: what would Mr Brontë do? It was the only guidance I needed. I knew just what Mr Brontë would do. He would fill his soul with the divine spirit and raise his eyes to the skies. He would preach with fervour on the abundant blessings of this life and the joyous prospect of the life to come. He would seek out the brightest lights of faith he could find, however dim and, by close personal attention, kindle them into flame, and he would lead by right example, living the selfless life of the disciple of Christ. So, all these things I tried to do and, after determined application and effort, I was able to see some lights of faith start to flicker across the pews.

It was a lonely road I was treading but I felt, after a few weeks, that I was making progress and doing a little good and that knowledge did me good too. I was receiving the occasional nod in the lanes, and people began to call on me with their problems, at first their personal problems but then their public ones too. The 'problem' of gleaning turned out to be a simple one to resolve and it marked my first intervention into public affairs.

The poor had enjoyed gleaning rights since earliest times and they did not see why enclosure should curtail them. The farmers were used to turning their livestock into the fields to eat off the stubble as soon as the corn was cleared, then the Badsworth Hunt wanted the livestock out again so that they could start cubbing. All of this put pressure on the gleaners to get into the fields as quickly as they could and the perennial complaint from the farmers was that the gleaners were taking corn even before the stooks had been cleared. It was an annual ritual and conflict was part of it, but it seemed to me wholly unnecessary. I spoke to the farmers and they agreed that if the gleaners kept out until the last stook was removed from a field, they would hold off putting in their livestock for three days. The only loser by the scheme would be the hunt whose season would start three days late. Mr Cator was an officer of the hunt and I put the proposal to him. At first he was against it but, when I told him that it was the will of all his Kirk Smeaton tenants, and as it was their interest that he had cited as paramount, he had no option but to agree.

I received a letter from Grant towards the end of September inviting me over to Oxenhope. He was eager to show me his new vicarage but, that apart, his news was not good. Since his second seizure, Mr Brontë had become, in Grant's words, 'almost childishly dependent on Charlotte', his moods oscillating between 'petulant irascibility' and 'solicitous fawning for her attention' while Charlotte, for her part, had left him to holiday in Scotland with some friends of Miss Nussey's. Add to these woes Mr Brontë's exasperation with his new curate and it was clear that my departure had done nothing to leaven his lot.

I put down Grant's letter and looked into the fire in my hearth. I saw Mr Brontë again, standing before his own hearth. From our first meeting to our last, he had stood there, facing me, sometimes blind, sometimes bronchitic, sometimes bereaved, but always erect and collected. I didn't like to think of him now, all alone, without Charlotte or even a curate. He must be feeling let down, I thought, as I watched my coal flames dance. Had I let him down, I wondered? He seemed to think I had, as did most of Haworth. As time went on, would I even think so myself?

I picked up Grant's letter and looked at it again. He was inviting me to view his new vicarage and I would have to reply. I was extremely reluctant to go back to Haworth – more than reluctant – I could not go back but, I could hear Grant say, Oxenhope is not Haworth, it is two miles away and, unless I wanted to lose him, I would have to go sometime. I looked out of my window at the mud-mired village. It was quiet, the harvest was home, and I was comfortably on top of my work. I decided I would go.

CHAPTER FIFTEEN

Return

It felt strange to be back in Oxenhope, so close to Mr Brontë and Charlotte while, at the same time, distanced from them by my months in Kirk Smeaton. The visit would be cathartic, I told myself, it would force me to face my past and lay it to rest.

Grant's new vicarage was handsome. Built in the vernacular style with mullioned windows and an oriel over the porch, it stood on a knoll overlooking a shallow valley on the southern edge of Oxenhope. It was comfortable and homely and just across the road from Grant's new church. Joseph and Sarah loved the place and I was happy for them.

Sutcliffe Sowden came over on the second day and we passed a cheerful afternoon exchanging news of our parishes and the wider world but if I thought, for a moment, that by talking about the present I could suppress the past among those haunted hills, my faith was tested on the following day, when I ran into Charlotte. I think it was inevitable. I was drawn to the western moors the minute I saw them and when the weather was fine, there was always the chance that someone would be out there with Flossy.

I set off after an early breakfast, heading up Moorside to the valleys of the Sladen and the Worth – those twin vales of solitude that had nourished me for most of my adult life. Passing Waterhead Lane, I walked along Enfieldside intending to cross the Sladen Beck at South Dean. White cirrus were streaking an azure sky and the sun sparkling silver off the dew on the heather. The air was still and, but for the crake of the occasional grouse, quiet. I walked the familiar paths and, with only my thoughts for company, memory and imagination mingled. I saw Emily sitting by the stream below Waterhead Lane and Branwell, hands in pockets, marching down Hill End, and in every shadow and every movement at the tail of my eye, I saw Anne, head down and hidden in the hood of her cloak. I saw Keeper, and so, when Flossy appeared in front of me, I was not in the least surprised. He came out of the heather just as I was approaching the clapper bridge in South Dean. He looked at me cautiously and sniffed the air, then he took a step back and put his chin on the ground. I called to him.

"Flossy!" He barked and wriggled his stiff old hips. He rolled onto his back and, while I gave him a fuss, Charlotte appeared round the bend in the path. She was wearing a heavy cloak and a winter bonnet and her cheeks were flushed from walking.

"Mr Nicholls?" She screwed up her eyes to see me.

"Miss Brontë." She came closer to me.

"You are wearing a beard. I thought you were in Kirk Seaton."

"Kirk Smeaton," I corrected her. "It's in the Deanery of Doncaster."

"Then why are you here?"

"I am visiting the Grants. They have moved into their new vicarage." Flossy ran across the bridge and barked. He was impatient to get on but Charlotte remained, standing, looking at me. 'So', I thought, 'here we were'. After all those months of anxiety about what Charlotte was thinking and what she might feel for me; and then the further months at Kirk Smeaton, striving to put Charlotte behind me – after all that – here we were, together, in South Dean, and I could not believe how easy it felt. Charlotte remained looking at me, saying nothing. She seemed at a loss so, after a few moments, I tipped her my hat.

"I shall bid you a good day then." I was about to walk past her and continue along the path but then Flossy, from the opposite bank, suddenly threw himself into the shallow beck and splashed his way across to me. I dragged him onto the bank and, while he shook himself all over my boots, Charlotte finally spoke.

"It seems we must return together." She stepped onto the clapper bridge. "Either that or I lose Flossy to Kirk Seaton."

The hillside on the north side of the bridge is steep so, while Flossy ran cheerfully on, Charlotte and I climbed in silence, pulling ourselves up by the tuft grass. At the summit, the path passes round the back of Virginia Farm and then opens up to an immense view across Haworth to Leeds and the Plane of York, twenty miles beyond. We settled into our stride along the ridge and, as we regained our breath, Charlotte talked. She asked me about Kirk Smeaton and its people and the state of the parish – questions I enjoyed answering because my new life was interesting to me and I was happy to tell her. Flossy brought me a stick which I threw for him; the sky was high and the landscape wide and as the rhythms of our talking and walking combined, I felt positive and Charlotte picked up on it.

"You bounce back like an India ball, Mr Nicholls." She turned up her face and smiled at me. "I am glad."

"God has been kind," I told her. "I have my health and my ministry and the support of my family and friends. I have much to thank Him for." Charlotte returned to the privacy of her bonnet and her eyes to the path. Too late, I saw how crass my boasts had been. Charlotte had no family to sustain her; neither she nor her father enjoyed good health and although she had a career, it was a solitary one that only compounded her sense of loss. We walked on in silence. Flossy brought me his stick again and dropped it at my feet. The old dog was panting hard but his eyes were bright and he would not let me be so I threw it again.

"And how is your father?" I asked, he being foremost in my mind.

"He is tolerable," Charlotte replied, from inside her bonnet.

"No lasting damage from his seizure then?"

"No. I think he is now over it." Charlotte, accustomed to walking with taller companions, was taking long strides to keep pace with me.

"And yourself?" I asked her. "How have you been?"

"Tolerable."

We walked on in silence for a few minutes more, each with our own thoughts, and then out of nowhere Charlotte asked me.

"Have you read *Villette* yet?" I had hoped she wouldn't ask.

"I have." I didn't elaborate.

"Perhaps you found the plot weak. Not enough incident."

"I may be a provincial curate," I told her, "but I do not require all novels to follow Fielding's pattern."

"Well, I am very glad to hear that." Our eyes met and she smiled, then she returned her gaze to the path. "Then you did find some merit in *Villette*?" I had not found any merit in *Villette* but, feeling bold, I decided I'd be frank.

"A story does not need to teem with incident, but it should have a purpose surely, and I am not sure I understand what *Villette's* purpose is. Your heroines seem to be retiring by degrees from society and I don't know where you can go after *Villette*." Charlotte shot me a glance.

"What do you mean?"

"Well, in *Jane Eyre*, your heroine struggles against social injustice and in the end triumphs because of her moral strength. In *Shirley* too, you treat with social issues, but now in *Villette* you do not even address social concerns, your heroine is interested in nothing but herself, and society and morals seem not to exist."

"And you disapprove of this progress?"

"I believe – as your sister Anne did – that those of us who are possessed of an education have a duty to contribute something positive to society and I see nothing positive in self-absorption. You dwelt on your heroines' anxieties in *Jane Eyre* and a deal longer in *Shirley* but in *Villette* they suffuse the whole work and there is neither happiness nor salvation nor any social good to be gained by it." Charlotte looked up at me.

"Happiness, salvation and the social good?" These are the sum of life's purpose are they?"

"Doesn't our Lord tell us that happiness in this life and salvation in the next depend on social engagement? On loving our neighbours?"

"And what of the inner life? You must own that you also have an inner life?"

"Of course. Through my prayers I commune with God."

"And contemplation?" I sensed the old fire building in Charlotte but I was not going to be intimidated.

"Our Lord spent forty days and nights in the desert but he did not go there to examine his *self*, he went there to learn how to give his *self* away, to God. That is Christ's message, isn't it? Give your *self* in faith to God, give your time on earth to the service of your fellow men, and salvation will be yours." Charlotte continued to walk with her head down. I was enjoying our conversation. It was liberating, after so long, to be out on the moors and talking as an equal with a Brontë.

"Did you perceive the promise of salvation when you were ministering to the intransigent inhabitants of Haworth?"

"Yes I did. When I abandon myself to God I do feel exhilaration in my faith and besides, it is only through engagement with others that we know ourselves at all."

"You must hold your integrity cheaper than I," Charlotte chided. "But then you are a man in a man's world, I am merely a woman in a man's world, not permitted to engage in it as you are." She looked up at me. "I cannot minister religion or engage in public life. The great seats of learning that you and Papa enjoyed are all closed to me; I cannot practice a socially useful profession or hold public office so the greater part of a woman's life must perforce be her inner life; her *self* is all that she has and if she values her integrity she will cherish it."

We had arrived at the point where our paths separated at the top of Dimples Lane. This would be the parting of our ways.

"Is that what *Villette* is about?" I asked, looking down at Charlotte. "Knowing your self? All those characters appearing in different guises and changing their names?" Charlotte moved a little closer, narrowing her eyes to see me.

"A work of art, Mr Nicholls, like any man or any woman, is the product of a single creator and yet perceived differently by everyone who meets it. Sadly, most people see only what they are looking for."

"But your heroine does find her true self in the end, doesn't she? And she finds it through her relationship with another, with her teacher, Paul Emmanuel." Charlotte stepped back and smiled.

"Is that how you see it? Or is Lucy Snowe abandoning her true self and deliberately exchanging it for Paul Emmanuel's version of who she is?" Charlotte took a piece of twine from inside her cloak and strung it through Flossy's collar, then, as she set off down the path, she called back: "Write to me again."

I returned to Kirk Smeaton confirmed in my resolve to put Haworth behind me. I did not want to enter into correspondence with Charlotte. She and I had met and we had talked as equals but the depth of our history and the scar of her father's rejection would not be skimmed over by the occasional exchange of our news and gossip. I was pleased with the way I had handled myself but I had been expelled, I had started a new life. I had met Charlotte and survived the experience. That would have to do.

My duties in Kirk Smeaton were considerably lighter than I'd been used to in Haworth. There was already a school with a competent master who was not answerable to me. Apart from a scattering of farms, the village was the parish, there were no outlying hamlets to organise and although the

Methodists were established, the contest for congregations, that characterised the religious life of Haworth, was long ago lost and won and the lines of loyalty drawn. But, with bible classes, an expanded choir and some private teaching, I did manage to broaden my portfolio of duties to a degree that absorbed me and my efforts were rewarded by stronger congregations and the approbation of my rector.

Mr Cator and I got along very well together. He was not the fiercely principled mentor that Mr Brontë had been, but then I was no longer the debutant who needed one, but Mr Cator and I understood each other and, through a mutual willingness to accommodate, we settled into a comfortable working routine – a routine that was only once disturbed, when my previous life intruded.

I used to meet with Mr Cator at Skelbrooke on Tuesday mornings to discuss the business of the parish. Round about the middle of October, a month or so after my return from the Grants, Mr Cator and I were concluding our meeting when he suddenly mentioned in a 'by-the-by' sort of way that he had had a visitor.

"I had an acquaintance of yours call by on Saturday," he told me with a wry smile, "wanted to know how you are getting on."

"Oh," I replied, "and who was that?" We were standing in the middle of the morning room waiting for my coat to be brought.

"Richard Monckton Milnes." The name was familiar but I could not place it. "Monckton Milnes." Mr Cator repeated. "Member of Parliament. Man of letters. He has the Fryston Hall estate up at Ferrybridge." I shook my head. I knew the name from the newspapers but I was sure I'd never met him.

"Well, he knows you well enough. He wanted to know how you are getting on. Said he had a sympathetic interest after all your troubles in Haworth."

"I beg your pardon, Sir." I wheeled on Mr Cator. "Would you mind telling me just what Mr Milnes meant by *troubles* and what business it is of his?" Mr Cator stepped back. He raised his hands in a gesture of submission.

"I am sorry, Nicholls. I have absolutely no wish to be indiscreet. I understood from Milnes that you were acquainted. Clearly, I misunderstood him."

"I shall be obliged to you, Sir," I told him through my teeth, "if you will tell me everything this man has told you about me." And Mr Cator, in simple terms, related the circumstances of my departure from Haworth. I was devastated; not because what he told me was true, I hope I will always face up to the truth however hurtful, but the perspective of Mr Cator's telling of the story and the accuracy of its detail were such that it could only have come from one source and that source Charlotte. I thanked Mr Cator for his candour and, helping myself to my coat from the footman, left him without ceremony.

I think I ran the two miles back to Kirk Smeaton. I had a right to my privacy and to Charlotte's discretion. I took up my pen the minute I got home.

The Old Rectory,
Kirk Smeaton.
18th October 1853

Dear Miss Brontë,
I write to seek your co-operation in preserving my good name. This morning, I was told by my rector that

a gentleman whom I have never met, whose name, in eight years, I never heard mentioned in Parsonage Lane and whose connection with your family can therefore be, at best, remote, knows every detail of our proceedings during the early months of this year and is broadcasting them to anyone he thinks will listen. My rector's informant is Richard Monckton Milnes M.P., a local grandee living eight miles from here. He is a man with wide and influential connections, and the way that he described to Mr Cator the details of what passed between your family and myself earlier this year, leaves me in no doubt that Mr Milnes' informant could only have been one of the principals.

I believe that I have the right to defend my privacy, and I am surprised that you are less concerned to preserve your own. Whatever gossip has already seeped into the public domain will have to circulate there for as long as anyone is interested to listen to it, but I must ask you – indeed, I think I have the right to demand of you – that you make no further revelations touching my personal affairs in the future.

I regret bitterly that I have to write to you in these terms, but the good name of a man in my position is essential to the conduct of his ministry and I owe it to the cloth, as well as to myself, to defend it.

Yours faithfully,
A.B. Nicholls

Charlotte replied by return.

The Parsonage,
Haworth.
19th October 1853

Dear Mr Nicholls,
If, for a moment, I ever doubted Bulwer-Lytton's assertion that the pen is mightier than the sword, I never can more, for your words have wounded me deeply.

Your reputation – your name – stands as high in my estimation as any man in these islands. I firmly believe that you are incapable of a base or selfish act, and if I were to speak your name to anyone it would be in those terms. When my father rejected you, you were accepting; when he insulted you, you praised him, and when he scorned and humiliated you, you silently left the field. You have behaved to my father, and to me, during these last twelve months, with a degree of stoic loyalty and good manners that I may have imagined but never thought to witness first hand. You have conducted yourself heroically, Mr Nicholls, and whatever the Fates have prepared for either of us in the future, I shall always regard you in that light.

I know who is Mr Richard Monckton Milnes. He is one of a group of gentlemen who cruise the periphery of the London literary pond and have, in the past, sought the acquaintance of Currer Bell. In Yorkshire, he has invited Papa and me to Fryston Hall but we have yet to accept one of his invitations and he has never been invited to Haworth. I have not seen Mr

Milnes in two years and plead innocent to any charge in that quarter.

I will own to you however that, since the loss of my sisters, I have sought the company and the confidence of close friends. Miss Nussey has been such an intimate, I have re-established the friendship of my former schoolmistress, Miss Wooler, and Mrs Gaskell too has become a sympathetic companion. Mrs Gaskell is acquainted with Mr Milnes, I know, as Miss Wooler and Miss Nussey may also be, for they are both well connected in that part of Yorkshire, but I will not believe that any of them has betrayed my confidence to him.

Nevertheless, you have been embarrassed when you had a right to feel secure, and in this you and I stand equally exposed. I expect, over the next month, to be with my friends in Ilkley and in London and I shall see to it that each of them reaffirms her discretion; it is the least I can do for a name that I would do much to defend.

Believe me, very sincerely,

C. Brontë.

It was a little late in the day to learn in what high regard I was held by Charlotte and not a little hurtful to be caressed with warm words when personal warmth had been withheld. For two days I allowed Charlotte's letter to upset me. I juggled hypothetical options with speculations on what might have been had some things happened differently or occurred at other times but then, after two days, I regained the mastery of my feelings and returned to the discipline of my work. I had noted however that Charlotte was still visiting London. I was sorry about that. I had hoped that the novelty of her doubtful friends would have worn thin by then, especially as her father needed her at home. And what was she doing in London, anyway? A year after *Villette*, and Currer Bell's name had slipped from the London papers. Other names, such as Thackeray, Gaskell and Martineau, whom George Smith had recruited on the back of Charlotte's success, were making the headlines now. Smith appeared to be prospering with or without Charlotte and I wondered if he still courted her as assiduously as he did when his business depended on her. It was a question I asked myself again, a month later, when I read of Smith's engagement to the daughter of a wealthy wine merchant and, a week after that, I received a second letter from Charlotte.

The Parsonage,
Haworth.
2nd December 1853

Dear Mr Nicholls,

I wonder how you spend these winter evenings in your rectory at Kirk Smeaton. Alone probably, like me. My life is so still. The time was when Emily and Anne and I would gather in the dining room after Papa had retired and share our thoughts and our feelings, but now, for want of airing, my feelings sour. You were right when you said there is no profit in self-absorption. I have sat in this room and examined myself until the silence has deafened my ears. Yes, our identity does depend upon its fellowship with others. Those that we grow up with shape us; those that we meet change us, and when we lose those we love we are scarred for life. I have stared into my self and found only void. My self does not talk back to me; it does not praise or chide me; it does not anger me, make me laugh, stimulate or provoke me. Solitude is a hollow vanity, and it can only make us sad.

I know that you too have known loneliness because you told me so but while my spirits corrode in Haworth, yours are tempered to a brighter edge and remain keen. You might have perished when my father cast you down into the flames, but you did not, you passed through the fire and emerged a purer and a stronger man. This year has been hard for you but take comfort, for there is no joy in this life that is not hard won.

You offered, twelve months ago, to accompany me on what remains of my journey, and though we both know why, you received no reply. Papa, I now believe, can be tractable. It may be hard and rough work, but I have reviewed the disposition of his arguments and if you would but signal me to engage, I have the ordnance ready to counter them.

Papa is not aware that I am writing to you in these terms and I would ask that you maintain the confidence. The Grants' servant, Susey, comes most days into the village; if, as I hope, you feel moved to reply, she will bring me your message.

I remain yours very sincerely,

C. Brontë.

The letter had been waiting for me when I came home at teatime and I'd taken it to read at the windows. I read it twice, to be sure of its meaning, then I read it again after tea. All evening, I sifted the letter's implications, picking it up and setting it down, and it was not until the next morning that I knew how I should reply.

The Old Rectory,
Kirk Smeaton.
4th December 1853

Dear Miss Brontë,

Believe me, I am gratified that you approve of my conduct over the past twelve months but, while my heart remains constant, I have to face the world as it is. If I could offer you today the protection that I offered you twelve months ago, I should do so gladly and with as much commitment as I did then. If, by marrying you, I could support your father and secure his tenure of your family home, I should do it. If I thought I might one day succeed your father, securing thereby your home for you for the rest of your life – again, I should do it. But these things all depend on my being your father's curate, which I no longer am; another holds that office and will be building his career in Haworth as I am in Kirk Smeaton – and you know as well as I that a marriage that takes you away from your father is unthinkable.

So, please, let us not agonise over the unthinkable. You have your father, your friends and your successful career; I have my ministry and my faith in God's Providence. It can be enough and, where there is no alternative, it must be enough.

God be with you always.
Your servant,

A.B. Nicholls

There was no point in my setting it down on paper but I felt cruelly ill-used by Charlotte. If she felt it so right to accept me now why could she not have twelve months ago? Charlotte was a strong-minded woman – then as now – and she could fight for what she wanted, so what had changed? Never mind. Whatever the reason, it was too late now. From whatever perspective I viewed our position – and I examined all possible – I could not see, since my removal from Haworth, how Mr Brontë's objections could be met. Charlotte and I had to accept that, we had to exchange vain hopes for attainable ones and look to our futures and besides, since November, something else had been gnawing at me.

I would have been interested to know what Miss Nussey thought about Charlotte's change of heart. That word *heroic*, in Charlotte's first letter, had troubled me. Miss Nussey once told me that Charlotte's great fault was to make a man into a hero and then be disappointed in him. She had thought, at the time, that Charlotte was making a hero of her publisher, George Smith. Now, George Smith was marrying, and Charlotte was eulogising me.

With Christmas upon us, I had more to think about than Charlotte Brontë. I had been looking forward to the festival as a chance to make my mark in Kirk Smeaton and I'd worked hard on the preparations. I'd organised hampers for the poor, and an old men's dinner and taken the choir out carolling. The choir had expanded since my arrival and improved greatly – quite a match for the Methodists – and I used the carolling to promote the Church in our weaker districts. In consequence of my efforts, the Christmas services were well-attended and that was noted. Senior churchmen invited me to join their families' celebrations and, on Christmas night, I dined at Skelbrooke Park. It was a large party and a splendid occasion topped off with the offer of a mount for the Boxing Day meet. It was an offer that, for want of a habit, I'd had to decline, but the offer sealed my acceptance in Kirk Smeaton, it helped me throw off the old year and usher in the new so when, in the New Year, I received another letter from Haworth, I opened it with more caution than pleasure.

The Parsonage,
Haworth.
3rd January 1854

Dear Mr Nicholls,
Matters have progressed since Christmas and the gentleman that you cast as the barrier to our marrying, Mr De Renzy, is now recast as our ally, for Papa is bitterly dissatisfied with his work and would be glad to be rid of him.

I have talked long and hard with Papa over Christmas concerning our marriage. At first he was hostile – very hostile, and bitterly unjust, but I am so convinced that our marrying is truly in Papa's greatest interest that I persisted, and I believe I have occasioned some movement.

Papa freely admits that having suffered De Renzy, he looks forward with apprehension to the prospect of replacing him with another stranger to the chapelry. Though at first only grudgingly, he now acknowledges your qualities – indeed, when I put it to him that you were the best curate he has had in thirty-five years, he would not deny it, and he had to agree that he would enjoy a deal more peace if you were his curate again.

Papa attempted all manner of objections to our marrying – many of them perfect nonsense – and I believe I managed to counter them but I have now done all that I can on my own and if the progress I have made is to be maintained, then your weight must be brought to the task. If you could come up to Haworth, I believe now that Papa would receive you, and there is of course much for you and I to discuss. Please try to come as soon as you can. You may write to me at the parsonage, I shall have no more secrets from Papa.

Believe me, yours very sincerely,

C. Brontë.

I believe now that Papa would receive you. The words flamed from the page. My new life, so carefully constructed, was instantly consumed by them because, however I tried to damp it, my love for Mr Brontë still burned and if Charlotte was right and he was ready to receive me, then I would go to him. I went straight to Skelbrooke to ask Mr Cator for seven days' leave and he granted it without question but, if I was minded to rush for the first train, the Fates were against me. Before I had even regained the Old Rectory it started to snow and it didn't stop until the evening of the following day, the Thursday, by which time the country was under three feet of snow. There was nothing to be done but go out with the rest of the village and dig. It was three days before a carrier got through and he reported that the Wakefield road was still blocked and no trains were running. I couldn't even get a message to Charlotte; I could only hope that Haworth was under the same blanket that we were and that she would understand. It was Monday before I got through to Wakefield and I was with the Grants by suppertime. I'd been expected. Charlotte had forewarned them, and she'd left a message that I could find her any morning at ten-thirty in Walled Lane. At ten the following morning, I set off to meet her.

Walled Lane is a section of the path that leads from the back of Saint Michael's to Marsh. It is a narrow footpath hemmed in on both sides by high stone walls. It is the haunt of young lovers in want of privacy, not the place that I should have chosen for our meeting, but when I arrived at twenty past ten, thankfully, there was no one about. The snow was well compacted by then and a freezing mist hung in the air. I was wearing my heavy coat and several layers of woollens but still I was cold and I stamped up and down, breathing onto my hands. As the church clock struck the half, I saw Charlotte coming. She was wearing a heavy blanket over her head and shoulders like a peasant but there was no mistaking her: the diminutive figure with the long, purposeful stride. She wasn't wearing her glasses and, as she drew near, I saw that her eyes were watery with cold, her cheeks pink and her brow scored with worry.

"You didn't answer my letter." She scowled. "I was beginning to wonder if you had received it, or if you would come."

"I'm sorry," I told her, "we've been under three feet of snow. The post and the trains were stopped." Charlotte was close to me, her warm breath condensing, like Anne's once had, on my coat.

"Shall we go to your father?" I asked, anxious to get on.

"Not yet." Charlotte looked up at me. "Do you not think that you and I have things to talk about first?"

"Why, Miss Charlotte!" I attempted a laugh. "Wasn't that my mistake last time? I'm not making it again."

"But you cannot go straight to Papa. He is not expecting you." I felt trapped.

"Why is he not expecting me?" The high stone walls were closing around me. "You told me you would have no more secrets from him."

"And nor do I. Papa knows that we are here. He has given me his permission, and he will see you in due time." This was not what I had expected, nor what I would have expected Mr Brontë to approve, and it must have shown. "Do you doubt me, Mr Nicholls?"

"No, I do not *doubt* you, but we both know how your father feels about paternal consent."

"We all three need to consent, don't we?" Charlotte's wide eyes were willing me to agree with her, but agree with what? My consent was declared; it was Charlotte's that was new.

"And would you have consented?" I asked her. "Last year? If your father had?" She did not answer, but remained looking up at me. "I do wonder," I went on, thinking of Miss Nussey, "how well you think you know me." Charlotte stepped back.

"How well I know you?" She savoured the question. "You do not think that I have observed you over the past nine years? Nine years as my neighbour and my father's right hand? You do not think that the observation of his fellowman might be the *sine qua non* of the novelist?" She smiled. "Mr MacCarthey?" She rested her hand on my arm. "I have observed you in the schoolroom, in the village and in the pulpit, and I know you. I know that your judgement is balanced, your heart kind and your principles sound. I know that you are wise, conscientious and benevolent." Her hand tightened on my arm. "And I know how you loved my family." A chill shivered through me. Did Charlotte know I'd loved Anne? Whether she did or she didn't, I wasn't ready to talk about her. I drew back. I'd had enough of Walled Lane. I released myself from her grasp and, thrusting my hands in my pockets, stamped at the ground.

"We must quit this alley before we are frozen solid and the talk of the village. I shall walk you to the end of the lane."

"What?" She pulled her blanket forward over her forehead. "And become the talk of the village?"

"Ah, no."

"Ah, no." She repeated, then added, "I shall speak to Papa. Meet me here again tomorrow."

The meeting in Walled Lane had unsettled me. It was far from what I had expected from Charlotte's letter and her manner had thrown me. I could not help thinking about Miss Nussey. Was this Charlotte raising me up on her pedestal now that George Smith was deposed? Her polished exposition of my qualities, with its perfectly measured metre, had done nothing to reassure me. Did Charlotte really know that my judgement was balanced? Did she know that I was kind, principled, wise, benevolent and conscientious? Had she, over those nine years, ever got close enough to me to know? The qualities that she listed may or may not have been mine but they were certainly the qualities of a Currer Bell hero. I did not want to be set upon a pedestal just to be knocked off it. If Charlotte was going to accept me, I needed to be sure that she was accepting me for the man that I really was while I, for my part, needed to know I was talking to the real Charlotte Brontë. I had no interest in marrying Currer Bell.

Charlotte and I did talk. We met again the following morning, when Charlotte told me that her father would see me on the Saturday. That was good news and I looked forward, albeit with some trepidation, to re-establishing our former relations. In the meantime, Charlotte and I walked and talked and began to get to know one another. For the next three days, we met at the end of Walled Lane and walked out together with Flossy over the snow-clad hills of Penistone and the Sladen Valley and all the time that we walked, we talked. We discussed literature and music, politics and the Church, dogs and birds and the power of landscape – in all matters Charlotte insisting that I express my opinions before she then chimed in with me. Charlotte asked me about Ireland and my life with the Bells. She wanted to know about Aunt Harriette and my late uncle and the role of the clerical wife; Charlotte asked many questions, but when I asked her for her own views, she contrived to pass the subject back again to me. There was a distinct list in the balance of our exchanges and I put it to Charlotte that I was being examined.

"You do not think it prudent", she'd answered, "to learn who it is I shall be expected to be?"

On the Saturday morning, I walked over to Haworth for my meeting with Mr Brontë. Wanting to avoid Parsonage Lane and Sexton House, I approached from the back, via Penistone Hill, but I could not avoid Martha when she answered the door.

"Why! Mr Nicholls!" She exclaimed with mock surprise. "Have yer come to make up?"

"Now-now Martha," I gave her a smile with my coat and hat, "but you can wish me luck."

Mr Brontë was standing before his hearth, as ever he did, but he looked thin. His close-cropped grey hair exposed his skull; his cheekbones were shelves and his eyes, sunk in their sockets.

"Good day to you, Mr Nicholls." He did not offer me his hand but indicated the chairs by the window. "Be seated if you wish." I went and sat down, only to feel awkward again when Mr Brontë remained where he was. "I appreciate your courtesy in calling on me but I hope you will understand me and not think me rude when I tell you that our interview must be brief. I have a deputation of weavers from Merrall Brothers calling in connection with the strike. An important matter. You will understand." I had heard about the strike at Merralls. It was the latest skirmish in the weavers' battle to resist the two-loom system. Passions were running high and Mr Brontë was supporting the weavers against the Church's principal donor. I told Mr Brontë that, of course, I understood his priorities.

"But you will tell me how you fare in Kirk Smeaton now you are here; I hear only good." I told him in broad terms how the Church stood in Kirk Smeaton and what initiatives I had been able to introduce in my short time there. "Mr Cator is a fortunate man," he replied. "You served me well here. I knew so at the time and I know it now." He addressed me slightly over my head. I don't think he could see me properly.

"It takes time for a new man to take up all the reins," I suggested.

"Ah! Not this man! He does not believe in taking the reins. He thinks it his place to sit in the back of the carriage and command others. He thinks the care of Church properties beneath him, he requires a horse rather than walk – no – the man has not the spirit." Mr Brontë shifted uncomfortably. "You do not want to hear about Mr De Renzy. We must see what will happen." And then he moved towards the bell. "I thank you for calling, Mr Nicholls." He was concluding the interview. We hadn't talked about Charlotte. I couldn't leave it there.

"Mr Brontë!" I jumped to my feet and he halted at the bell. "I never intended … I never wanted to take Charlotte from you, you know. That was never in my mind. I hoped – I still hope – to make Charlotte happy and at the same time secure your comfort and your peace of mind here in your home." I was standing in front of him. "I still want that opportunity, Sir." Mr Brontë stood very still and then, when I had finished, he said,

"I believe you are honourable, Mr Nicholls, but you do not command destiny. There are more ways than one that a daughter can be taken from her father."

I left Haworth that afternoon confused and despondent. After the years of cold indifference, Charlotte had been warmer and more pliant than I could ever have hoped. The change was so dramatic. It had been wonderful to see her buoyant again, and to enjoy her company and conversation, but I couldn't help wondering, as I rumbled through the snow-clad landscape, how much of her warmth had been heart-felt, and how much self-delusion, because she was certainly deluded about her father. He had given me no indication that he was ready to consent to our marriage – none whatsoever – and yet, the following Tuesday, I received a letter from Charlotte reporting that he had spoken well of me. She wrote in high spirits and wanted to hear that I, too, was optimistic. I hadn't known how to reply and, two weeks later, I received another letter from her.

The Parsonage,
Haworth.
1st February 1854

Dear Mr Nicholls,
I have made great progress with Papa since my last
letter and am close to breaching all of his objections.
He has made up his mind to release De Renzy and
admits that he could do no better than replace him
with you. I have had plans drawn for the conversion
of the lumber room into a study for you, so that Papa's
own domestic arrangements need not be disturbed,
and I have ideas about the disposal of my royalties that
I would discuss with you, so that any fears Papa might
entertain on that account may be allayed. In short, Mr
Nicholls, I have been working tirelessly to show Papa
that all our interests are consonant and I cannot see
him holding his position for many days longer.

Please, for all our sakes, have patience and keep faith
with me.

Very sincerely yours,

C. Brontë.

How many more bombardments? How many despatches
from the front? I had met Mr Brontë and he was entrenched.
My visit to the Grants had shown me that Charlotte and I
could be happy together, happier than I'd imagined, but
Charlotte came with her father and his consent could not be
beaten out of him. I admired Charlotte's energy and I wanted

to support her but everything I had seen in her father was of a man standing firm. It took me a day or two to compose my reply.

The Old Rectory,
Kirk Smeaton.
4th February 1854.

Dear Miss Brontë,

I write from the bottom of my heart to plead caution. If bombarding with arguments could change your father's mind then your earlier campaign over Christmas would have achieved its end then. I too wish that your father would sanction our engagement, but it seems to me that his objections are so far beyond argument that harrying him will do more harm than good.

My proposal of marriage has already caused a rift between your father and me, and, I believe, been the cause of his last seizure. Please, do not now annoy him to the point where you cause a rift between the two of you and risk a third seizure from which he may never recover. That would be the worst possible outcome for us all and a responsibility that I could not bear.

I pray for a happy resolution, and I urge you to pray for it too. Put your faith in Providence and do not further upset your father.

As ever, your obedient servant,

A.B. Nicholls

The Parsonage,
Haworth.
10th February 1854

Dear Mr Nicholls,

Every time that I go down on my knees I pray for Papa's change of heart, but there are hours in the day and the long nights when my mind in its freedom cannot help but plan for the outcome for which I pray and is there not a vanity in wishing that pales before the duty of trying?

Perhaps our marriage is more important to me than it is to you. You, a man, as you have more than once told me, have a career that gives your life purpose, whether you marry or not, whereas I, a woman with an ageing father, and perhaps someday completely alone, am denied any such purpose. 'But you have your fame, your successful career as a writer', I hear you say, 'that surely is sufficient absorption?' Perhaps, once, it may have been, but since the loss of my sisters, writing has become only self-absorption – a lonely, bleak and joyless pastime – and if true domestic happiness replaces fame, the exchange will be for the better.

I know that you think me forward, organising and unsentimental. These things, by necessity, I have had to become, but do you think that because I have won some success in the world, achieved independence, and erected a serviceable façade against unwelcome intrusion, that I am now become heartless? You would be wrong. I would put down my pen and abandon independence tomorrow for the chance to depend on a virtuous and superior spirit – for though I crave companionship, I do not crave the companionship of an equal – I crave a master, a man to whose will I should be pleased to bend, whose approbation would give me reward and whose displeasure, punishment – a master whom I would feel it impossible not to love.

Your strength and your virtue are the walls of my anchorage, and I will the day when I can lay myself up within them, but for that day to come I must exert myself a little yet with Papa, and if, in that, I cannot rely on your approbation, at least extend to me your forbearance.

Believe in me and trust me,
Your servant,

C. Brontë.

On the day that I received Charlotte's letter, George Smith was married in London to Miss Elizabeth Blakeway and a month later I was accepted by Mr Brontë. Charlotte had triumphed. To this day, I do not know what changed her father's mind. Was it the sheer persistence of Charlotte's attrition? Or was it his despair at having to try once more to find a new curate? He had not liked my successor any more than my predecessor and the older he got the more he needed support. Was it then my familiarity with his ways and the chapelry that was the attraction? I don't think I shall ever know how much of my change of fortune was due to Mr Brontë, to Charlotte or to George Smith but when, at the beginning of April, Mr Brontë received me in his parlour with a good grace, I dared look forward with hope to the future.

Mr Brontë had wanted me to come back immediately, so eager was he to replace De Renzy, but commitments in Kirk Smeaton made that difficult. My replacement there would have to be found and Mr Cator was used to staying in London until June. I had kept him from the London season the previous year and I did not want to upset his arrangements again and, besides, De Renzy too had to be considered.

I went to see De Renzy, once the engagement was announced, to discuss the transition, and when I saw him I realised I knew him. We'd been at Trinity together. The name is not a common one but, with so much else on my mind, I had failed to make the connection. He had been one of the Wicklow set and not the most serious of students but I remembered him as a decent fellow. We had graduated together in '44. It was a bond that only slightly eased a difficult interview.

He was indignant that he was being uprooted 'through no fault of his own', as he put it, 'to make way for his employer's daughter's fiancé'. He himself had just got married and taken a cottage at Providence on the other side of the Worth Beck – major commitments to the Haworth cure and he felt ill-used. I found it difficult not to sympathise with him, especially after I heard John Brown's view of the matter. John had disapproved of my engagement to Charlotte, he'd made that brutally clear, but John was a straight-dealing man and when he ascribed Mr Brontë's disaffection with De Renzy merely to his over-attachment to my habits of working and, more worryingly, to Charlotte's whispering against De Renzy, I was left with a bad taste about the business.

Charlotte was impatient to be married as soon as possible. Public interest in her could not be avoided and news of our engagement soon spread but we were both determined to keep the ceremony private. I approached Dr Longley and he agreed to grant a waiver on the reading of our banns, which helped keep the secret in Haworth. We set the date for the 29th June and determined that no more than had to would know.

Charlotte had planned everything. By the third week in April builders were converting the parsonage lumber room into a study for me. The room required a new window and a fireplace and chimney. These were major works at Charlotte's own expense and she tried to involve me in them but I had too much to do in Kirk Smeaton and, as I told her, the plans were hers and I was happy for her to execute them. Charlotte also tried to involve me in a programme of visiting to introduce me as her fiancé to her friends. She prepared the itinerary of a progress through the homes of Mrs Gaskell, Miss Wooler, Miss Nussey and the Taylors of Hunsworth with whom she had holidayed in Scotland. I did not particularly want to be paraded in front of Charlotte's friends and, in any case, I had too much to do in Kirk Smeaton and, on those grounds alone, I declined, but there was another reason: I wasn't feeling well. I had had a bad head cold since February that I could not shake off and my limbs and shoulders ached. I thought it was the rheumatics again and when, in May, I still felt no better, I made an appointment to see Dr Teale in Leeds. Dr Teale was the lung specialist who had attended Anne and I had confidence in him – in his skill and his discretion. Dr Teale examined my chest and my back, listening to my lungs through his stethoscope. He looked down my throat and held a lamp to my eyes, he manipulated my joints and in the end when he had examined me thoroughly he told me that he could find nothing physically wrong with me beyond a common cold; I was, in his opinion, suffering merely from 'an overwrought mind' consistent with the symptoms of other young men on the eve of marriage. I left Dr Teale very disappointed. My pains were real. They were not in my mind.

Mr Cator found a replacement for me sooner than expected and I said good-bye to Kirk Smeaton during the third week of May. There was a small ceremony and reception with a generous speech from the chairman of the vestry committee but Mr Cator wasn't there, he had had to go back to London, and I slipped out of Kirk Smeaton as quietly as I had arrived.

In Haworth, with a month to go before the wedding, I put myself at Charlotte's disposal but her plans were, by then, so far advanced that, apart from attending a brief legal ceremony, she had nothing for me to do. One of Mr Brontë's supposed objections to our marriage had been the idea that I might covet Charlotte's fortune. It was of course nonsense, money had never been a consideration, so when Charlotte proposed a marriage settlement in her father's favour, making him her heir in the event of her death without issue, I had no objection. I signed the deed in the parlour on the 24th May in front of Mr Brontë and Charlotte, Charlotte's Hunsworth friend, Mr Taylor, and Mr Metcalfe, the Keighley solicitor. I signed with perfect equanimity but I could see how Messrs Taylor and Metcalfe might have wondered at my abnegation of traditional rights, and I did not attempt to read Mr Brontë's mind. The fact was that Charlotte believed the settlement necessary to win over her father and there was nothing she would not do to that end. Charlotte was a powerful and a persuasive woman and I the object of her desire; I was at once honoured and unnerved.

Charlotte went off to Leeds after that, to meet up with Miss Nussey for a tour of that city's drapers and haberdashers, so I took the opportunity to take leave myself. I caught the train from Keighley on the Saturday morning, the 28th May, arriving in Scarborough at about two o'clock. The summer season was under way and, as I walked from the station down to Woods' Lodgings, the town seemed bigger and busier than when I was there last. I had never been in Woods' Lodgings and I wanted to see the room. The lady who received me was sympathetic but the room was already taken, she told me. She remembered Anne as a regular member of the Robinson party and she remembered her passing – 'vividly' – as she told me, but the room was occupied and her lodgings were full. She was sorry.

I found a room at an inn and spent the rest of the day walking along the shore, as Anne had, on that last day of her life, five years before to the day. On the following morning, I walked up to St Mary's, through the woods, where I found some late bluebells. They had been Anne's favourite flower so I picked some and took them with me up to the grave. It was fully grassed over by then and the headstone had been corrected – by Charlotte, no doubt – when she had visited in '52. I arranged the bluebells at the base of the headstone and sat down on the grass beside it, looking out, with Anne, to the sea. I did not pray: being so close to her, I did not need intercession. She told me she was at peace, and that Branwell was at peace, although Emily still had not settled. She asked me to make Charlotte happy.

I returned to Haworth on the Monday. I wanted to start work in the chapelry but De Renzy had still not departed and I was not allowed to mention the wedding so there was little for me to do and, anyway, I still felt unwell. As the day of our nuptials approached, the aches in my limbs grew worse. I had headaches and stomach cramps, I lost my appetite and when, on the morning of our wedding, I looked at myself in Grant's full-length mirror, the suit that had fitted me eighteen months earlier, hung on me, and my beard framed a face of wax. Grant was to stand for me and Sutcliffe Sowden officiate so, at a quarter past seven in the morning of Thursday the 28th June, the three of us set out for Haworth.

It was a long two miles. The sky was overcast and the air humid so, walking up the fields in my serge, I felt nauseous and my head throbbed. When we arrived at St Michael's, there were no bells and no onlookers, just Joseph Redman waiting to usher Grant and me to our pew, while Sowden went off to the vestry. As my eyes grew accustomed to the gloom, I saw that Tabby and Martha were sitting in the sexton's pew with the rest of Martha's family, including, I was pleased to see, John. There was no one else. The secret had been kept.

Charlotte arrived on the stroke of eight. I heard her by the rustle of her dress, but when she drew up beside me, there was no Mr Brontë. Standing in his place on Charlotte's arm was Miss Wooler and behind them, Miss Nussey. I turned and looked round the church but Mr Brontë was nowhere to be seen. I looked down at Charlotte for an explanation. She was dressed all in white: white mantle, white bonnet and a white veil that covered her face so she could not reply. Miss Wooler leaned to Sowden and whispered to him that she would be giving Charlotte away and so it was: Charlotte married me supported by her friends.

After the short ceremony we repaired to the parsonage for breakfast and Mr Brontë was out on the step. I was relieved to see him and he was in good spirits. He congratulated me and shook my hand and played the glad host and, if he harboured misgivings, they did not show. His absence from the service he blamed on his bronchitis but if he had other reasons for staying away then I think I understand what they were: it is one thing to congratulate a bride and groom at a wedding breakfast, it is quite another to swear oaths before God in His house:

"*Who giveth this woman?*" Sowden would have asked Mr Brontë and, standing upon the flagstones that covered the mortal remains of his wife and four of his children, he would have had to give his last child away.

"*And forsaking all others,*" Charlotte would have pledged, and her father would have had to sanction before God her passing from his care to mine. I believe I understood Mr Brontë's absence, and I sympathised.

Toying with boiled ham and Madeira cake, Charlotte and I accepted the congratulations of our friends and by ten o'clock we were changed and in the back of Michael Pickles' landau rolling down Parsonage Lane towards Keighley and the start of our honeymoon. Just how much of myself Charlotte had married and how much of some fictive hero, I did not know, but I never worried more who was

Charlotte or who Currer Bell – Mrs Nicholls gave herself to me completely.

CHAPTER SIXTEEN

For as long as we both shall live

Our wedding day ended beneath the walls of Edward Plantagenet's fortress at Conway, in the Castle Hotel, and we arrived tired. Three connections and baggage for a month had made the journey arduous. We had trundled along side-by-side in the carriages, watching the landscapes go by, saying little, and so the day ended. Charlotte had her head cold and I my aches and pains, and with the accumulated strains of the past months gnawing at my apprehensions I was relieved, after supper, when Charlotte asked if she might write to Miss Nussey. I told her 'of course' and that she need not ask. I bid her a good night in the residents' parlour and left her to go to my bed.

We spent four days at Conway, driving up the Conway Valley and exploring the coast down to Bangor. It was indeed a strange sensation to be alone with Charlotte, without the support of family or friends and, while I tried to allow Charlotte every liberty to do what she pleased, she would not, insisting always that we do whatever I wished to do and see what I wished to see. Charlotte was herself unwell and yet she constantly attended to my aches and pains and my comfort. Her ministrations were flattering and kindly meant but they did nothing to buttress my sense of self-worth and by the time that we left Wales, my anxiety ran deeper than ever.

On the fifth day, we took the packet from Holyhead across the St George's Channel to Kingstown and then on by train into Dublin. Alan was on the platform to greet us and he had brought a surprise with him: my cousins Joseph and Mary. Joseph was still at Trinity, completing what had been a brilliant academic career, but Mary had travelled down especially from Banagher and it was with some pride that I introduced my brother and my two favourite cousins to Charlotte. She was impressed.

"What a courteous man your brother is," she'd remarked once we were alone. "So well-informed, so sagacious." My cousin Joseph had 'a brilliant mind' and Mary was 'so pretty, so lady-like, and with such gentle English manners.' Just what, from the models of her father and me, Charlotte had expected of Irish manners, I did not ask.

I had planned that we would spend a week with my brother in Dublin but matters so fell out with my sister-in-law that we decided to curtail the visit after only two days. Caroline had social ambition which Alan was proving able to fund. He was still agent for the Grand Canal Company but he was now acting for other shipping companies as well and he was venturing into insurance. He had taken new offices at Eden Quay and when we arrived by landau at his new home in Great Charles Street, off Mountjoy Square, it was clear that Alan and Caroline were well on their way. Caroline's welcome was effusive. She was 'delighted beyond measure at our marriage' and 'so proud' of me. I accepted her congratulations as a normal expression of familial goodwill but I should have noticed her true interest when Alan told me that their new baby, a second daughter, was to be christened Charlotte Brontë Nicholls.

Caroline took immediate possession of Charlotte. From the moment we arrived she was over her like a swarm of wasps so that, after only ten minutes, Charlotte had to plead weakness from the journey and retire to our room. At dinner, Caroline made it clear that she was going to ride roughshod over all my plans. Though she couched her intentions in less stark terms, the essence of them was that she was going to trumpet her connection with the celebrated authoress, parade her around her acquaintances, and throw a house-warming party at which Charlotte would be the prize attraction. Alan knew full well what I would make of these arrangements and, while he was suitably embarrassed and apologetic, he seemed powerless to rein in his wife and so it fell to me to gainsay her. Over the next two days, Joseph and I conducted Charlotte and Mary round Trinity and Dublin's other major sites. I had plans for the following four days as well but Caroline was so insistent on her own arrangements – arrangements that Charlotte resisted – that, after two days, I decided the combined pressures of city, head cold and Caroline were oppressing Charlotte and we must leave. Caroline was not pleased to let us go but Charlotte and I parted on good terms with my brother and that would have to be enough. We moved on with Joseph and Mary to Banagher.

If Charlotte had been pleasantly surprised by my cousins, she was no less surprised by Cuba House, although it was no longer so grand as it was. Pupil rolls had declined at the school through the famine, a trend my cousin James had been powerless to reverse. Grand houses need maintaining and Aunt Harriette had neither the money nor the energy of former years so if there was an air of grandeur about the old place, it was an air of faded grandeur and I think that appealed to Charlotte. We stayed with my aunt for a week, during which time Charlotte got to know one or two more of my cousins. The household was in festive mood because my marriage to Charlotte was only one of three being celebrated that summer: James was about to marry a Miss Elisabeth Tyrrell and Harriette, John Adamson, one of Aunt Harriette's nephews.

"Your family is so amiable," Charlotte told me, "the men so thoroughly educated and the young women strikingly pretty." We had been walking in the garden before tea and, as we approached the steps to the house, Charlotte added, "Mary is so diffident but obviously clever. She is another inscrutable."

"*Another* inscrutable?"

"She reminds me of Anne."

Aunt Harriette took Charlotte to her bosom and, again, Charlotte was surprised at the consonance of interests between herself and my family. Aunt Harriette had attended school in London and spent her life in the twin orbits of teaching and the Church. She also read widely and, although she was more familiar than most with Charlotte's literary achievement, she treated her no differently from any other member of the family. By the end of the week, Charlotte was rested and her cold much better, but when I thanked Aunt Harriette for her kindness, I received more in reply than I'd expected.

"It has taken you a long time, Arthur, but you have found a good woman. I hope you will cherish her." I was sitting with my aunt on the steps of the east terrace, shelling some early peas.

"I will cherish her," I told her. "Charlotte is spirited and she has a powerful intellect but I am aware that her constitution is weak." I looked up from my peapods. "I shall be very careful of her." Aunt Harriette raised her eyes to me.

"As a husband?"

"Yes. As her husband." Aunt Harriette returned her attention to the basket of peas. We each split three or four more pods and then my aunt looked up at me again.

"I hope you will soon reassure Charlotte of that." She gave me a level look. "Don't leave it too long, Arthur." I felt the blood rush to my cheeks because I knew what she was saying.

"I don't know what you mean," I blustered. "Charlotte knows full well of my regard for her."

"I mean, Arthur, that a priest can minister to a woman's spirit, her friends to her mind and a physician to her body but I hope I do not have to tell you that she also has needs for which matrimony is ordained and it is plain to me that those needs have yet to be met." I jumped to my feet but my aunt caught hold of my hand. "What is it?" she asked, "Is it Anne?" She tightened her grip. "Anne is dead, Arthur, dead these five years. You have married Charlotte." I wanted to get away. Tears were pricking at my eyes. "Didn't you once tell me that you had begged Anne to put the dead behind her? Her curate, Weightman? To embrace life, however imperfect?" She stood up and faced me. "You miss Anne, I know, and Charlotte will miss her too, but you are both still here and life goes on." Tears were streaking my cheeks, by now, and my aunt took my face in her hands. "Charlotte has married you, Arthur, she wants you, and she needs you to want her." She brushed at my tears with her thumbs.

"So show her. Then you will learn what happiness is and Charlotte will love you."

I had given a lot of thought to our honeymoon. I wanted Charlotte to learn about me, my family and my home and, in the last two weeks, I wanted to show her my country. From Shannon Harbour, we took the steamer down Lough Derg passing beneath the Mountains of Arra to Limerick where we lodged for one night. From there we took the ferry around Loop Head for the short sail beneath the Cliffs of Moher to Kilkee. After the lakes and mountains, I wanted to show Charlotte the ocean, and the small resort of Kilkee, with its white sands, high cliffs and foaming waves crashing in off the Atlantic, was the perfect place. I had taken lodgings at the West End Hotel. Our room was simple but clean and it overlooked the bay. On the morning of our first full day, I took Charlotte out for a walk.

We set off north out of the town, up the steep coastal path that leads to the top of the cliffs and The Point. From there we had panoramic views of the ocean and the George's Head rocks while, at our backs, were the hard rocky grasslands of County Clare. This was the Ireland I had brought Charlotte to see. In Haworth, we both enjoyed the freedom of the open moors but, at Kilkee, nature works on a different scale: the landscapes are wider, the rocky ground harder, the Atlantic winds stronger and the rain-laden skies fly faster over your head – and then there is the ocean.

A stiff westerly had blown up in the night, driving banks of thunderous clouds in off the sea. The wind was strong on The Point and, as we approached the cliff edge, it blew harder, flecking our faces with salt-spray and deafening our ears. Holding on to one another we looked down over the cliff. Wide lines of foam rolled in from the ocean, they pounded the cliff shooting up sheets of spray, they drew back and came back and pounded again, their white waters seething with foam. Charlotte was entranced.

"Come further back!" I shouted against the wind. Charlotte looked up at me. She was clutching her bonnet, her escaped hair flying, and the tears streaking her cheeks. There was a small rock behind us and I indicated that we should move to it. Charlotte sat down and I placed a rug across her shoulders then I stepped back to admire the show of God's power and I could not help but think about Anne. On that cliff above the ocean I thought of that other cliff that slopes from a headland to the harbour at Scarborough and I remembered some lines.

I wish I could see how the ocean is lashing
The foam of its billows to whirlwinds of spray:
I wish I could see how its proud waves are dashing,
And hear the wild roar of their thunder today.

Anne's lines were still in my mind when I led Charlotte back down the footpath where, to my amazement, she started reciting them. Had she been reading my mind? I felt naked and invaded but then, at the last line, she misquoted and without thinking I corrected her.

"*And hear the wild roar of their thunder,*" I shouted to her against the wind, and she stared down at me. "You said '*the wild roaring of thunder*'," I explained, "it's not that, it's '*the wild roar of their thunder*' – it refers to the waves." Charlotte was astonished.

"You know Anne's poem?" She came down to me and took hold of my arm. I shouldn't have corrected her. I wished I hadn't and tried to carry on down the path but she held me, examining me. She said. "I forget sometimes that you know my family. Anne would have loved this place wouldn't she?" Her eyes were shining and her escaped hair flying. I didn't want to talk to Charlotte about Anne, I wanted to get on down the path, but she came up close into my face and gripped my arm.

"When you took me, you also took my sisters." She gripped my other arm and turned me to her. "You do know that, don't you, Arthur?" She was inches from my face, her eyes wide, willing me to acknowledge her truth and I had to.

"I do," I told her and, while the words were still on my lips, Charlotte kissed me. She kissed me so hard I felt her teeth behind her lips and her breath came hard down her nose. I put my hands on her back to steady myself, her muscles were taut and through the joining of our lips Charlotte poured into me all the passion in her body and soul till I thought I might willingly drown. It was a transcending moment in a transcending day and that night, after supper, to the sound of the sea sighing on shingle, Charlotte became my wife.

We were almost a week at Kilkee and Charlotte loved the place. I had hoped she would. I had loved it since I was taken there as a boy, and for most of the week that Charlotte and I were there the skies were high and the breezes light. We explored the cliffs and the hinterland together and walked along the strand; we relaxed, we read and wrote our letters home and, like holidaymakers before and since, we enjoyed observing our fellows.

The West End Hotel was a modest establishment and no more than it pretended to be — although some of the guests wished it otherwise. I might not have noticed the Dowager Lady O'Brien's party if I had been on my own but I was not on my own, I was with a woman more attuned to the minutiae of human behaviour than anyone I ever met. In the drawing room or at dinner, Charlotte would raise an eyebrow at me or touch me with her foot beneath the table to draw my attention to the O'Brien ladies. Nothing seemed to satisfy them: the food was too plain, the plumbing too noisy and the service inferior to that at the Dunleary Royal Marine. Mrs Shannon, the proprietor, and her daughters ran themselves ragged to try to please their guests but nothing they did seemed to suit. The noble ladies carped and clucked and turned what ought to have been a few days' pleasant vacation into a constant vexation and they vacated ahead of their time. Unkind, I dare say it was, but Charlotte enjoyed the O'Briens' antics and she made sure I enjoyed them too. Charlotte and I were happy at Kilkee; happy in the moment and happy in the knowledge that the rest of our lives lay before us.

After Kilkee, we went on to Killarney before spending a few days at Glengarriff at the head of Bantry Bay. Our honeymoon was drawing to its close and our thoughts homeward so we did not linger in Cork or Dublin but pressed on, arriving in Haworth on the evening of the 1st August. We had been away for five weeks and if, through the years of my concern for Charlotte, I had imagined that the task of restoring her to happiness would take yet more years, then I could not have been more wrong. Even before we arrived back in England, Charlotte was blossoming with confidence and a new self-assurance. Not the old self-assurance. Not the acerbic self-assurance that sought always to do battle and to dominate. In Mrs Nicholls, I met a new Charlotte: a woman content first with herself and so at peace with the rest of the world and far from wanting to dominate, Mrs Nicholls leaned, with confidence, on me.

Charlotte had been away from Haworth for five weeks but I had been away for fourteen months and while the work I was returning to was familiar, my personal circumstances were wholly changed. I was married to Charlotte. I lived with her under the same roof as her father, I shared her bedroom, across the landing from his, I managed the affairs of the chapelry from my own study across the hallway from his and, although to all outward appearances my father-in-law accepted me and pretended to the close relations of former times, I sensed tension in his attitude to me and hoped that, with time, it would dissolve.

Charlotte did not pick up on these tensions; she was too happy and all Haworth knew it. Charlotte was not, by nature, a sociable woman. Before marriage, she had engaged as little as she had to with village affairs: duty calls on behalf of her father and the short spell of teaching in the school had been about the sum of it, but after marriage, to everyone's surprise, she embraced with zeal the life of the clerical wife. Suddenly, as a married woman, Charlotte wished to be on terms with people she had known for years but never acknowledged. The minute we got back, she set to arranging a party in the schoolroom for hundreds of people. It was a 'thank you' for the avalanche of congratulations we had received. The event passed off very well, there was a festive atmosphere and warm speeches but, although I enjoyed the day, I could not help reflecting that the people who were fêting us then were the same people who had, in the same hall, only the year before, shown me a very different aspect at the presentation of my retirement watch. But Charlotte was happy, perhaps even surprised to be happy and, after all that she had suffered, small wonder that she wanted to share it.

Charlotte filled the parsonage with visitors that autumn. The Grants came over with Charles, who was by then a strong-backed five-year-old. Then Sutcliffe Sowden came for a few days with his brother George (also in Holy Orders) and then, at the end of September, Miss Nussey came up from Birstall and she stayed with us for two weeks. Apart from the briefest encounter at the wedding breakfast, I had not seen Miss Nussey for two years. I had always liked her. She was a down-to-earth, plain-speaking Yorkshirewoman and I think we had got on well enough, but over the period of my exile from Haworth, I had noticed a shift in Charlotte's attitude to her, and I remarked on it while we were in Ireland.

"Oh I think we are firm friends again now." Charlotte had assured me as we walked along the wooded shore of Bantry Bay. "You saw that she was my bridesmaid."

"So there had been a rift to be bridged?" I suggested. Charlotte had not answered immediately, but looked down at her feet on the well-trodden path. After a few moments she said,

"I think Ellen is a confirmed spinster and perhaps she took comfort in the prospect of my remaining one too."

"Do you mean she is jealous of me?"

"Ellen and I have been close for a long time. My marrying demands adjustment from her as it does from others to whom I am close."

"And has she adjusted? Is she pleased for you now?" Again Charlotte thought before she answered.

"It is a pity that you declined her invitation to Birstall. And you did not acknowledge her at the wedding breakfast."

I had felt Charlotte's reproof but I said nothing at the time. I had told Charlotte at the beginning of May that my commitments in Kirk Smeaton made visiting impossible and as to the wedding breakfast, that had been so brief and bemusing that I cannot remember whether I paid attention to Miss Nussey or not, or whether Miss Nussey paid any attention to me. I did my best, while Miss Nussey was with us, to be friendly and make amends for any past error. Miss Nussey was, and would remain, Charlotte's closest friend and so must be accommodated but, despite my best efforts, Miss Nussey remained chilly with me throughout her visit. I was sorry, but I felt I had done what I could.

Charlotte's and Miss Nussey's friends, the Taylors, followed close on Miss Nussey's heels with their little three-year-old Emily, known to the family as Tim. The Taylors were part of Miss Nussey's Birstall circle and Charlotte had known them for years but it was the first time I had met them and I have to say that I was charmed with Tim. She liked the men. Mr Brontë used to join us after tea in the dining room and Tim chattered away to him, telling him all her business, and Mr Brontë answered her back, giving as good as he got. He told Tim that she reminded him of Charlotte when she was that age, coming out with the unexpected and an answer for everything. Tim was fascinated by Mr Brontë's white hair and he bent his head forward so that she might run her little fingers through it. He asked Tim what she thought of my black hair and she looked across at me with a serious expression.

"I shall have to hold it as well," she declared, and she jumped off Mr Brontë's lap and came and climbed onto mine. She pushed her fingers into my hair and then into my beard.

"This black hair is nice," she decided, "but you should go straight to the barber's and cut off those whiskers." We all laughed loudly and Tim, overawed by the response, ran off to the skirts of her mother. I sprang to my feet.

"Ah well!" I wailed with an air of dejection. "I have become quite attached to these whiskers but judgement has been passed." I swept dramatically towards the door. "To the barber's!"

I ran from the room and collected a razor and then went into the kitchen. Tabby was sitting by the range with some tatting.

"Have you any hot water, Tabby?"

"Now what do yer want with 'ot water, Mr Nicholls?"

"Have you got any?" I whispered urgently.

"Kettle's boiled ten minutes since." She nodded towards the hob. I quickly poured out a bowl of hot water and, shedding my coat as I went, I ran into the scullery. In quick time, I shaved my moustache and all the whiskers around my mouth and throat, leaving only the sideburns on my cheeks. I dashed back into the kitchen and Tabby's jaw dropped. I threw on my coat and ran back into the dining room, re-entering with a flourish. The room erupted. Tim ran to me squealing with glee, her mother gasped in astonishment, Mr Brontë roared with incredulous delight and Charlotte, blushing and smiling broadly, put her face into her hands, for she knew what no one else could, that she had complained of my whiskers ever since we were married.

More visitors followed in November. Sir James and Lady Kay-Shuttleworth were not so much friends of Charlotte's as admirers of Currer Bell. They had, in the past, entertained Charlotte at Gawthorpe Hall, their seat near Padiham, and at their holiday home on Lake Windermere. Sir James had been a pioneering public servant before he retired and, as 'The Father of English Elementary Education', he was something of a hero of Mr Brontë's, but Sir James' mission was not entirely benign. He took me aside on the second day of his visit and offered me the lucrative living of Habergham on the Gawthorpe estate. I declined the offer out of hand. Not only for Mr Brontë's sake, but because it was clear to me that it was not me that Sir James wanted in his pocket but my celebrated wife. I thought the offer an abuse of Mr Brontë's hospitality and kept clear of Sir James for the rest of his visit.

At the end of her stay in September, Miss Nussey had invited Charlotte and me on a return visit to Birstall. I had never been to Miss Nussey's home and Charlotte was keen to reinstall me into her favour but, with the Taylors and then the Kay-Shuttleworths following on, there had been no time, and then Miss Nussey's sister, Mercy, caught typhus fever. The poor woman was very ill. She was being nursed at home by her mother and her sisters and Charlotte was ready to go but I urged caution, in fact I insisted on delay because this was the first autumn, in all the years I had known Charlotte, that she had not been ill and I was not going to put her at risk. I asked Charlotte to decline Miss Nussey's invitation until Mercy was better, adding that if any disappointment were caused by my edict, then she was welcome to blame me.

Marriage was suiting Charlotte and me. We had, in a few short months, found consonance in our tastes and an ease of companionship beyond anything I had hoped for and our constitutions responded accordingly. I had put on twelve pounds in Ireland and by November a deal more, for I was again filling my suits. My rheumatic pains had left me, I was stimulated by my work and fulfilled in my marriage, I had never felt so well and Charlotte too was blooming; it had been years since I had seen her so well but then, at the end of November, she went down with a chill.

One of the pleasanter routines of our married life was the walks that we took together. We went out three or four times a week and, on a day following the thaw of some early snow, we took Flossy up to Lumb Bank to see the waterfalls in spate. The weather had been fine when we set out but, while we were at the falls, the rain started and by the time we had covered the two miles home we were thoroughly soaked and shivering. I put Charlotte straight to bed with brandy and beef tea but by morning she had all the symptoms of a developing cold and we left her in bed for two or three days. Sad to say though, Charlotte was not the only victim of the Lumb Bank excursion; we lost Flossy.

Like us, Flossy had come home bedraggled. He was about twelve, which is a fair age for a water spaniel and, apart from some arthritis in his hips, he was reasonably fit, but the day following the walk he was listless and during the night he died. Martha found him. She was waiting to tell me when I came downstairs in the morning, and I went in to him in the kitchen. He was laid out where he always slept on the rug in front of the range. He looked peaceful but very still and when I bent down to him his body was cold and already stiff. I lifted him into my arms and looked at him: my companion of seven years and Anne's from a puppy. He was the last living breath of Anne and I loved him. It was the start of a sad season.

Charlotte's cold persisted throughout December. It left her tired and weak and then at the turn of the year she told me she was feeling bilious and her stomach was losing its tone. Charlotte was familiar with biliousness but she was adamant that this was something different, something new and besides, her usual monthly troubles were, by Christmas, late. The news moved me deeply. I had never expected this. I had always enjoyed children, but given Charlotte's age and her frailty I had put aside any thoughts of having a family of my own but in the teeth of all reason, I could not help but hope. Charlotte too was excited, I could tell, but she urged caution. It was, she said, very early days and her sickness could be symptomatic of any number of things; she was not going to admit to so unlikely a condition as pregnancy until she was sure. I told Charlotte she must rest, and Tabby and Martha to make sure that she did, but Charlotte had, as an indulgence to her father, accepted a return invitation to the Kay-Shuttleworths. I told her that it was now out of the question and that she must decline but she was reluctant. She was continuing, at my insistence, to put off the visit to Miss Nussey but she argued that two or three days at Gawthorpe Hall would in fact be warmer and more comfortable than staying in Haworth. I protested. I put it to her that she was putting herself – and possibly her unborn child – at risk, merely to humour her father, and I was ready to over-rule her, but then Tabby went down with acute diarrhoea and, as such cases can be infectious, I decided that Gawthorpe might indeed be the safer option.

We took the train from Keighley to Rose Grove where Sir James's closed landau was waiting to drive us the two miles to the hall. Charlotte was right, Gawthorpe was a well-managed household, and even in January I found the house over-warm and my abiding memory of the visit is of oppression. I was oppressed by my worries about Charlotte and I was oppressed continually by Sir James. Sir James is small and lean with a polished dome and side whiskers; he looks like a clerk but his looks belie an exacting and domineering personality. Sir James 'told' Charlotte and me – his captive audience – all about himself: his career, his successes, the great men he had known, his plans for the estate and, sitting in his over-heated parlour after an over-large dinner, he told us all about the novels he was writing and he read from one of them at length. Gawthorpe Hall was the ancestral home of Lady Kay-Shuttleworth's family. It was a gloomy Jacobean mansion on which Sir James had recently lavished a small fortune extending it and restoring it in a style that was a pastiche of the original and so now even more oppressively gloomy than ever. Sir James conducted me over every inch of the house, its offices and grounds and then over the new church at Habergham where, at least, he had the sense not to renew his offer.

Our three days with Sir James felt more like a week and with Charlotte vomiting several times a day I was angry with myself for going at all but then, with Tabby's diarrhoea at home, I had had to make a decision. On the way home, we both hoped we should find Tabby improved but when we arrived she was not, and there was a further harassment waiting for us: my cousin James. My heart sank. It was not that I dislike my cousin James, far from it, but Charlotte needed, above all things, rest, and I would have resented any visitor. Charlotte, of course, dutifully pulled herself to her full height and played the perfect hostess to James, just as Aunt Harriette had done for her, and he could not have guessed at her condition. Nor was I going to tell him. Not at that stage. Even when James announced that Elisabeth was with child and he was about to become a father I held my tongue and, besides, I did not know how much Mr Brontë knew.

Mr Brontë was enjoying my cousin James. It was clear, when we arrived back from Gawthorpe, that Mr Brontë had taken to him and James to Mr Brontë. They shared a common view of politics and the Church and found a level of erudition in one another that impressed them both. Mr Brontë hadn't met my family as Charlotte had, and I think James's visit, unwelcome though it was in its timing, helped him appreciate his son-in-law a little more.

James stayed with us for four days and the minute he was gone Charlotte relapsed. For more than a fortnight Charlotte had been persistently vomiting and it was getting worse. She could keep almost no foods down, she was exhausted and there was no more hiding it from Mr Brontë. Mr Brontë had had six children of his own and seen much. I told him of Charlotte's suspicions and asked him if he thought her symptoms normal.

"No," had been his curt reply, his manner more worried than pleased. Charlotte agreed that we should send for Haworth's latest physician, Dr Ingham, and also for Dr MacTurk, the senior physician at the Bradford Infirmary. We were also, at the time, worrying about Tabby of course who, after a month of eating nothing without it going straight through her, finally retired to her bed in the next room to ours. Poor Martha was running the household and nursing two invalids, one of whom she had to share broken nights with in the servants' bedroom. Under similar circumstances in the past, Mary, or one of her girls, would have come up to the parsonage to help but, by the beginning of '55, John Brown was himself chronically ill with dust on the lung and requiring constant nursing so, to relieve Martha, and also, if I am frank, to address my worries about cross-infection, we made hurried arrangements for Tabby to be taken to her great-niece in Stubbing Lane. It is a decision that, in hindsight, I regret, but it seemed the right one at the time.

Dr MacTurk arrived in Haworth on the day following his receipt of our note. He examined Charlotte thoroughly and his opinion confirmed Dr Ingham's that Charlotte's sickness was indeed symptomatic and that after a few weeks of complete rest she should, if she were careful, get through the sickness and proceed. Neither Dr MacTurk nor Dr Ingham saw any immediate danger.

Miss Nussey, whom Charlotte was by now putting off because of her own indisposition rather than Mercy's, sensed a crisis. Charlotte had been too weak even to write to Miss Nussey since my cousin James left so I was answering her letters for her and putting myself in the position of the bearer of sad news. Ever since October, Charlotte had been putting back putative dates for our visit to Birstall but I had to tell Miss Nussey plainly now that, although Charlotte was in no immediate danger, Dr MacTurk was insisting on complete rest and so there could be no thoughts of visiting in the foreseeable future. Miss Nussey's response was to ask to be allowed up to Haworth but Charlotte did not want that either. I kept in touch with Miss Nussey, writing to her every few days, keeping her appraised.

By the middle of February, Tabby was so frail and wasted that it was clear her time was near. I went down to see her in Stubbing Lane and, though her body was by then emaciated, her mind was still sharp.

"Eeh, Mr Nicholls," she'd smiled at me from her bed, "what yer doin' down here botherin' wi' me for? Yer should be with your Charlotte." Tabby's bedroom was small but airy and it looked out over the roofs of the neighbouring cottages to the wastes of Brow Moor. I pulled up a chair and took her hand. "How is she, Mr Nicholls?" she asked me.

"She is poorly, Tabby. Still poorly, but no worse I think." Tabby examined me, frowning.

"Hang onto her," she gripped my hand, "for t'Master's sake, hang onto her."

"Dr Ingham is with her twice a day and we have the best doctor from Bradford," I told her, but the tears were streaking her cheeks.

"Oh we've lost some childers haven't we?" she wept, attempting a brave smile. "Maria — cleverest child ever — that's what Master used to say. She'd sit and read paper to him and then they'd argue toss over politics and she only ten." Tabby looked out of the window to the hump of Brow Moor. "Sharp as a pin, she was, like Branwell and Charlotte, only nicer with it." She was seeing them again when they were young. "She was kind was Maria, like Elizabeth and Anne, but not as pretty as them. They took after their mother." Tabby looked at me. "They should have lived to be mothers, them two, Elizabeth and Anne." Then smiling sadly, she added, "Whoever would have thought it'd be Charlotte?"

"And Emily," I said, evading talk of Charlotte, "you haven't said anything about her." Tabby eyed me cautiously.

"Emily's seen the Guytrash," she confided. "She saw its shape and heard it roar over Withins Heights on a full moon — and she's seen fairies playin' in the beck above Griffe Mill." Tabby watched me to see that I grasped the importance of what she was saying. "There were fairies up and down all them streams in the old days, before the mills broke up the waters an' scared them off with their churnin' and their din." She withdrew her hand and looked sadly at her fingers. "There'll be none of us sees fairies again. Not round here. Emily was the last." Then a wide, proud smile spread over her face. "A visionary. That's what t'Master called Emily: a visionary and a genius. And he liked her best."

Tabby died that night. She was eighty-four and she had been at the parsonage since Charlotte was eight. The following evening, Charlotte made her will.

When Dr MacTurk told us that Charlotte's sickness was symptomatic, we expected that she would gradually get better but she did not, she got worse and, by the middle of February, MacTurk himself was worried: 'nature', he told us, 'would take its course'. I took McTurk aside and asked him what he meant by that but he merely shrugged and repeated, 'I can do no more', then he went back to Bradford, leaving Charlotte in the care of the novice Dr Ingham. My worries darkened. Surely, Charlotte was not going to die from this? Not after Anne? Not bearing our child? Because of her illness, Charlotte would not allow herself to look beyond it to a happy resolution but I couldn't help it. My heart had soared at Charlotte's news. It was such an unexpected turn of events that it could only have been providential − a pregnancy that was meant to be − my child and Mr Brontë's grandchild. Since Charlotte told me, I had been basking in the golden promise that all I had been through − my desolation after Anne, my loneliness, my empathy with Charlotte's loneliness, the proposal, rejection, humiliation and exile and all the stresses of Charlotte's brow-beating her father − all of that would now be justified because, as Charlotte herself once said: 'there is no joy in this life that is not hard won'. And this child would be a joy; it would bind Charlotte and her father to me and the seed of that joy would be mine, but if the child died, or worse, if the child and Charlotte died, where then was I? How, in the court of history, would I then be judged? Or, more urgently, how by Mr Brontë?

'There are more ways than one that a daughter can be taken from her father.' That was what he had said. Was this then what he had meant? That to a thirty-eight-year-old woman with a slight frame and a delicate constitution, pregnancy would be fatal? Was that, all along, the reason why he rejected me with such force and resisted so tenaciously Charlotte's campaign to change his mind? Because he foresaw this? Charlotte must not die. How could I face him? How could I live under the same roof with him? Or even work with him? But equally, how, after all he had suffered, could I leave him entirely alone? It was an impossible prospect. With or without the child, Charlotte must not die, for her own sake, for her father's sake and for mine because, after our few short months of marriage, I loved Charlotte. She, more than the child, was who I needed to live and hourly I prayed that she would.

I continued to fulfil my duties as best I could. Among them was the conduct of Tabby's funeral which, on a wet February afternoon, was a grim ordeal but honour demanded that one of us take it and Mr Brontë wasn't up to it. I was still taking some bible classes in the mornings and visiting the sick in the afternoons and there were, of course, all the services to conduct because, as Charlotte deteriorated so did her father and his duties devolved upon me. We hardly spoke. The only thing on both our minds was too painful to talk about and when we did speak, I saw the fear in his eyes, the fear that he was about to lose the last of his family and I was the cause of it. The strain was oppressive and I was finding it harder each day to function so when, in the middle of March, Joseph Grant offered to look after the chapelry, we gratefully accepted.

Charlotte drifted in and out of consciousness, for long periods occupying a twilight state of low, wandering delirium. Dr Ingham came every day. He gave her medicines and tried to look positive but he was young and I don't think he had the full grasp of Charlotte's condition. I sat with Charlotte, watching her and talking to her, and during her periods of lucidity she did eat and drink a little: some beef tea, and spoonsful of wine and water, sometimes a light pudding, but the portions were tiny and would not have sustained her even if she had been able to retain them, which she could not, and so she weakened.

By the fourth week in March, Mr Brontë could not talk to Charlotte any more, it was too upsetting for him and he felt he would only depress her if she saw him continually praying and so he prayed alone in his room. I talked to Charlotte whether she were lucid or not, and read to her, and

I prayed of course, when I thought she would not hear, oh how I prayed because 'what', I asked in my fervent appeals, 'had we done?' What vile displeasure had I and Mr Brontë given to God that such a brilliant life as Charlotte's should be ripped from us? Had I not paid my tithe of suffering after Anne? And now, having been allowed to love, was I again to be denied? Nine months. Was that to be my meed of happiness?

Charlotte hardly spoke towards the end but, when she did, it was to console and to thank me. I remember our last coherent conversation. Martha and I had lifted Charlotte in her bed and banked pillows at her back to support her head for some beef tea. She was pitifully small by then, five stones at the most, and her face was grey with the constant pain. Martha had offered her the cup.

"Here y'are now," she coaxed her, "it's not too hot and not too strong. Just as yer like it." But Charlotte was not listening.

"I'm sorry," she whispered, her thin lips quivering.

"Nay, just try a bit," Martha tried to insist but Charlotte was not looking at Martha, she was looking at me.

"I have let you down." She nipped tight her lips to stop them trembling and the tears spilled from her eyes. She moved her hand across the bed and I took it. It was brittle as a bird's bones.

"You haven't let me down." I smiled, stroking her hand.

"I so wanted to give you your child," she continued, "I shall not know now shall I? What it is to be a mother?" I leaned forward and took Charlotte into my arms and, while Martha sobbed over her cup, we wept and embraced so tightly that even today I still feel Charlotte's cheek. "Look after Papa," she whispered.

"I shall." I pulled back and wiped my eyes. "Although he has cause to resent me."

"How so?" said Charlotte, surprised.

"If you and I had not married ..."

"But you are the blessing of my life," she insisted, "how can Papa resent you?" She looked to Martha who pulled an awkward face then she closed her hands around mine. "You have been the tenderest nurse, the kindest support and the best earthly comfort that ever woman had. How can Papa not love you?"

When Charlotte died, in the early hours of Saturday 31st March, I was not with her. It is a regret that I shall live with all my life. I was asleep in the nursery next door. I had sat with her for most of Friday until sometime after dark when Martha found me asleep at the bedside. She told me I should get some rest and so I lay down in the nursery. Then Martha was waking me again.

"Yer'd better come, Mr Nicholls," she was saying. "I think she's gone." I threw off the blanket and rose from the bed.

"You should have wakened me."

"I just popped down to t'kitchen. I were only gone two minutes an' when I come back Miss Charlotte were very still an' I just knew she were gone an' that were just a minute since ..."

"Where is Mr Brontë?"

"In his bed. Have I to get him?"

"No, Martha, I shall do that." I went through to Charlotte and Martha stayed by the door. The room was dim and the air heavy with stale warmth. A patchwork quilt lay on the bed and beneath it, barely discernible, was the faint outline of a wasted frame. Charlotte's head was on the pillow, very still, the face turned towards me and, though the eyes were closed, there was the trace of a smile on the lips and the crazed lines of pain that had etched Charlotte's face for the past months were gone.

I went round the bed to the windows and threw back the curtains. The first shafts of dawn were glowing behind Brow Moor even as the stars still sparkled in a cloudless sky. The wind was light. It would be a fine day. I lifted the sash to clear the stale air then returned to the bedside. I had looked on the dead before and for the past two weeks I had reconciled myself to Charlotte's death but at that moment, looking upon her peaceful face, I could not believe it. She would wake. Her eyes would open and she would look at me and smile. I put my hand to her cheek. It was still warm but the skin was stiffening. The life had gone out of it. My beautiful wife. My best friend. She was gone. I turned from the body and looked out of the window beyond the church and the houses to the distant moors and the light of the rising sun.

"I am the resurrection and the life," I said aloud. "He that believeth in me, though he were dead, yet shall he live, and whosoever liveth and believeth in me shall never die." Without looking at the body again I went out past Martha and into Mr Brontë. I lit a candle and touched him on the shoulder.

"Mr Brontë." He opened his eyes but I knew that he would not know me and so I said again, "Mr Brontë." He looked at me blankly for a moment while he came to his wits and then he cried out,

"Oh my poor Charlotte!" He pushed back the covers and, in his nightshirt and cap, stepped onto the floor. "God have mercy! God have mercy and bless my dear Charlotte!" He took the candle from me and went through to Charlotte's bedside and, falling to his knees beside her, he cried out, "Oh, my Charlotte, Charlotte, Charlotte." I left the room and pulled the door shut behind me then I put on my coat and boots and set off for the moors.

I had no thought of where I was going. I did not pray, I did not think, I was impelled only to walk and, as I walked, my tears sprang and the tide of my grief bore me on. For an hour I walked unaware of the world or even of myself, my senses drowned in a welter of bitterness and when, after an hour, I did find myself again, I was standing on Ponden Kirk, four miles from home, looking out over the valley of the Worth. The air was fresh and above my head, in the clear blue sky, a single curlew was circling the rocky outcrop, screeching at me. She was trying to draw me away from her nest, a nest that I would not have been aware of had she not been screeching. Springtime. The whole valley was moist with life. Everywhere, stiff new shoots were shoving themselves up, cutting through the detritus of last year's life that in death was compacting, returning to earth, to Demeter's earth, the mother of life and of death. For the Greeks, the afterlife continues below the earth. Demeter's earth. Demeter's grasses. Demeter's people. The same recurring cycle, turning for man just as for the plants. It was a notion of recurrent life that, in that place, on that morning, had the clearer ring of truth for me than any one of eternal life. Branwell would have trumpeted the notion on his way to Eleusis as Emily had in her poems.

The valley was stirring. People were loosening hens and geese from their coops and turning out beasts. I watched

Robert Heaton leading out his heavy mare. He was walking her slowly down the avenue from Ponden House, her powerful hind flanks rolling languorously at the start of another working day. Would Charlotte be with her family today? Mother and brother and sisters reunited? All bar the father left alone now with me. I shivered in the damp air. How could I face him? What could I say? What was he waiting to say to me? God forbid that he should have another seizure. I had to go back. I stepped off the rock and set off back to the parsonage.

Martha must have been watching for me because, when I turned up the garden path, she was out on the step.

"How is Mr Brontë?" I asked her.

"He's in his parlour," she whispered. "He's got Mr Wood with him. You know, for t'coffin."

"Is he all right?"

"What do yer think?" Martha shrugged and dropped her head. She looked exhausted.

"You get off to bed and get some rest, Martha. I shall see to Mr Brontë."

"But someone's to sit with Miss Charlotte."

"Martha, Charlotte is gone." Martha looked at me in disbelief as if I had slapped her. She started to cry. "Would you rather go down home?" Martha nodded. "Off you go then, and go straight to bed."

I went to my study to write to Miss Nussey. Mr Brontë had written to her the day before, to prepare her for the worst, and now that the worst had happened, it was right that she should hear it from me. It did not take me long, my note was only brief, but by the time I was carrying it down to the post office, the passing bell was already tolling. In the post office,

Mr Hartley was kind. He had known the family for years and was a good neighbour: he admired Charlotte's 'gifts and spirit', as he told me. Out in Kirkgate, other parishioners saw me. Some were kind and some asked impertinent questions and all the time the ten-second toll was summoning me back to face Mr Brontë.

At the parsonage, I found Martha in the garden. She was cutting boughs from the lilac and the pussy willow.

"What are you doing here?" I asked her. "You are supposed to be at home in bed."

"Yer've got a visitor." Martha nodded towards the house. I went in and saw Miss Nussey's portmanteau lying on the hall floor. Miss Nussey herself, still in her travelling cape and bonnet, was descending the stairs.

"Ah! You are here!" she cried, and as she reached the hall floor she raised her gloved fists to her throat. "Charlotte is dead!" Miss Nussey was shaking and her face was twisted with grief. "I got Mr Brontë's letter and caught the first train." She rolled her head and cried out again. "Charlotte is dead!"

"Miss Nussey," I said quietly, stepping towards her, "please, come into the dining room. You will disturb Mr Brontë." I took Miss Nussey's arm but she cast me off. She bustled past me into the dining room and I followed her, closing the door behind us. Miss Nussey went to the window and put a handkerchief to her face. "Won't you sit down?" I suggested, but she remained looking out of the window. "I am sorry, Miss Nussey …" I was about to appraise her of the sad events but then she turned on me.

"Why did you keep Charlotte from me?" Her tear-filled eyes were burning with rage. "Why did you forbid her from visiting me? Why did you forbid me from coming here? By what right?" her body was shaking. "I don't think you *ever* understood." She dabbed at her eyes. "Charlotte and I were friends for twenty-five years – *twenty-five years!*" She threw down the words like a gauntlet. "And the closest of friends through childhood and womanhood sharing our tragedies and Charlotte's triumphs – we were *as one.*" She glared at me, her eyes level as spears. "Nobody knew Charlotte Brontë as I did. Nor loved her so well."

I felt sick in the stomach. I had not the strength to resist such an attack. I wanted to sit down but could not while Miss Nussey stood and so I leaned with both hands on the back of a chair.

"We are all in a state of shock, Miss Nussey." I began again to try to calm her but she seemed determined to hear nothing from me.

"A strange sort of shock that leaves a wife not yet cold all alone in her soiled deathbed. Not a servant in the house. Not a soul to perform the obsequies. Just poor Mr Brontë left to grieve all alone the passing of his last …" Miss Nussey faltered, her shoulders shook and she started to cry noisily into her handkerchief. Through the window I glimpsed Martha, her arms full of boughs, crossing the garden towards the house.

"Did you go down to Sexton House for Martha?"

"In *bed!*" She spat out the word. "Your one servant laid in bed on such a day as this!" Crying into her handkerchief, Miss Nussey rushed from the room. In the hall she met Martha and, with a lot of bustle and fuss, she conducted the poor woman up the stairs as if she were herself now mistress of the house. I remained in the dining room leaning on the chair. I heard the women enter the bedroom above me. They would be performing the rites with which both were so sadly familiar and decorating the bed with the lilac and willow that Martha had brought from the garden. I remained, motionless, in the dining room – the dining room that had been Charlotte's sanctum, only now it was empty. I left the room and went to Tabby's kitchen, which was empty. I went into the scullery where there were no dogs, Martha was stolen from me and, after my encounter with Miss Nussey, I had not the strength to face Mr Brontë and so I left the house.

I walked down Parsonage Lane, drawn, I think, by the old warmth of Mary, but Sexton House was no longer my home, it hadn't been for two years and, in any case, did not Mary have her hands and heart full with poor John dying from dust on the lung? I walked past Sexton House and into the church. That was empty too. I walked down to the tablet let into the wall at the east end, the tablet that would now have to be replaced because it was already full. I read the names. I did not know the older girls, Maria and Elizabeth, nor the mother and aunt after whom they were named. Were they watching me? Were they blaming me? 'Patrick Branwell Brontë'. 'Emily Jane Brontë'. I expected no sympathy from them. Both of them would be blaming me for putting their sister in an early grave. 'Anne Brontë.' Would Anne blame me? Her dying words had been 'take courage Charlotte' so I hoped not. And now Charlotte herself. Do you blame me, Charlotte, for cutting short your life? What a price we have paid for love.

"Oh almighty and most merciful father," I prayed aloud. "Take unto thy bosom thy daughter Charlotte departed this day, forgive her her sins and admit her to thy Grace. For the sake of our lord Jesus Christ."

"Amen." Mr Brontë's resonant baritone rang out at my back. I turned. He was standing two yards behind me, shaved, groomed and erect in his best black suit, facing down the world, even on such a day as this. I was in awe.

"Mr Brontë …" I fumbled for something to say. I think 'I'm sorry' fell from my lips but then, I think to quieten me, my father-in-law opened his arms. I stepped forward and gave myself up into his embrace and as his arms closed around me he whispered,

"My dear boy."

Postscript

Nicholls stayed on in the parsonage for another six years, looking after Mr Brontë with Martha until Mr Brontë's death in 1861 at the age of eighty-four. Nicholls had been expected to succeed to the cure but the trustees of the Haworth Church Lands, the body that found the stipend, voted by five votes to four with one abstention in favour of the Vicar of Bradford's nominee, John Wade. Nicholls went back to Banagher. His cousin James, as Master of the Royal Free School, was still living at Cuba House with his wife and growing family but his Aunt Harriette and Cousin Mary had moved out, to Hill House, a smaller property nearby with twenty acres of land. Nicholls joined his aunt and cousin there, living quietly and looking after the farm and, after three years, he married his cousin Mary. Nicholls was forty-five and Mary thirty-four, their marriage was childless and Nicholls never sought another cure in the Church.

Nicholls remained close to Martha Brown who never married. They maintained a regular correspondence and Martha visited Hill House at least five times between 1862 and 1878, each visit lasting up to several months. Always protective of his privacy, Nicholls nevertheless came out to defend publicly the reputation of any member of the Brontë family, whenever he felt it threatened, and his second wife seems to have accepted his abiding loyalty to his first wife's family. Martha Brown died in Haworth in 1880 at the age of 52. Aunt Harriette died at Hill House in 1902 aged 101, Nicholls himself died there in 1906 aged 87 and Mary in 1915 at the age of 85.